STORIES FROM THE SHERIFF'S DAUGHTER

Stories from the SHERIFF'S DAUGHTER

a novel

LAREIDA BUCKLEY

TCU Press

FORT WORTH, TEXAS

LIBRARY OF CONGRESS CATALOGING-IN-PUBLICATION DATA

Names: Buckley, Lareida, - author.

Title: Stories from the sheriff's daughter / Lareida Buckley.

Description: Fort Worth : TCU Press, [2023] | Summary: "Stories from the Sheriff's
Daughter is a fictional collection of stories following the life of a 9 year old girl who
moves into a small town Texas county jail when her dairy farmer father is elected
sheriff. The stories, sometimes funny, sometimes tragic, evoke small town Texas
in the 1950's and 60's where readers can explore the impact of her growing up in
the jail's environment of lawmen, prisoners, and politics. In the jail, she bumps up
against some of life's worst tragedies, including murder, rape and suicide while her
parents try to maintain her innocence.

Though the stories are fiction, the author actually did grow up in the Burleson County
jail in Texas, where her father, and eventually her mother, served as sheriffs of the
county"— Provided by publisher.

Identifiers: LCCN 2022048660 (print) | LCCN 2022048661 (ebook)
| ISBN 9780875658346 (paperback) | ISBN 9780875658414 (ebook)

Subjects: LCSH: Children of police—Texas—Fiction. | Fathers and daughters—Fiction.
| Jails—Texas—Fiction. | Criminal justice personnel—Social life and customs—
Fiction. | Small cities—Texas—Fiction. | LCGFT: Novels. | Bildungsromans. |
Fictional autobiographies. | Prison fiction.

Classification: LCC PS3602.U2655 S76 2023 (print) | LCC PS3602.U2655 (ebook)
| DDC 813/.6—dc23/eng/20221028

LC record available at https://lccn.loc.gov/2022048660

LC ebook record available at https://lccn.loc.gov/2022048661

TCU Box 298300
Fort Worth, Texas 76129

Design by Julie Rushing

———

FOR MY FATHER AND MOTHER,

THE DEDICATED SHERIFFS IN THESE STORIES, AND

THE WONDERFUL PARENTS THEY WERE IN REAL LIFE.

———

ACKNOWLEDGMENTS

Thanks to my parents for making growing up in a jail so very normal, and for keeping the trauma of that upbringing to a minimum, and to my brothers who made such great characters for my stories.

Thanks to all my writing group friends who heard these stories and encouraged me over the years. Special thanks to Junko Weeks. Heartfelt thanks to Cheryl Anz, who grew up with these stories and just would not let them die. Thanks to Kate Evans, editor and adviser, for that final push. Thanks to my husband, Byron, who always believed in me.

NOTE

This is a work of fiction. Names, characters, places, and incidents either are products of the author's imagination or are used fictitiously. Any resemblance to actual events or locales or persons, living or dead, is entirely coincidental. However, the prevailing attitudes in small Texas towns during this period are accurately portrayed and include offensive language that in no way reflects my respect for other races and cultures.

—*Lareida Buckley*

For its part, TCU Press actively promotes civility, respect, tolerance, consideration, and professional conduct. TCU Press does not tolerate bigotry of any kind, but occasionally does publish works of authors who employ racist language that exposes the bigotry of particular places and times.

One

Alongside Evil

*T*he day had come. I was finally going to see a prisoner, and not just any prisoner. This was not a disturbing the peace, or a drunk in public. This was murder, and the murderer was on his way to our jail.

I'd been hoping to see a real prisoner ever since we'd moved into the jail. Every day of those three weeks, I'd been picturing what he'd look like in great detail, and I had it clear in my mind. He'd be skinny and hungry looking, with long greasy hair and a mustache. He'd have the bad posture I'd always been warned against, and his clothes would be dirty and look like he'd slept in the trunk of his car. He'd have a tattoo, or maybe several of them. A skull with dripping blood. A coiled snake or some really bad words. He would, of course, be missing teeth, and those remaining would be brown and discolored from smoking cigarettes or chewing tobacco. And this scary character was about to be locked up in our jail, right across the carport from our house. I had moved a chair up to the front window of our living room, where I could see everything when I pulled back the curtains.

Finally, the black-and-white police car barreled into the driveway, slinging gravel as it skidded to a stop. The highway patrolman leapt from the car, opened the back door, and dragged the prisoner out, leaving the car door swinging open. He was handcuffed, so I knew he was the murderer, but I couldn't believe my eyes. He was just a kid, no more than sixteen or seventeen years old. He had excellent posture and looked fit like an athlete. He wore pressed Levi's and a button-down collar shirt. His hair was blond and short, like my brothers', and he was obviously too young to grow a mustache. Even worse, he was crying. I never expected to see a prisoner cry.

We'd moved into the jail three weeks before, two days after my ninth birthday. It was one of those sunny, warm winter days common in Texas, and we'd been carrying cardboard boxes in from the car, when I heard my grandmother, a no-nonsense farm woman who always spoke her mind, say to my mother, "Is it wise, girl, moving in alongside evil?" We laughed, but my grandmother's face showed she didn't think it was a laughing matter. She stopped walking and eyed the jail with an expression I'd not seen before. Wise or not, it got me to thinking about prisoners and criminals living so close. My stomach tightened up, like it did when Daddy let me ride on the hood of his truck in the pasture, as I looked at the barred windows. I was about as excited as maybe only a nine-year-old can be.

Moving to town was excitement enough. I'd lived my whole life on our dairy farm on the hill just outside of town, in the big farmhouse my daddy was born in. Our neighbors were distant. I could barely see the roof of the Barnetts' hay barn across the north pasture, and if Mr. Barnett wanted to talk to Daddy, he'd ride over on his tractor. They were not, as my grandmother said, yelling distance. Despite the cows and my two brothers to play with, the creek to fish in, the tank to swim in, it was all too familiar, maybe even boring. The jail, though, was right in town, a block down the hill from the courthouse square with all that downtown Caldwell, Texas, in 1956 had to offer. The drugstore, the picture show, the Perry Brothers five-and-ten cent store. The bank, the Chevrolet dealership, the post office. Doc Skrivek's office. Now I could walk to all of this, by myself, on my own. I could not believe my good luck. When Mama said we could hear every car that went by, I wondered why she didn't sound happier about it. I was celebrating town life, and jail life, too.

During those first few weeks, though, the shine had faded from the jail. I had not seen a single prisoner, even though some passed through. Mama and Daddy were shielding us kids from the prisoner side of the house. We were out to school in the mornings before any activity with the courts, and off to Sunday school early on Sundays before the Saturday night revelers were freed. Before we ever moved into the jail I'd seen Wooly Hearne, the town drunk, staggering around downtown all the time.

I wondered what good was it living in the jail if you never saw any desperados, or witnessed any shootouts, or experienced any excitement at all?

Daddy, whom I had begun to refer to as "My father" (as in "My father is the sheriff"), had not even fired the pearl-handled pistol his friends had given him after his election in November. Mama hid it in the dresser drawer every night when he took it off. He'd unsnap the big buckle that held it on his belt, well hidden under his suit coat, and hand it over. The Texas Ranger who came down to the jail to welcome Daddy into office had been dressed in a suit and tie, with no star or badge at all where you could see it. He looked like the First State Bank president. Even Daddy's badge, a little gold star, was worn on his shirt pocket under his suit coat. Jail life was not living up to my expectations.

The jail itself looked nothing like jails I'd seen in Western movies, where they were always big and scary. Instead, our jail was brand-new and modern, made of pink brick, long and low. You had to look hard to even see the bars on the windows. It was a radical change from our farmhouse, with its high ceilings and huge drafty rooms. The sheriff's house was the jail's twin, the two separated by an open carport. From across the street, it looked like a duplex, a living arrangement I had only recently become aware of. Two families sharing opposite ends of the same house seemed odd to me, a country girl. Maybe not so odd as a sheriff's family and the county's prisoners sharing opposite ends of the same building, but that hadn't yet occurred to me.

The jail side was small, only eleven cells and a shower. That was apparently big enough, because on the day we moved in it was empty, so Mama let my two brothers and me go in to look around. My grandmother, the evil of the place still in her mind, wouldn't set foot inside, but stood guard by the door. There was a hallway down the center, with cells on both sides. The doors were solid steel, not open bars like I'd imagined, or what I'd seen in *High Noon*, my all-time favorite movie. Each solid steel cell door had a little barred door about five feet up to pass things through. My brother Walter, five years older than I, closed a cell door on me. He and my other brother Bill, three years older, held it shut while I protested loudly. I was used to this kind of treatment from my brothers, so I didn't panic. I figured they would soon get bored, so I just looked around. The cell was small, not even half the size of my new bedroom on the other end of the building. It had a metal bed with a thin striped mattress, really more of a quilt than a mattress, a sink, and a toilet. All of it was already dirty and smelly, despite the newness of the jail. There was hardly enough room to pace back and forth. Something about it made the hair stand up on my arms. Being locked away in there would be bad; I could tell that after two minutes.

Bill got tired of harassing me and stepped inside the cell. I could see he felt the creepiness, too, saying, "Well, at least it has a window to look out of." That was about the only good thing to be said. I was just surprised that Bill would see it. I didn't think him to be one to appreciate the finer things. In the years to come, those jail windows would be where prisoner after prisoner stared out, yelled out, and cried out. They became our windows into a darker world.

Mama came in, wrinkling up her nose at the smell, already full of plans to clean the place up, to replace the mattresses with better ones, and to get the county commissioners to pay for decent linens. She measured the little doors to decide on food trays for the meals she would prepare. Mama was a little person, not much bigger than me at age nine, but really pretty, with dark curly hair that she hated, and smooth peachy skin she put cream on every night. Her eyes were gray and showed whatever she was feeling, for everybody to see. She was feeling that this smelly, dirty place was not fit, not even for criminals, and she would see it made better. I thought that cleaning the place up wouldn't do much to make those small and scary cells bearable. I was glad to walk out to join my grandmother in the sun.

There was, at least, one new thing I was enjoying. I'd heard it said a few times, and it made me feel almost famous. "Isn't that the sheriff's daughter?" I'd heard it at the drugstore, and around town, and I was proud.

My father could quote poetry in the Old English while milking a cow and teach Masonic secrets to lodge members on the back porch. He taught me to read the funny papers long before I started school. He told jokes at the breakfast table. He could plow a field, plant it, and bale the hay. He could fry eggs he'd gathered from the hay barn and bacon that he'd smoked himself. He could churn butter, make cheese, and freeze the best peach ice cream. He could brand a cow, dehorn a cow, or castrate calves. He could doctor a sick cow and pull a calf when the cow was in trouble. When the nearest veterinarian was in the next county, he went out day or night to doctor cows for farmers all over the county, in return for eggs, a bushel of corn, or a couple of watermelons. He milked the cows, carried the milk up from the barn, strained it and bottled it with Mama, and delivered it in his pickup truck. He could fix that truck, or a tractor, or a broken-down windmill. He was on a championship football team in high school, played at Baylor, and for a semipro team in San Antonio during the Depression years. Though shy, he could speak to a political rally or a school assembly, always about working hard and treating people right. He was the softest of touches. Whether it was big loans for family members, cash for a needy stranger, or quarters for kids. His dairy was always sorely in need of money because he was sure people would pay their milk bill if and when they could. I never heard him raise his voice. With his soft tone, he could calm an injured cow, or a raging drunk, or a crying child, as I could testify myself. He might cuss at a recalcitrant cow but prayed every Sunday night in his favorite pew at the Methodist Church. His khakis were always starched, even in the dairy barn. He steam-ironed his suit lapels just so. He was kind to one and all.

He was handsome and big and strong. But best of all he would tell me I was special.

So when somebody said, "Isn't that the sheriff's daughter?" I was glad it was me.

The night I finally saw the prisoner was our third weekend in the jail. Mama and I were playing cards at the kitchen table, a long-running mother-daughter tournament which she was winning. She always did. I told her that some parents let their children win, on purpose, just to be kind. She threw down her winning hand, laughing out loud and saying, "Gin, baby girl. Your deal." Mama was competitive.

The police radio that sat on top of the refrigerator, its long black mike cord coiling down the side, crackled in the background. Though in time we would get used to the radio blaring day and night, three weeks in I was still listening to every word. I heard all the police chatter from the neighboring towns, about forty miles in all directions, and there was a lot of it. Often though, all we heard was where the police in four counties were having their coffee. It didn't matter to me, I still found it fascinating. Mama, in the interest of a "normal" life, was trying to ignore the radio, and to get us kids to ignore it, too. Later, the police radio made me popular for sleepovers, as visiting kids loved listening to it all night long.

Our county was about thirty miles of rolling farmland east to west and forty or so north to south, which might seem large, but in Texas, big is ordinary. The Yegua Creek runs along the county line on the Dime Box side and on the Somerville side as well. Toward Bryan, the Brazos River marks the line, so when you cross any one of those bridges, you know you're back in Burleson County. That was always a lot more satisfying to me than when crossing an imaginary line like you did coming from the Milano side. Every time we'd cross the bridges, Daddy would say, "Breathe that Burleson County air, Dolly." (He called me Dolly, and I prayed nobody I knew would ever hear him do it.) "I drew my first breath in Burleson County, and hope to breathe my last one here, too," he'd say. He loved his home county, more than most people would ever say out loud. When you'd get up on top of one of those hills, and see fields and farms spread out for miles in the distance, morning dew shining in the sunlight, or covered with a purple carpet of bluebonnets in the spring, you could see how he'd feel that way. Mama said he was a homebody, but the way she said it made it sound like a good thing, even if she did like to see the world outside Caldwell much more than he did.

Caldwell sat right in the middle of the county, with the courthouse on a promontory, visible for miles around. We could pick up radio traffic from the bigger towns in the counties around us: Bryan, Brenham, Giddings, Rockdale. Suddenly, in the middle of our card game, we heard the Bryan dispatcher yell, "Brazos County Sheriff's Office calling all units in or near Snook!" Her panicked tone was unusual on the radio, where everybody tried to sound professional and calm. And this was a regular deputy dispatcher, not a sheriff's wife who happened to be taking calls in her kitchen like Mama did. We laid down our cards to listen.

"Texaco gas station in Snook just robbed! Two white males driving a dark blue '55 Chevy. License unknown. Armed and dangerous! Repeat: Armed and dangerous!"

She was yelling, and even I could see why, this being the most serious crime I'd ever heard on the radio. Soon, though, she calmly relayed details, calling in highway patrolmen. We heard her talking to my daddy in his car when he joined in the hunt for the blue Chevy on our side of Snook. I was proud to hear him sounding like a real sheriff. Not so much like my smiling daddy, more like a lawman.

Mama didn't look proud, though. With her lips pressed tightly together, she looked worried. Our phone was ringing, as more people called in about the gunfire. Mama roused Daddy's deputies from their beds to help in the search of the county's backroads. I got to answer the phone when she was busy on the radio. Finally, jail life was getting exciting.

The whole thing turned sad when the news came in that the gas station attendant had been shot dead. He was an old man, and he should have given them the money, but resisted. He probably felt safe there in Snook where he'd lived his whole life and never seen anybody kill anybody outside their family.

Late in the night, two highway patrolmen from Bryan found the robbers parked in a cemetery near Tunis, not more than ten miles from the scene of the crime, as people would later call it. Dozens of lawmen had gathered around the cemetery, shouting and surrounding the blue Chevy. The robbers refused to answer the demands for their surrender. When one jumped from the car, gripping a gun in his hand, he was shot, many times, by more than one officer. No one ever knew who fired. Mama and I heard the shots because one of the deputies used his radio mike calling his office. It was the shootout I'd been picturing, maybe hoping for, but my heart sped up and tears filled my eyes. Neither Mama nor I had ever heard a gunshot fired at a real person, with deadly intent. Mama had to sit down. I wanted to hear Daddy's voice. I exhaled when he called in, asking Mama to call the ambulance for the dead boy at the cemetery in Tunis. Mama seemed to get a little color back, but her hands quivered as she made the call.

An hour or so later, while I watched the other boy being dragged to his cell, tears running down his face, Mama came up beside me, blinking back tears of her own. She always cried when one of us kids cried, and now I thought maybe she cried when anybody did. If that was true, jail life was going to be hard on her.

It turned out that he was a high schooler from across the river in Bryan. He had only been the driver, he'd said, and that the other boy, the dead one, had done the robbery and shot the old man, accidentally. The highway patrolman told us that was what the guilty ones always said. Daddy had set the gun (everybody was calling it the murder weapon!) on our kitchen table, already covered black with fingerprint dust. It was a big gun, even bigger than Daddy's revolver. I could hardly take my eyes off it before Mama sent me off to bed.

Nobody slept much that night in the jail, not on either side of the carport. Daddy made calls from his office, Mama walked the floor, the boy cried in his cell, and I listened to it all.

Next morning, I walked out the kitchen door headed for my dreaded piano lesson with the long-suffering Miss Bea, who, like me, knew I'd never be a piano player. I considered my lessons a success when I could get Miss Bea to play classical music herself, while I sat and listened. But Mama wasn't quite ready to give up on the dream yet, so I was off, bundled up in my heavy coat. It had come a norther during the night. I had to walk past the jail yard to the street. The yard surrounded the jail side of our place, enclosed with a tall chain-link fence, topped with barbed wire. I'd always thought it a little too much for Caldwell, but not this morning. We had a murderer in there.

Even if he was evil, like my grandma said, I wanted to get another look at the boy. There he was, at the window, hanging his arm out the bars as far as it would go, waving at me furiously. I would have thought he was trying to get out the window if I didn't know it was impossible.

"Little girl! Little girl!" His voice sounded hoarse, and he was crying. "Please," he cried, "please call my mother for me. She'll get me out of here! I'll give you the number. Just call her for me."

Here I was, talking to a murderer. Or maybe the next best thing to a murderer. He was all the way across the jail yard, but I could see and hear him. I clutched the fence, squeezing the impression of the chain links into my fingers. I could feel my heart beating up in my neck, like before I went to the dentist, and my teeth were clicking together. I couldn't find my voice.

The boy seemed calmer, now that he had my attention. He went on, "I know my mother will get me out of here. I have a science paper due on Monday. I promised her I'd finish it today, if she'd let me go out with . . ." he trailed off. He must have been remembering the night before, because he started to cry again. He looked me right in the eyes for the first time, and though I wanted to look away, I didn't, because, here he was, talking about his science paper and his mother. My heart started to shift out of my ears, back into its rightful place.

"Is Kyle really dead?" he asked. He asked it like a question he already knew the answer to.

"If Kyle is the other guy with you last night, then, yeah, he's dead." I tried to be gentle. How strange to be worried about the feelings of a near murderer, but then he'd lost his friend, but then his friend was an actual murderer. I loosened my grip on the cold fence and warmed my hands with my breath.

"We didn't even know if that gun was loaded," he said from the window. "We wanted to make sure it wasn't loaded, but we didn't know how to get it open to look inside. We never meant to hurt anybody, we just wanted gas money."

I didn't say a word, but I was thinking he was sounding pretty far from a murderer. He sounded like a dumb kid who didn't know how to figure out if a gun was loaded, something even I could do.

"I've never been in trouble before," he said, like he didn't want me to think bad of him. Not much of a desperado.

"Do you have any tattoos?" I asked him.

"No." His lips lifted into a small smile. He not only had all his teeth, but they were also white and straight. He probably hadn't had his braces off for very long.

He looked past me out to the blue Chevy that the tow truck had pulled into the feed store lot behind the jail. Even from here, you could see a bullet hole in the driver's side door. He held onto the bars with his hands real tight, and I could see his fingernails were clean and clipped short. He pointed to the car with a lift of his chin. "Kyle let me drive last night, and I opened her up on that straightaway past the river. Kyle was afraid to drive fast." He looked like he was about to grin, but instead started crying again.

"Call my mother, please, please." He sounded like a little kid now, sniffling and whining.

Me, I was thinking how even Kyle didn't sound like your usual murderer, and I was wondering if there was even such a thing. While he cried and cried, my throat tightened. I felt like I might cry myself. I turned away, back toward the kitchen door. Over my shoulder, I said, "I'll talk to my Daddy." I hadn't seen desperation before, and I wanted to get away from it fast. Even being afraid of the prisoner had felt better than this.

The kitchen was warm and cozy, with Daddy at the table pouring coffee from the percolator like any morning. He was dressed in his usual suit and tie and didn't look like he'd been up all night. His black wavy hair was still damp from the shower. It was longer than most men wore it and had a permanent crease where his Stetson fit around his head. Even after the terrible night before, his gray eyes were clear. The wrinkles all around them, which Mama said were from smiling too much, were deeper than usual, but softened as he smiled at me.

"That boy wants us to call his mother," I told him.

"I was just going out to talk to him," Daddy said, maybe sad, too. "I called the boy's parents last night, and again this morning. His daddy said they'd tried everything to keep him away from Kyle Westerly, and that he wouldn't listen. He said the boy had made his bed, and he could lie in it."

"What did his mama say?" I asked.

"She just cried," he sighed. He put his hand on my shoulder and gave it a little squeeze. I thought again that there was going to be a lot of crying around here.

We walked out together, slowly, into the cold. The sky was gray now and threatening rain. I could tell Daddy was dreading talking to the boy by how slow he was moving, how quiet he was, not teasing me about my piano playing like he usually would. I hurried on up the street, holding my music book, *Easy Melodies for the Right Hand*, against my mouth as a shield against the north wind.

I knew when Daddy told him, because I heard that boy wail out loud like he'd been hit hard and was using his last breath to cry out. I'd never heard anything like it. My breath caught in my throat, and the chill I felt running through my body wasn't from the cold wind.

Late that night, I lay awake in my bed, listening to the boy sobbing and crying for his mama who never did come. My own mother was walking from the hall to the kitchen and back, every now and then looking in on me. Daddy went out to talk to the boy several times in the night. I started thinking about what my grandmother had said that first day, but I think we all knew by now that we weren't going to be living alongside evil, we were going to be living alongside pain.

Two

Fool for Love

*O*ur crying prisoner, accused of murder, was named Billy Ewell. It turned out he was the most popular boy in his high school. The boys wanted to be his friend, and all the girls, we would soon find out, wanted to be his girlfriend. He had indeed been an athlete, a football star, caught the winning touchdown pass in the district title game. But in our jail, he was merely a crying boy that Mama was trying to comfort with her macaroni and cheese and chicken and dumplings, and my daddy with a kind word when it looked like his mama wasn't coming for him. My brother Bill began standing for hours at Billy's cell window in the jail yard, and, like most people did, had gotten to like him. He ran errands for Billy, tried to call people for him, got cokes from the feed store (with his own money!), listened to his story, and repeated it around the breakfast table. But, at the first, Billy was beyond comfort, and cried and cried, right up until the reporters came.

The *Bryan Daily Eagle* had discovered that Billy Ewell, football star, was in our jail, and from their first day's coverage, he was "Billy the Kid" Ewell, and featured in articles almost every day, most with a favorable slant. The fact that he was charged with murder was overshadowed by his football career, and, in his own words, he'd only been "along for the ride." After the articles appeared, carloads of girls from Bryan drove by the jail every day, pulling up in the feed store lot, yelling at Billy through the fence. Finally, after Mr. Seifert at the feed store complained, Daddy moved Billy to Cell #3 on the street side so the girls could park on Fawn Street, right by the fence. My mama worried that these girls' mothers didn't know they were hanging on a jail fence in the next county, talking to an accused murderer, even if it was a big mix-up, like the papers said. Even more worrisome to Mama, some mothers drove their daughters up to the jail to see the prisoner, smiling and laughing with him themselves. There were so many phone calls for Billy in those first days, like they thought we'd go out and get him to come into our house for a chat, or like he might have a phone in his cell as if it were a hotel. I myself took several messages for him, writing them out on a message pad, like I did for my daddy. Finally, Daddy put a stop to all the phone calls. Only emergency messages were to be taken for the prisoners, not the likes of "Will you be out in time for the prom?"

It wasn't long before they all lost interest, anyhow. The *Bryan Daily Eagle*, the carloads of girls, the phone calls all slowed, and finally stopped. There were three or four diehards, girls Billy probably wouldn't have been interested in as a free man.

Finally, after his arraignment, and after the papers quit writing about him every day, one girl remained. Loretta. She was true blue. She had come the first day, and every day after, waiting out the carloads of Bryan girls when they were hogging all the room at the fence. And now finally she had the place to herself.

She even tried to bail Billy out of jail. She worked after school at the CannonBall Café, and had more money than most girls her age, money of her own. She went to area preachers to see if they would help, but with the shine worn off Billy's story, they wouldn't help her. She contacted a big city bail bondsman from Houston but couldn't raise enough cash. She made a last-ditch effort, going to Billy's absent parents, begging them to put their house up as collateral. They refused, and never once came to visit their son.

Loretta's efforts failed. So he became our first long-term prisoner in the months before his trial. Our whole family got to know him pretty well. Mama knew he liked his eggs over easy in the morning with grits and bacon. Daddy kept up with his court dates and lawyer visits. Bill stood vigil at the cell window. Even I said "hi" as I passed his window.

We all got to know Loretta, too. She bought Billy Marlboros and Snickers, his favorites. She came every single day at lunch and right after school. She'd drive up after work at the CannonBall and stay late into the night to keep him company. Despite her attentions, Billy Ewell did not seem grateful.

I'd hear him talk real mean to her. Even my brother Bill thought Billy was rough on Loretta, and my brother was far and away the meanest talker I'd ever come in contact with, at least when he and I fought, so I thought him a fair judge.

At the cell window, Bill asked Billy why he was so mean to Loretta.

"She don't mind," Billy said. "She don't expect any better. She's that kind of girl." Bill wanted me to know he was quoting Billy, so I wouldn't correct his grammar.

I was hurt for Loretta. Everybody, even a fool, likes a kind word, and I told Bill as much. Then Bill said something that made me think he might not be a lost cause after all. He said, "Well, that Loretta is a fool for love."

Even though Loretta kept on spending her waitress tips on him, Billy got more and more surly as the days went by. He'd snap at her if she brought the wrong cigarettes (he was a chain-smoker by now; his teeth were even looking a little brown), and call her moron or trailer trash, or even worse if she let his hamburger get cold before she got it up there after work. It got so bad that Mama sat me down for a talk about how I should never let anyone speak to me in that way. She was so upset, she had Daddy talk to Billy about how other people could hear him.

But one late night when the jail lights were off, I heard Loretta by the fence in the dark.

"Don't worry, Billy, I'll be right here. It's all going to be okay. I'll be right here. I love you."

It was the sweetest talk I thought that that jail yard ever heard, or would ever hear. Billy must have felt it, too, because he called out "I love you." The words rang across the yard where Loretta was hanging on, you might say, for dear life. From my bed, I imagined she might go right over the fence, barbed wire be damned, to get closer to the boy she loved.

When Billy's trial finally came up, he wouldn't let Loretta attend. She'd sit in her car pulled up by the jail yard fence, waiting for him to be brought back in handcuffs to tell her about his day in court. Loretta talked to Daddy: "Do you think his lawyer's any good?" To my mama: "How does it look for him?" She even asked me and my brother Bill for reports, and we knew less than she did.

If the truth be known, it was going exceptionally well for Billy Ewell. He had a good lawyer who'd been a football fan of Billy's and was working pro bono. There was not a lot of evidence against Billy himself, and he told his own story convincingly. And people liked him, seemed to believe what he said. They'd go off talking about what a good kid he was, too bad he was in such a bad scrape. Some of the old gang of girls started showing up in court, including Sara Seeley, a rich girl he'd been going out with before this whole ordeal started. She could have bailed him out of jail with her makeup money alone, my grandma said.

Billy Ewell didn't seem in the least surprised to see these people at his trial, these people that my mama called his fair-weather friends. But he must have been expecting them all along, smiling and chatting as he was in the crowded courtroom. I was quick to realize if these were fair-weather friends, that made Loretta a rainy-day friend, parked as she was out by the jail fence all day every day after court, all day during court, and every single night since the whole thing started, no matter what the weather was. As I got to thinking about it, I could remember seeing Loretta out there in a headscarf and a raincoat, under a leaky umbrella, more than once. Rainy-day friend, indeed.

The jury was out only an hour before coming back with the verdict "manslaughter." The judge gave Billy Ewell time served and told him he was free to go.

And go he did.

None of us, not even Daddy, knew where he went, or who drove him away. We'd only seen the back of the expensive herringbone blazer his lawyer had bought for him, as he hurried out of the court room. Billy Ewell was gone.

Later, as we walked down the hill to the jail, Mama said, "Oh, my goodness. That looks like Loretta's car."

"It sure is," I said, "and I can see her sitting in it." Loretta had the front door open, and I could see she was dressed up. She had on fancy shoes, and her hair was curled real pretty.

"Billy's been gone for over two hours," Mama said. "He should have already come down here for Loretta, and to get his things from his cell."

Mama tried to hide it, but I could see the doubt and worry flashing across her face.

Mama went over to tell Loretta that Billy was free. Loretta was crying and so happy and hugging Mama. Mama didn't have the heart to tell her that Billy had been gone from the courthouse for hours, and I think she was hoping for Loretta's sake that he'd turn up any minute.

Loretta sat there until dark, when Daddy couldn't stand it any longer. He went out, knocked on her window, and told her, gentle as he could, that Billy had been free since just after noon, and did she want to come in and call someone? "No, Sir, thank you," she said. "Our plan was I'd wait here, and he'd come get me. I'll wait. He's probably taking care of some things."

Daddy slid into the seat next to Loretta, consoling her as maybe only he could. When he finally came in, Daddy said she didn't cry. In fact, he said she remained hopeful. Daddy hardly ever cried himself, but he looked as though he might do it tonight.

Mama kept watch on the car all evening, frowning like she was the one waiting on someone who most likely would never come. She said it was like watching someone's heart breaking real slow.

I jumped out of bed the next morning and rushed to the window to see if Loretta's car was still there. There it was, her brown Pontiac still parked by the jail yard fence closest to Billy's cell. I could see her long hair hanging against the window, yesterday's curls gone. At ten that morning, we heard the engine roar to life, and Loretta slowly pulled out onto Fawn Street and disappeared up the hill. The next week, she drove by three times, gazing at Billy Ewell's cell window. And then we didn't see her anymore.

Each time she drove by, I'd worry about Loretta. I hadn't seen many relationships up close, but I knew this one was different. What made Loretta come every day, and then wait so long when it was clear Billy wasn't coming back for her? What made her drive by, when she knew Billy was long gone?

I remembered the night I'd heard Billy Ewell call out into the dark, *I love you.* I wondered why he'd said it when he didn't mean it. Why did he make promises he never meant to keep? Why did he break Loretta's heart?

Weeks later, I wondered if Loretta had heard like we all had heard, that Billy Ewell was happy and free and selling cars for Sara Seeley's dad in Brazos County.

I wondered if she was happy for him. Knowing her as I'd come to, I was pretty sure she was. My brother Bill had had it right. Loretta was a fool for love.

Three

Caldwell Cowboy

*M*ama and Daddy were fighting, if you could call what they did fighting. They didn't yell, or talk loud, or even sound angry. Mama held her lips between her teeth, and Daddy looked pained and said as little as possible. Then after some long silences, they'd hug. My brothers and I could judge how bad a fight was by how long it was before they hugged. How long they held each other after it was over said a lot, too.

They didn't fight much, but this one was an old one we'd heard many times before. Mama wanted to take us someplace, and Daddy said we couldn't go. We'd been hearing versions of this fight our whole lives. The places might change, but it was always the same result. This time, Mama wanted the whole family to go to Daddy's family reunion at Camp Creek. The lake at Camp Creek wasn't that far away, but the annual reunion was for a whole weekend, and we'd never made it to one yet. It would be for two whole days, and there would be cabins for the grownups and tents for the kids, and we were meant to stay two nights, or at least one. Mama really wanted to go, almost as much as us kids did. She wanted to go every year. In fact, she wanted to go lots of places but was married to Daddy, who liked to stay home, and got himself into situations that kept him right there, no argument.

"We could go Saturday and be back by Sunday afternoon," she said, already giving up on Friday. But like last year, and the year before that, it didn't look promising, judging by the look on Daddy's face. He kept his eyes closed for a really long time. He was torn between giving her what she wanted, and doing what he had to do, and the hurt showed in his eyes when he opened them. Years before, we couldn't go because cows had to be fed and watered and milked every single day. Now I heard Daddy telling Mama about deputies' time off, and prisoners to be fed, and response time when people needed help. From the look of resignation on Mama's face then, I knew she was thinking that people needing Daddy's help were going to be a bigger obstacle to her going anywhere than those cows had ever been, and they'd been huge. Mama managed a little smile and reached out to touch Daddy's arm.

The fight was over, and the hug was beginning. I thought that much as Mama wanted to go to Camp Creek, it would take a long hug to get it done.

I knew how she felt because I wanted to go, too. Like her, I wanted to go anywhere, anytime. Maybe I got the urge from her. But even if we weren't going to Camp Creek, and even if I hadn't really been anywhere yet, I did have a travel plan, and I'd had it for a long time.

My brother Bill and I were going to ride around the world on horses. We never sat down together to make a plan, but I had pictured it clearly in my mind, since I was five years old, when my older brother Walter introduced me to maps and the globe. He agreed to keep a record of the trip for Bill and me, putting pins in the map as we went. Bill and I would ride out in the wide-open spaces, never through towns or on highways, and we would hardly see any other people, unless they were American Indians or cowboys like us. We'd camp under yellow cottonwoods like down by the creek at the farm, and there would always be a full moon at night. The sky would be clear blue like the Texas sky, no matter where we rode. If it got cold, I'd wear my blue jean jacket that Bill had outgrown. I didn't take oceans into account, never having seen one.

The idea for the ride was Bill's. He was only three years older, but he got around all on his own, and had for years. He rode his horse Starlight, day or night, anywhere he wanted to go. He never had to wait for Mama to take him places, but he'd get in trouble for not coming home when he was supposed to. I thought he could do no wrong, and I wished I could come and go like he did. When he started wearing cowboy shirts and boots when he was eight or nine, I had to have the same. When he said he was going to ride around the world on a horse, and that he'd take me with him, I got so excited I jumped up and tried to hug him, my eyes flashing, but Bill was not a hugger. Despite no return hug, I floated around for days with thoughts of horses, and roads and rivers to cross.

Starlight was meant to be mine. Like Roy Rogers's Trigger, she was a palomino with white stockings and a white star on her forehead. That's what Daddy called it, a *star*, not a blaze or some other marking. And I got to name her. My brothers and I always watched the evening sky for the first star. Whoever saw it hollered out, "Star light, star bright, first star I see tonight. I wish I may, I wish I might, have the wish I wish tonight." That, and her very own star, made her Starlight.

Starlight may have been my horse, but I could not catch her. I would go out in the pasture with a bucket of feed and her bridle hidden behind my back, just like Bill did. I'd get close, and she'd shy away. Bill could go out there and catch her in a minute, even without the horse feed. So little by little, she got to be his horse, and that made him so free.

Bill used our ride to get me to do anything he wanted. He'd say, "Go get me a Coke," and if I was slow to move, or just didn't want to do it, he'd say, "I'm not going to take you around the world with me." I'd carry in the firewood, even though it was his chore, lie to Mama and Daddy about where he was or what he was doing, or even give him money, if I ever had any, which I hardly ever did.

Our real inspiration for the ride was James Kincaid. James was a cowhand who used to work at our dairy before Daddy got to be sheriff. He wouldn't do dairy work, only cowboy work, like herding or rounding up cattle, or branding, which he told us he liked, or even castrating, which he said nobody liked. James Kincaid was so thin that his skin looked like weathered cowhide stretched tight across the bones of his face, and you could really see the bones right through it. It looked like those bones might poke through if he smiled just right. The muscles on his body looked so hard and tight they made you think of gristle. My grandma used to say that if James was a chicken, he wouldn't make good eating. He wore a cowboy hat with the brim turned up sharply on both sides, pointing down just as sharp front and back, nothing like any fancy cowboy hat you ever saw in the movies—and nothing at all like Daddy's clean and blocked Stetsons. He was always chewing on a matchstick that he had to move around to talk.

Much as he looked like a cowboy, we were more amazed by one thing: he was the only adult we'd ever known to ride a horse everywhere he went. In town, on the country roads, on the highway, no matter the weather. When he rode in the rain, the water would run down off his hat onto his yellow slicker, and down onto his saddle, and he didn't seem to notice. He was always talking to his horse, leaning down and whispering in a pointed ear, patting underneath the mane. It was as though that horse was his best friend, or maybe his only friend.

Once, we passed him riding over in the next county.

"Hey, kids," my mama called to us in the back seat, "we're about to pass James Kincaid on his horse."

We got up on our knees and watched out the back window until James and his skinny appaloosa disappeared from sight.

"He's a long way from home," Mama said, a little catch in her voice.

My brother Bill and I kept staring out the window, and I was thinking that James had probably ridden that horse around the world. Mama might have thought so, too, because, when I looked back and saw only her eyes in the rearview mirror, she had the same dreamy look in them that Bill and I had in ours.

Caldwell was the county seat in farm country. In years past, on Saturdays, farmers would come to town to sell produce and buy supplies. Out of habit, or tradition, people still came to town on Saturdays, whether they had business or not. Mama and I would drive up to the courthouse square and try to find a good parking place in front of the drugstore, where we could watch people walk by. She'd talk about how they looked, who they were with, who their people were, on and on. Mama was from Deanville, a small community five miles out, and had lived there or in Caldwell her whole life. She knew everybody and had a story on just about every last one of them.

"There's Margie. Margie Schmidt," she'd say. "She went to Red Hollow school with Sis and me. She was burning match sticks to blacken her eyebrows in second grade and set fire to the schoolhouse." She might mention that Harry Klein "has a metal plate in his head," or that Mavis Cox and July Watson were once married to each other. It was fascinating.

This Saturday, my mama's friend Maedell had come to sit with us. Maedell was thin, with a long neck that she craned out in front of her, bird-like. Her hair was brown and blond-speckled like a sparrow wing, styled in what Mama called a feather cut. She had a cackle of a laugh that she used freely, and anybody my mama didn't know or have a story on, Maedell did, because she was a Caldwell girl, born and raised, too. They'd talk and laugh, and I'd know more about people walking by than a person should, especially a little kid like me.

There we were, Mama and Maedell going on about people like always, when a car pulled up beside us, right in the next parking space. Maedell looked first, crooking her long neck around and out the car window, and then she laughed her laugh. "Would you look at that," she squawked. "I didn't even know James Kincaid could drive."

I jerked my head around to look, and couldn't believe my eyes, but there he was behind the wheel of a dark green Ford, a 1950 model, according to Maedell, who knew cars. He wasn't wearing his hat. His hair was thinner than I'd imagined. His face was sunburned brown, right up to the hat line, where it turned to what my grandma called grub-worm pale. He wasn't chewing on a matchstick, though several were scattered on the dashboard. He looked plain and ordinary, like any other grownup. I was struck dumb, something my mama said hardly ever happened.

Maedell craned her head out the window. "James, you've got a new car?"

"Yes'm," he drawled. At least he still talked like a cowboy. "My cousin Frank died and left me a little money, so's I could finally afford one. Got rid of that horse."

Just like that, he said it.

"Got rid of that horse."

I couldn't believe my ears.

He rode his horse all over the county . . . because he had no money?

I felt like I had just seen the bad guy shoot the good guy in one of my favorite Western movies. James wasn't a unique John Wayne kind of person; he was just a poor man who couldn't afford a car.

I thought I ought to be happy for James. But I wasn't, and when I told Bill about it, which I did the moment I saw him in the kitchen eating watermelon off the counter, he didn't believe it.

"It can't be. James Kincaid loves his horse, like I love Starlight," he protested, cutting a big slice right out of the heart of the melon.

But he saw James in his car soon enough.

And we stopped talking about the trip around the world.

Bill came up with other ways to get me to do his bidding and to talk me out of any money I happened to come into, and he was good at it, I must admit. Still, there were times when I would tell Mama about the ride, how I'd be bedding down in soft sand under those yellow cottonwoods while Starlight fed in good grass beside a running creek. She liked to hear about it.

A few months later, I was with Daddy out at the farm. Although he was the sheriff now, he still loved to go out to the farm to look over his cows. We were out of the dairy business now, but he kept a herd of cattle to sell off the calf crop each year for extra money. County sheriffs did not make a big salary. As always, we'd taken his patrol car down into the pasture, noisy as it could be, police radio blaring as it had to, and here came those cows, gathering up around him like he was a cow magnet. If I walked out there by myself, quiet as a ghost, even carrying feed or hay, they would scatter. I asked Daddy about it, and he said it was like he was their daddy . . . he fed them, doctored them when they were sick, looked out for them, like he did me. Those cows loved him, like I did.

All his cows had a name, some named for whoever owned them before, like the "Barnett cow." Some had the sweet names we kids gave them as calves, like Nubbin and Tiger and Twister, even though my grandma was always warning us never to give a name to something we might eat someday. Daddy checked them all out, doctored them if needed, and relaxed into their herd. It had been a wet spring, and there was plenty of grass, and the cows were already looking fat. Daddy was smiling in that way he did out here at the farm. He had me take a count of the cows to see if any were missing, and as I worked at it, a call came in on the two-way radio.

"Sheriff's Office to One-Twelve." One-Twelve was Daddy's call number. The jail, usually Mama, much as she hated to talk on the radio, was One-Eleven. This call was from the office at the courthouse.

Daddy answered, "Go ahead, Sheriff's Office." It was Daddy's deputy and his best friend for all his life, Bub Wallis, a really funny man who kept us kids and even the prisoners laughing much of the time, with his stories about what he always called "the calamitous times we live in." Bub was tall, taller than Daddy, and had such a serious face, strangers were caught by surprise when he made them laugh. He raised appaloosa horses and didn't really need to work, but always said he liked the company, which always got another laugh. Best of all, Bub was a whittler, always with his pocketknife, too sharp for us kids to touch, going at a piece of wood. I had several of his carved horses, including one of Starlight, on the shelf up over my bed.

"Colonel," Bub drawled. "There's a bad accident out on Highway 21 west at Cade Lake Turnoff. Two cars, probably some people hurt." Bub called Daddy Colonel. Nobody ever knew why, and he never used the ten codes on the radio, preferring to tell the story of what happened in his own color-ful way, sometimes with a joke or two thrown in for good measure. Today, though, he was pretty quick and to the point, and that made the situation seem more serious. The accident was only a couple of miles from our farm, so we were off, clods from the pasture flying out from under the patrol car, and cows scrambling out of the way.

As we drove, the closer to the accident we got, the more cars we saw stopped beside the road. Daddy said these were the gawkers. A smashed-up car sat farther up along the road, broken glass spread around. And beyond that lay a crumpled car in a heap, gas spreading like dark puddles all over the highway, the smell burning the inside of my nose. That car looked especially bad. You couldn't even tell what type of car it had been. One whole side was caved in. I could see that the car was dark green, even though the sunset there on Highway 21 West splashed red rays all over the scene.

"Stay here!" Daddy said, as though it was an order, a tone he hardly ever took with me. But I'd already seen a lot, enough to last me for a long time. I rolled the window down so I could listen to the people nearby talking.

"That's James Kincaid's car," said a tall boy propping up his motorcycle against the highway sign. "He's probably dead in there."

When I'd first seen it, my throat tightened and I'd shivered a little and I'd thought it was his car. I'd hoped it wasn't. But now I knew. And maybe he was dead. But then, deep inside, a thought came to me: *This is what he gets for selling his horse and driving a car.*

I felt even worse for thinking that.

Daddy came back my way, and he hardly got within hearing distance when I was calling, "Is it James Kincaid? Is he dead like they're saying?"

"It is James," Daddy said quietly when he got close enough. "He's unconscious, but we don't think he's dead. We'll know more when they get him cut out of there."

I could see the sparks of the blowtorch already cutting a hole in the crunched-up metal to get James out of there. I wanted to watch, but Mama had come to take me home and was adamant about it. We drove away as the fire truck washed the gas off the highway, making iridescent rainbows flash all over the pavement. Looking back, I said a little prayer for James.

———

Daddy came in late that night and told us that James had survived the crash but was in serious condition at Goodnight Memorial Hospital. Both his legs were broken and his head was cut up and he'd been knocked around terribly. There was talk about scars.

I was relieved to hear he was going to be okay. Mostly I didn't feel mad anymore about his driving a car and not riding a horse. I think it was beginning to sink in that James riding in a comfortable and dry car was none of my business. Bill said he was sure that when James Kincaid finally died, it would be by a horse, kicked in the head or something. Mama told him not to say such things, which I could tell made him want to say them more, Bill being the kid he was. But for the moment he shut up.

I forgot about James Kincaid for a while. But one night I had a dream where James was galloping alongside the highway in the rain, his yellow slicker flying out behind a big horse, its tail standing straight out. He was racing with a green '50 Ford running fast on the blacktop—with my mama at the wheel. Suddenly James turned and the horse bounded over a barbed wire fence, disappearing in a field of green rye grass. It was the greenest rye grass ever, green like might only happen in a dream. Mama kept on driving until she was out of sight.

The Saturday morning of the Camp Creek reunion, Bill came running into my room, having what my grandma would call a conniption fit.

"Come out to the yard! You gotta see this!"

I knew it had to be something for Bill to make such a fuss, so I raced out after him. There, hitched to the jail yard fence, was the most beautiful horse I'd ever seen, Starlight included. From Bill's slack jaw, I could tell he agreed. The horse was bright red. "A Blood Bay," he said. The horse was tall, maybe seventeen hands. He looked like he could leap over tall buildings. His coat shone like it'd been curried and brushed for such a long time you could see the sunshine in it. His tail and mane were long and blond. All the tack was new, still looked a little stiff like it might rub on your legs if you rode too long, but it was oiled up and had little silver inlays that shined like mirrors. The horse seemed to enjoy the spotlight, all glistening as he swatted flies with his silky tail.

"He must have cost a pretty penny," Bill said and patted the horse's hindquarters, looking what my grandma called dreamy-eyed.

There in the carport, talking to Daddy, stood James Kincaid, spiffy in a starched white shirt and what looked like new boots, fancy ones, polished up bright. He had on jeans, still dark blue like new, and except for one bum leg that now bowed out sideways at the knee farther than it should have, he looked like the old James.

Bill walked right over. "Mr. Kincaid," he said. "Can I ride him?"

"Sure, Bill, take him around the block. Real easy though."

Bill mounted up and walked the big red horse up the hill by the Seifert feed store. I knew he'd be running him as soon as he was out of sight, probably even on the pavement. Bill was not one to ride a horse slow and careful. I imagined him galloping across the neighbors' yards lickety-split. I could not help picturing it as me.

James Kincaid's words to Daddy brought me out of my thoughts. He was looking for work. Daddy was always finding work for people, and when he couldn't find something, he was apt to hire them himself. Wooly, the town drunk, lived out at our farm, doing caretaker work that really didn't need doing for almost two years, until Daddy finally found someone to hire him on.

"So, if you need anybody to work cattle, I'm ready to hire out," James was saying. "My leg was busted pretty bad, but now I can ride just fine, and 'course I have Red."

"He's a fine horse," Daddy said.

"Bought him with the insurance money from the wreck. Best thing that ever happened to me."

"Are you getting another car?" Daddy asked, and I was glad he did since I wanted to know myself, and was sure Bill would wonder, too.

"Nah," he drawled out. "I could have gotten a couple of cars for what Red cost me, but I think I'll ride from here on out. Little skittish about cars nowadays."

Bill, a grin on his face, rode up and hopped down off Red. I was checking close for signs of sweat so I could get him in trouble, but James and Daddy didn't even look our way.

"He's a beauty, Mr. Kincaid," Bill crowed. "A real beauty."

Daddy promised to ask around for James to see if anybody needed a cowhand, and James Kincaid, favoring his bad leg, climbed up on Red. He sat there in the Saturday morning sunlight, him and the horse shiny and bright.

Once James Kincaid was riding away, Bill started singing, and I joined in, "Back in the saddle again . . ." We watched him in the distance, looking again like a man who might ride around the world on a horse. Maybe he'd take off today, riding hard for some yellow cottonwoods.

Mama stood at the kitchen door, watching James through the screen, while Daddy watched her.

"I think I'll go catch Starlight today. You want to go for a ride?" It took me a bit to recover from the shock, since Bill never asked me to go anywhere with him.

Chapter Three

"Sure!" I said before he might change his mind.

That next afternoon, we all piled into Daddy's black Chevy and drove to Camp Creek, just for the one day. In the sunshine, we ate fried catfish with my daddy's family. Mama and Daddy rode around the lake in Uncle Merrill's boat of shiny varnished wood, Daddy smiling and Mama laughing loud enough so you could hear her on the shore.

It was just Camp Creek, and it was only one day, but we had traveled.

For that Sunday, and for a couple of years after, my trip around the world was on.

Four

Bill Gets Shot

"Bill got shot!" My cousin Carolyn ran out of my grandma's house to tell me. All the cousins crowded out onto Grandma's back porch to watch and listen.

I asked right back, "Did it kill him?" thinking she was trying to make me laugh with the story of my worst enemy, my middle brother Bill, getting shot.

"They don't know yet," she said. Her face crumpled, and she broke down crying. Carolyn never cried.

I saw my mother leaning against the other side of the porch with her hand up against her cheek like she'd been slapped in the face, and then I knew it was real. I stood there in my grandmother's yard, not crying or anything, just feeling empty and lost like that time in Austin when I was a little girl and got lost from my mother in a department store. But this time I was right where I knew I was, in my grandmother's yard, under the chinaberry tree, wearing my blue pleated Sunday dress with the rabbit pin, thinking I was about to eat Sunday dinner.

Yes, Bill had become my enemy that year. He had made torturing me his life's work. There was physical torture, which he dearly loved. He'd put what he called a "frog" in my arm, a little lump raised by a sharp quick punch with a knuckle. He'd have his friends check out the lumps. He liked to show me how a cow eats corn, which meant clamping down and squeezing on my knee until I yelled bloody murder. That was a favorite any time we had to sit beside one another, especially in the car. He instructed me in how a politician beats his wife, by grabbing my wrist and twisting the skin until it burned.

Worse than this, though, was the mental torture. He'd blab to any boy I liked that I wanted him to kiss me. He also told boys I detested that I loved them. When I stuffed my training bra with Kleenex, he told all his friends—and my true love, Donnie Smith. Of all the low-down things he ever did, that may have been the worst, keeping me hiding out in my room for a week before Mama forced me back to school, taking me there in the same car with the evil Bill.

My oldest brother Walter took part in some of this stuff, but being five years older and more like an adult, he didn't take it as far as Bill did. Having Walter know any of the naughty things I'd done was almost like having Mama and Daddy know them, since he hardly ever did any naughty stuff himself. He was class favorite, made all As, and when you got a teacher he'd had, she'd be likely to say, "I hope you do as well as your brother did," putting the pressure on from the start. It didn't bother me too much, but Bill sure did hate that "why can't you be more like your brother?" at school. It amazed me I could feel sorry for the likes of Bill, but times like that, I did.

Bill didn't turn out mean or anything like that, except of course to me, but he was a handful, Mama would say. He got into trouble, lots of it. Most of it was prankster stuff, trying to be cute or different from everybody else. He liked to run around free and loose, and not be what he called "cooped up." He rode Starlight all over the county with Mama and Daddy barely knowing where he was half the time.

Bill didn't like school and played hooky now and then. When he did go to school, he'd daydream, not get any of his homework done, and make jokes when the teachers called on him. It goes without saying they didn't think he was a bit funny. He was the first kid in Caldwell to have a Mohawk haircut in 1956, and a few teachers thought he ought to be expelled for it, but it didn't hurt anybody but himself, and that was because he looked silly. He took his school picture one year as a hoodlum, greasy hair and turned up collar, and a mean, pouty look on his face, eyes all squinty. My mother almost died when she saw it, knowing it'd be in the yearbook.

Bill was one to take chances and was always getting hurt. He had a cast on some body part every year or two throughout our childhood. And he did like guns. He had BB guns when we were real little, an air pistol for a year or so, and finally, he got a .22 rifle, and was out, he'd say, "reducing the rabbit population." He loved shooting at bull's-eye targets and cans or bottles, getting to be a real deadeye, to hear him tell it, and he liked to show off his skill when he got the chance.

A country girl herself, Mama was familiar with guns. But when it came to her children and guns, she worried. Long before we moved to the jail, she insisted that Daddy give us all lessons in firearms, how to shoot them and be safe, how to store them. Since we'd been in the jail, guns had come to be one of her biggest worries. Everybody who walked in the door had one on his hip, and there were a couple more in every car in the driveway. When a gun was confiscated or taken for evidence, it might sit around the house for a day or two. We knew better than to touch any of them, but they were there. With guns everywhere around us, Mama had kicked up the safety talks a notch or two. Yet Mama worried that Bill was gun crazy, as my grandma said.

The Sunday Bill got shot, he had taken a couple of boys out to the farm to shoot cans. They walked through downtown Caldwell, around the courthouse square and down past the fine houses on Buck Street, carrying the rifle. Nobody thought a thing of it. One of the boys was a neighbor of ours, Harry Perlick. Harry had a terrible complex because he stuttered, and he had a habit of standing with one foot on top of the other. He idolized Bill, which I saw as a serious character flaw. Harry's daddy told me himself that if Bill moved up on Cow Manure Mountain, Harry would want to move in next door.

The other boy with them was Pinky Taylor, a twin, and though I didn't know many, I thought the twins I knew were strange, and you could see why, what with somebody looking exactly like you, wearing the same clothes and all. It sounded like a nightmare. Why, you wouldn't even have your own birthday party. Nobody could tell me that two kids with the same birthday would get as many presents as one child would.

Pinky Taylor, and his twin Punky, really named Peter and Patrick, didn't look all that much alike, and didn't dress the same anymore. In fact, they didn't run around together much, so if you didn't grow up with them like we did, or if you weren't invited to their birthday parties, you might not know they were twins. You might think one of them failed a grade, forcing them into the same class. They were big boys, tall and skinny, getting close to six feet, and hardly weighing a hundred pounds apiece, and that's sopping wet with a gallon of sweet iced tea inside of them, so my grandmother would say. They didn't stand up straight, neither one of them, probably from being so tall so young. They had straight black hair with creepy widow's peaks in the front. They slicked it back with Brylcreem, and Brylcreem was not considered cool. The cool boys had Butch wax flattop haircuts. So, the twins were strange, but my brother Bill was friends with nearly anybody and everybody, so his going out shooting targets with Pinky and Harry wasn't odd, no more than anything Bill did. Even if Pinky wasn't the kind of kid you would like to see with a gun in his hand, I could have said that about half the kids Bill ran with, Bill himself included.

Bill and Pinky were shooting, and Harry was mostly standing around on one foot, watching the goings on. He got a turn with the gun only every now and then, since Bill and Pinky were competing. They were firing at paper targets on the barn wall but shot up those targets right away. They couldn't tell the old shots from the new and began arguing about whose shot was which.

So they decided to aim at cans up on the fence posts, walking around the pasture dodging manure piles and looking for just the right post, with Harry carrying a bag full of tin cans and coke bottles. He said later that he didn't mind carrying the sack, even if Pinky didn't carry anything. Harry was always a good sport. Bill and Pinky began to argue over which fence post to shoot the bottles off of. Bill did like to have things his way, I knew that, and he could be completely bull-headed about things. I guess Pinky could too. He was probably butting heads with Punky since before they were born, my grandma would mysteriously say later.

It turned out Bill thought they were shooting too close in the direction of the new housing project, down across the open fields. Daddy had taught him how far a .22 could shoot, so Bill told Pinky he was taking the bottle someplace else.

When Bill went up to the fence post to get the bottle, he turned around, and just like that, Pinky shot him right in the stomach.

"It was the biggest target," Bill said later, "probably all Pinky could hit."

A look of terror flashed over Pinky's face and he took off running. Bill could still walk but was in a lot of pain. "Gut shot," he said, as he and Harry started up the dusty lane towards the highway. The Harris boys came by in a pickup truck, lucky for Bill, and drove him right on in to the hospital. It was pretty scary, waiting for the doctors, Harry said. Bill still thought he was like a Western hero, gut shot and walking around to tell about it, but it wasn't long until he fell unconscious right there in the ER waiting room, and Harry was afraid he was dead for sure.

It took some doing to get our whole family to the hospital, spread out all over the county like we were that Sunday. Right before dark, Grandma and I arrived in her old black turtle-backed car she said was from before the big war. I knew she meant World War II, but Bill always teased her that it was the Civil War. All the things Bill said and did—like joking with our grandmother—were flying through my mind. I'd felt odd ever since my cousin told me about Bill, like I had too many thoughts in my head. As though there was no more room. I had seen myself in my grandmother's hall mirror before we left, and I looked hard at my image, to see what a person as scared as I was looked like.

When I arrived, Mama was leaning over Bill's hospital bed, unwiped tears running down her face. She stood and hugged me, and her usually soft body felt hard and tight. Bill had wires and tubes attached to his nose and stomach. His hair was slick across his forehead, and he looked white as the sheet covering him.

"Bill's going to make it," Mama said into my hair. "He will," she added, like I'd argued with her.

"I know he will," I said, even though I didn't know any such thing. I was scared Bill might die, and it made me sick to my stomach to see my mother in such a state.

When Mama released me, I went into the little bathroom off the waiting room. I felt better being in there by myself where I could pretend nothing happened and try to stop thinking for a few minutes. I washed my hands over and over and sat on the toilet hoping my stomach would settle. I felt off kilter, like when you're walking and step off the curb before you meant to and you're just crazy off balance for a while, struggling to get back on your feet. But when I heard loud voices from the little waiting room out front, I hurried out. Mama was holding Bill's rifle and was damning that gun and all guns, and my mother never cussed. Looked like Harry had propped the gun up against the wall by the door when the Harris boys carried Bill in. She was crying, holding the gun by the barrel with both hands, looking like she might smash the thing against the wall. Daddy moved in, taking the gun and handing it off to Walter, signaling with his eyes for Walter to take it outside. While Daddy held her close, she laced her arms around him, bringing one hand to rest on the pearl handle of his gun. She stroked that handle, her eyes looking like they were on fire, and I was afraid she might grab it and throw it through the plate glass window. Gradually, she closed her eyes, and melted into Daddy, seeming to hold on to him like he was the only thing holding her on the earth.

At last, a nurse came for Mama so she could see Bill before his first surgery. I sat on the arm of Daddy's chair and laid my head on his shoulder. I squeezed my eyes shut but couldn't stop the stinging tears. I felt as bad for Mama as I did for Bill. Daddy made a little humming noise in his throat. We all sat there in the dim light, nobody saying a word. That right there told you this was as far from an ordinary time for our family as it could get.

Even though I'd wished for it a time or two, said it out loud lots of times right to his face, I knew now that I didn't want Bill dead. He might torment me, frog me, embarrass me within an inch of my life, but I didn't even want him in the hospital, where it smelled funny, like cold alcohol on warm skin right before the needle goes in. It flashed through my mind how Bill had blacked out the teeth of all my friends in my yearbook last year, and I smiled like it was a good memory, which I guess it was now. They had looked pretty funny, especially Peggy Worsek, who had put on a great big fakey smile for her yearbook photo. Bill blacked out her two front teeth and made the others into little points. She would have laughed at it herself. I guess I wanted Bill home, tormenting me like always.

———

They brought in a doctor from Houston to work on Bill, the operation going on for hours that Sunday night. In a corner of the waiting room, Walter and I had found a fish tank. We got to know every fish in there while Bill was in the operating room, especially a big black mean one that picked on all the other little silver and blue fish. Harry, who stayed with us all that night, named him Big Bill, and we had to laugh. As the lights went low in the waiting room, I blinked in the dark, snuggled up next to Mama, who cried quietly nearly all night. Daddy came and went, with sheriff business and for a meeting with Pinky's dad and the Texas Ranger who'd been called in to handle the case against Pinky.

From what everybody said, Pinky was distraught. He first said it was an accident. But he finally broke down and admitted he'd been aiming at Bill's head but changed his mind and went for his body. It seemed like he wanted that clear so people would know he didn't miss his mark.

Pinky's father was terribly upset, waiting around in the hospital parking lot all night. Daddy agreed not to press charges, since Pinky was thirteen years old, and because he'd been having a hard time of it since his mother died. Psychiatric treatment was decided upon as the best plan. To me there was that twin thing, but it was never even mentioned. I guess nobody but me put any stock in my theory about twins being peculiar.

A message had been broadcast on the Bryan radio station that Bill needed blood, and people kept coming in all night to donate, a lot of them complete strangers. I studied them closely as they passed through the waiting room so I could see what kind of blood Bill would have running in his veins. They were mostly handsome Air Force guys from the air base across the river, but I concocted some stories to tell Bill about the scary, ugly horrors who'd mixed their blood with his.

Bill lived through the operation. I fell asleep right after they told us, even before Mama quit crying. We went home except for Mama, who stayed in the hospital for four days, sleeping in the room next to Bill's when she could. Bill wasn't out of danger for three days, three days that I spent making deals with Jesus over how I'd act, and what I'd do if he let Bill be okay. I was already getting a little worried about how I'd stick to these deals if Bill did pull through, but I kept on upping the stakes every day. I wasn't going to cuss. I wouldn't lie, even what Mama called white lies. I wouldn't call either brother names. I would do my homework without being told and wouldn't claim I did it when I didn't. I wouldn't talk about Jane Ann Dewars behind her back. I would never call Mr. Black "Moley" as he walked down the hall at school even though the mole on his chin was a favorite topic of every kid in school.

During those three days, the carnival came to town. I forgot about Bill as I threw baseballs for a blue teddy bear and busted balloons for a big pink dog. Late in the evening, I was going round and round on the Ferris wheel holding the stuffed animals, breathing in the diesel fumes, and I thought of Bill, of how I might never see him again, how he might die, how I was here, having fun. I got right off the ride and found Daddy to take me home. He saw my tears, and tried to make me feel better, saying there was nothing I could do, that it didn't do Bill any good for me to worry.

But instead of taking me home, he drove to the hospital. We stood at the door of Bill's room. He was pale and sheltered under a big plastic tent that Daddy said was filled with oxygen. I set the blue bear and the pink dog on the foot of Bill's bed, facing them right at him, so they'd be the first thing he saw when he woke up. If he woke up.

I lay in bed that night wondering about my deals with Jesus. If Bill's life depended on them, he didn't stand a chance.

Next day, Mama came home from the hospital, her eyes red but looking more relaxed, with the occasional smile crossing her face. She slumped at the kitchen table next to Daddy. Bill was awake. "Out of the woods," she said. They took out his spleen, part of his liver, and lots of other stuff, leaving the bullet there in his back, where we'd all get to feel of it later on. Mama stood at the kitchen table, as she told us this, and looking at Daddy, told how the bullet had ricocheted off his organs and around and around through his body. She was somewhat of an expert after three days with Bill's doctors, and she looked down at Daddy's gun, a .45 caliber, holstered onto his hip by his belt with the silver buckle. She told us all how much more damage a .45 bullet would have done, a bullet from a gun like Daddy's, it being more than twice the size of the bullet in Bill. She tried to sound calm and quiet, but I could hear tension, and maybe fear in her voice; could feel it, too, and I thought Daddy probably could, too, from the look of him. Bill didn't get shot because Daddy was sheriff and we lived in the jail, thanks be, but even I could see it looked like all guns were going to be a problem for Mama.

———

Bill stayed in the hospital for three weeks and got lots of presents, comic books, and candy, but he claimed he almost went crazy in there. First thing he said to me wasn't thanks or anything like that, but that he never had seen a blue bear, much less a pink dog. Bill never was much for gratitude. He got to stay home from school for three more weeks, but he couldn't go anywhere outside the house; he wasn't supposed to get out of bed. If I say he was a holy terror in those weeks, cooped up in the house like he was, I'm not giving him near enough credit. All that time, I was trying to keep to my deals with Jesus in spite of Bill's being what my grandma called a hellhound, maybe worse than he'd ever been.

I tried for a week or so not to get mad at him, let him pick on me without mercy and never once told Mama on him, but I knew I couldn't keep it up. I was soon canceling out on my deals with Jesus. So Bill and I were back to normal: enemies to the bone. I explained to Jesus that I would love my enemy as myself much as I could, but all our other deals were off.

———

After Mama and Daddy had some long talks, and hugs, in the bedroom, there were some new rules in force around the jail. Daddy's gun was not only hidden away when he took it off at night, it was locked in the drawer. Confiscated guns no longer sat on the kitchen table or on the wagon wheel coffee table in the living room, but were put in manila evidence bags soon as Daddy brought them in the house. I barely got a glance a Cody Crockett's shiny blue revolver the night he shot up the juke box at Charlie's beer joint before Daddy had it bagged and locked in the trunk of his car. It was a fancy gun, unlike any other I'd seen, and I was glad I got a look at it, even if Mama was eyeing me the whole time.

The gun cabinet in the living room, filled with hunting rifles and shot-guns, including the .22 Bill got shot with, was locked up tight, and nobody but Mama, and maybe Daddy (and I wasn't sure even he was privy to it) knew where the keys were. Over the next few weeks, Mama talked to each and every deputy, highway patrolman, city policeman, and Texas Ranger who came in the jail door, about guns and her children. A little crease between her eyebrows had developed when she was talking guns, and it was right about that time that I noticed it never did go away at all.

And Pinky? His family moved away soon as school was out that year. If Pinky went on to be a mass murderer or something, we never did hear of it.

Five

It Might Have Been Suicide

*W*alter, as older brothers like to do, was trying to get a reaction. He said, "Suicide is when somebody kills himself. The way some people do it is to slice open their wrists with a razor blade and let all their blood drain out." He looked at me real close to see if I was getting grossed out, and I was, but I wasn't going to let him see it. One of the things I'd learned in my short life was to never, ever let your brothers know when they got to you.

It was Saturday morning, and we kids were staying in to avoid the heat, hot enough to melt your shoes on the pavement and not even noon. Daddy had been out all night on domestic calls, twice to the same family's home. After only a few months, we knew these husband-and-wife fights were a big part of Daddy's job. It shocked me that people were so violent to family that they needed to call the sheriff, but they were and they did, some people over and over again. Rich part of town, poor part of town, didn't matter. The night before, it'd been the Millers, a couple Daddy had hopes for after bringing in their preacher for counseling. But that night, the neighbors on both sides of their house called, and Daddy went out around midnight and again at three a.m. Now Mr. Miller sat in our jail, Daddy had gotten no sleep, and from what I'd heard, Daddy was feeling sad he couldn't make peace.

Making peace was what Daddy told us being sheriff was about. Though not as exciting as arresting people, shooting at people and getting shot at, which I as a ten-year-old thought sheriffing was about, peacemaking was what he felt called upon to do. When I'd learned the Beatitudes in Sunday school a few months before, I felt good for him. "Blessed are the peacemakers: for they shall be called the Children of God." I thought my daddy might think it was worth the troubles of being sheriff, but I knew my mama didn't think it was even close.

Mama was cooking pinto beans and cornbread, prisoner food we were already calling it. It wasn't only beans, but, if we were lucky, onions and carrots and celery and sausage from the Manas Meat Market up on the square. Later, when Walter's wife got these jailhouse recipes, and I got a look at them, I realized they were not fancy at all. She used a cup of ketchup in the beans, rather than fancy sauces and seasonings. She made big pots of everything, especially on Saturdays when the jail might fill up overnight, what with weekend drinking and fights and such, her never knowing how many she'd have to feed. Anybody who was in our jail for any time at all gained weight and would start to ask Mama for their favorite meals, like it was a café or something. I think she kind of liked it, especially when they'd come back after being released, bringing their wives to get her recipes. I would later realize that all her recipes were meant to make as much as she could from very little, as she got pennies per meal from the county. Her one indulgence was on the occasional Sunday when she might go down to the Krueger brothers' barbecue stand for burnt ends and the cheaper pork pieces, giving herself what she called the Lord's day off. On those days, barbecue lovers on both sides of the carport could be heard to say "Praise the Lord!"

Mama turned from the stove to the phone on the first ring. She didn't want it to wake Daddy. She worried about him not getting enough sleep. We kids could see the call was serious from looking at Mama's face as she talked, eyes closed and lips tight. She hung up, hurried into the bedroom where we could hear her whispering. Daddy was up and dressed so quickly we knew something big was afoot.

"Who was on the phone?" I asked Mama while she helped Daddy into his suit coat as he hurried out the door.

She turned, closing the door, hesitated, and then sighed. "Oh, you'll know all about it in two minutes anyway. It was John Beaman who called. The man in his rent house is out in the yard threatening suicide."

The way she said it, "sooeyside," it sounded like a carnival ride, but her narrowed eyes gave lie to that idea.

"What's *sooeyside*?" I asked.

She turned away, picked up the phone, and said, "I better find Doc Skrivek. They may need him, and it's his day off." I recognized this as a stall. She'd do that when she wasn't ready to talk to me about something, putting it off until she could get ready for a Big Talk sometime later.

I knew I'd get nothing more from Mama, so I turned to Walter. As Daddy raced out of the driveway, screeching his tires on the pavement, Walter told me about the razor blades and the slashed wrists, with Mama frowning her disapproval. Once I recovered from the images in my head, I asked what I later realized people always ask when there's a suicide, "Why? Why would he do that, Walter?"

Now, Walter saw I was undone by the idea, and if I didn't know brothers better, I'd think he was being kind. "I don't know, kid, and probably nobody ever knows. There must be lots of reasons."

Much as I loved to see my brothers unsure and confused, it was not a very satisfying answer.

I heard my mama tell Doc Skrivek that the man had a gun to his head, and as bad as that image was, I was glad to hear it since it let me put an end to the razors and bloodletting Walter had put in my head. Once off the phone, Mama didn't want to talk about it yet, and really, by that time, neither did I, so I let her be, and took off to the movie matinee, like I always did on Saturday afternoons.

But I had suicide on my mind. I only half-watched the Western, sitting in my regular seat at the Matsonian Theater, which all us kids called the Ratsonian because it was so run down and was supposed to have rats, even though I never saw one. I would have loved it if I had. I always sat in the same broken seat that leaned back like Daddy's recliner, looking high and low during every movie for sign of a rat, my feet safely off the floor. Today, though, I kept thinking about how all the cowboys in the movie were trying their best to stay alive and here we had this guy trying to kill his own self, right here in Caldwell.

Even at ten years old, I knew about death. For as long as I could remember, on Sundays my whole family would drive out to the Masonic Cemetery, on the next hill over from our dairy farm, and stop at the family lots all through the graveyard. My brothers had already told me, happily, that our granny was there, under the big pecan tree, rotting like a dead cat would on the roadside, except that her fingernails were probably still growing even now. My daddy told me that all our dead kinfolk were spirits up in heaven, which brought to mind white robes and angels with wings. It was just as hard to picture as the rotting granny in the ground.

Why anyone would want to be a spirit or to be rotting under the ground, on purpose, by shooting himself in the head? I turned this question over and over in my mind, as I walked down the hill from the courthouse to the jail, past the feed store. Then I saw Daddy come up in the driveway, driving slow like a funeral procession, with a prisoner in his car. He got out to help the man from the back seat. Daddy's jacket was off, his sleeves rolled up, his shirt wet with sweat. The man looked hurt, walking unsteadily on wobbly legs, leaning on my daddy with all his weight. He needed a shave, his clothes were wrinkled and dirty, and they did not match, like something my brother Bill would put on when Mama wasn't looking. I got closer and could see the man's eyes looked funny. The pupils were really big, hardly any of the colored part of his eyes showing at all, and a bandage covered half his face and the side of his head. He turned away and groaned audibly when he saw me looking his way.

I went in the kitchen door real quiet, like I always did when I wanted to listen in on Mama and Daddy, hoping this time that I could figure out what had happened and why, just by hearing what they had to say about it all. He always told her everything, and usually it made me want to ask more questions, but I knew better. Mama hated how small our house was here at the jail, making it easy for us kids to listen in. She was always saying, "Little pitchers have big ears," when she thought we could hear them, which made me try even harder not to miss a word of what they might say next.

"Did he point the gun at you?" Mama had that shaky, worried voice I was getting used to hearing from her. Though she never said such a thing out loud to us kids, she was always worrying that Daddy would get himself killed in this dangerous job. She was sitting on the arm of his chair, like she did sometimes, her hand on his shoulder. I liked to sit there, too, on the other arm, but I had to hide out in my bedroom right now, close enough to hear them talking, but so they didn't know I could. I knew the living room was dark, the curtains closed like always.

"No, he never did threaten me," Daddy said. "He had the rifle held right up under his own chin. Had his finger on the trigger from the time I got there until he did it." My heart jumped in my chest. What had he done? "He yelled and raged, and then was crying at the end. It was pretty hard to watch, him sitting there on an old rusty tricycle in the yard, crying like a baby."

"Would he listen to you?" Mama asked.

"It looked like he was. I thought I had him talked into laying the gun down, right when it went off."

"Was he hurt bad?"

"Well, not so's you could see, but there was a heck of a lot of blood. The bullet cut a gash right up through the side of his face. Doc Skrivek took lots of stitches. Hard to believe he could miss his own head, but he'd been holding the rifle up there for over an hour by then, and it was heavy. It was hot out there, too. No trees at all, and the yard's burnt brown." Daddy was talking slowly now, stopping between each sentence, like it was hard to go on. "I kept trying to stay in the shade at the side of the house myself."

"Rita Jones said his wife ran off with some other man," Mama said. Rita Jones was my mama's friend who knew everybody's business or claimed to. My mama liked her talk, but my daddy didn't and chose to wait and see what was true. I liked her, too, with her tall, teased blonde hair and a mole drawn on her cheek, because she didn't seem to care a bit what people said. It was like she knew that maybe they were just gossiping, too. I got the feeling that if she didn't know what happened or how things turned out, she made out like she did. Making up a neat ending to things when there really wasn't one seemed like a talent a person could use, especially around the jail.

Daddy said, "Well, that's just talk, but John Beaman did say he owes everybody, so it could have been the money. His wife is gone off, that part's true. He kept telling me she'd left him. House was a mess. I could even smell it in the yard in that heat."

I kept on listening in, but by this time, I could see that really Mama and Daddy didn't have any more idea about why this happened than I did. I had known for a while that they didn't know everything, and would even admit it out loud, in front of just about anybody.

"Daddy! Daddy!" my brother Bill came running in, loud like always, swirling in a cloud of dust from the driveway. "Is it true some guy tried to shoot himself and missed? Everybody's laughing about it on the square. They say he's going to have a scar like Zorro!" Bill loved Zorro, even had a cape and sword for a while before he thought he was too old to play like that. "Is it true, Daddy? Is he in our jail?"

"The gun slipped," Daddy said, "but it's nothing for anybody to laugh about. He meant to do it. You go out there to the jail yard and make sure nobody bothers him from the fence, Bill." Giving Bill a job to do was Daddy's way of keeping Bill out of trouble, and it worked really well. I'd tried it with Bill myself, but I guess I didn't have the knack. He wouldn't listen to a word I said. But, for Daddy, Bill was out the door.

"Had he quieted down when you put him in the cell?" Mama asked.

"Doc Skrivek gave him a shot, but he was still pretty desperate. He's upset that I came over there today, angry he's here in jail. He's mad at himself for not even doing this right. That's what he said, 'Can't even kill myself.' Poor fella." Daddy was sounding downright tired now. "You know he came to our church a time or two." Daddy shivered out loud, and I guessed that his sweaty wet shirt was getting cold in the air-conditioning by now. He liked to keep it freezing cold in the living room, what with his wearing a suit in the summertime and all.

Mama tried to make him feel better, even if she didn't sound so good herself. "They'll be able to help him in Austin. You'll take him up to the state hospital tomorrow?"

"Yes," Daddy sighed, sounding downright sleepy now. "Doc should have the commitment papers by then, and I don't think he ought to have to stay here in jail any longer than he has to. So far, he's only hurt himself."

I had heard the old-timers who played dominos up at the old First National Bank building say that Daddy coddled the crazy ones. I knew there were people who seemed normal, but who would go crazy every couple of years. When Mama gave us the Big Talk about some raving lunatic in the jail, she'd say they forgot to take their medicine. Daddy said things got to be too much for them, but he'd never tell me what those things were. Daddy never liked to put those people in the jail like criminals. He'd drive off up to Austin on the weekend or in the middle of the night and wait for hours in the parking lot of the state hospital, talking to the crazy people while they waited for the psychiatrists to open up the hospital.

––––––––

First thing next morning, Daddy and the suicide, slumped in the back seat, rode off to the state hospital. I knew the back seat had no door handles and the windows didn't roll down.

The man stayed at the Austin state hospital for three months, till one day during an outdoor exercise period when he walked off the hospital property onto Guadalupe Avenue. I loved to ride down that street when we went to Austin because it was so busy what with all the college students and the mental patients. Sometimes, it was hard to tell them apart, and when I said that, my mama laughed. The suicide's name kept on showing up on the state hospital bulletin of escapees, but he was never heard from again. Nobody ever knew for sure what happened to him, but we all wondered, especially me.

Wondering was something I was doing a lot of. Here in the jail we bumped up against lots of stories that didn't have neat endings, or if they did, we didn't know what they were, just like this suicide. I spent hours staring off into space, pondering what might have happened. Mama might tell me to "snap out of it!" when she walked by, and then she'd mutter something like "damned jailhouse." And Mama never cussed.

I'd had some practice wondering, even before the jail. Ever since I could remember, we'd all have Sunday dinners at noon, at my grandma's house in Deanville. The times Daddy could get away, he'd join us out there. After dinner, he would sit napping on the porch (my grandma called it the gallery) in the shade of the big chinaberry tree, in a straight-backed chair, leaning against the railing. When he'd wake up, he'd tell me what his dreams had been about.

"I dreamt," he'd start out, and then he'd tell me a fine story that I suspected he was making up as he went along. In one of my favorites, he met an

Indian princess at the feed store in town, and she offered him beautiful beads that would cure all his ills, if he would bring her bird feathers, especially blue ones. That day, he sent me off searching for bird feathers, probably so he could get back to his nap, I now realize. I liked the dream princess with shiny black hair so long she could sit on it, offering the secrets of health and long life in exchange for bird feathers. But this dream, like all Daddy's dreams, didn't end. Instead, he'd ask me what I thought "might be" and I'd have to make up an ending. I thought up a big, beautiful blue jay, a tame one that talked like a parrot for the Indian princess. My endings were always happy. Daddy said I was real good at it. He'd give me dark, sad dreams that were hard to end happy, to test me.

"It might have been that way," he'd say after, and it made me feel good.

Daydreaming was what Mama called this, smiling. If riding around town looking at big houses, with no jailhouse attached, picking out which one she wanted to live in was daydreaming, then I knew she had done it, too. But if daydreams were supposed to make you feel better, they didn't seem to work on Mama.

Coming by daydreaming from both my folks, I thought it might be that the suicide did just fine when he left the hospital. It might be that he was happy and went to hall dances where pretty girls looked at the scar on his cheek, thought it was mysterious and wanted to touch it. It might be that he danced all night with the prettiest girl who threw back her head laughing when he spun her around.

Maybe they got married and had kids and he thanked the Lord every day for the near miss in the rent house yard in Caldwell.

Six

Jody

*E*verybody in town said Jody was simpleminded. Her own mama had called her stupid and would grab her by the ear and twist it hard right in the grocery store where anybody could see. Years later I thought, uncomfortably, that it was lucky for Jody that her mama died young.

Miss Ella Darwin, Jody's social worker, had her office next door to my daddy's in the courthouse. She told me that Jody was slow to learn and born that way, that she couldn't anymore help the way she was than any of us can, and that she ought to be treated the same as the next person. Miss Ella, known throughout the county as The Welfare Lady, was tough as nails about money matters, but when it came to looking out for people who couldn't look out for themselves, she was as sweet and caring as she could be. It seemed to me that Miss Ella's job was just like Daddy's, without the gun.

Jody's mama had died of cancer years before. And now that Jody's daddy had taken sick and was in the hospital, Miss Ella and everybody else in town was wondering what was going to become of the girl. I worried myself that a person could lose their entire family. My brother Walter remembered when Jody had tried to start the first grade after he did, although she was older. Walter said her daddy even rode on the bus with her, something nobody had ever done before. She didn't last too long in school, even with her daddy coming down to help her learn her way around. Kids teased her, Walter said. He remembered the cruel word "retard" had been whispered, and even said out loud.

Jody was a pretty girl, tall and slim, with thick blond hair pulled back in a long ponytail, but it was usually unkempt and uneven. When I saw her,

I always thought it was sad she didn't have a mother to cut it off straight across the bottom like my mama did. When I would see her at Miss Ella's office, she would tell me stories, mostly about her chickens. She seemed to be frightened of people in general, but I was just a little kid, hanging around the courthouse. She knew her chickens all by name, and she would tell me what they ate, how much, where they laid their eggs, everything, down to the last detail.

Word was that Jody's daddy wasn't long for this world. Their neighbor, Al Sorenson, a chicken farmer with no family of his own, offered to take Jody in. She'd been staying with him ever since her daddy had been in the hospital. Jody's daddy planned to appoint Al as Jody's legal guardian. Miss Ella thought that a fine plan, especially when Al, who hardly ever said a word, gave her a long and detailed story about how Jody had been coming over to visit his chickens all her life, happily spending time with them and gathering their eggs. Jody herself told Miss Ella much the same thing, and how she was thrilled to be moving into the little house out behind Al's big house. The fact that Al's little place had once been a henhouse made it even better.

Al had another chicken house now, fancy, brand-new and air-conditioned, with more chickens than any other farmer in the county. He had hired hands and everything. People called him The Chicken Man, and they called his hired hands chickenboys. Even my brothers had been chickenboys for a few days one summer, debeaking chickens. This is when chickens are grabbed up by their feet and carried out squawking to a machine that burns off the tips of their beaks so they can't peck each other. I saw a few debeakings, even smelled the beaks burning when we went to pick the boys up. It was an awful thing, even for me, and I didn't especially like chickens, except fried with cream gravy. Walter said Jody would hunker down in the back corner of the chicken house, as far away from the debeaking as she could get, comforting the chickens when they came back in without their beaks. He said she looked sad and heartbroken all during the chickens' ordeal. Al told Miss Ella that Jody wouldn't eat a chicken, or even a turkey for that matter, and since she'd been staying at his place, he'd quit eating them, too. I thought that was probably a real hard thing for a chicken farmer to do.

Though it seemed a good solution for Jody to live with Al, some people felt it not proper for a girl her age. I wondered why, but my mama told me "Don't even ask." They seemed worried but nobody else was offering to take her in themselves.

In the end, Miss Ella told Daddy that Al's guardianship was legal. She said once Jody's daddy was dead and buried, the talk would die down like talk always does.

We all went to Jody's daddy's funeral. Jody bravely threw in a handful of dirt at the graveyard. She left with Al carrying flowers. The gossip would have stopped except that Sudie Ripper, the Episcopal preacher's wife, wouldn't shut up about it. She kept calling Daddy, asking what a sheriff is good for if he can't keep things *like this* from happening. She bothered Miss Ella, too, what with her concern for Jody and Al and their souls, and for the souls of anybody who might come in contact with them. My daddy and Miss Ella got to where they dreaded answering the phone and would cross the street or duck into a store if they saw Sudie Ripper coming their way. She even cornered my brother Bill and me at Skrivek's drugstore one Tuesday and went on for ten minutes about how our daddy was not doing his job. Miss Sudie was one of those ladies who didn't have any eyebrows of her own. She drew hers on with a pencil in a sharp arch, which my grandma said made her look like she'd seen a rat. Her tea-breath hot on my face, she went on and on—and I wondered why Al's and Jody's souls were in peril. Bill and I tried to back away, but she kept stepping forward until we bumped the pharmacy desk with our backs. I was so unsettled I'd forgotten to lick my strawberry ice cream cone, and it melted down onto my arm. Later Bill admitted she'd scared the bejesus out of him, too.

Mama didn't like the idea of Sudie Ripper challenging her kids and called her up on the phone to let her know that her children were not involved in any of the sheriff's business. In her sugar-coated voice she said, "I'm sure you understand." But when she hung up, she said, "Damn that interfering woman," and Mama never cussed.

Daddy told Mama that Sudie was out to Al's farm a couple of times during those months, driving up and giving Al a good talking to at any time of the day or night. I felt sorry for him and Jody, if she gave them half the scare she did me.

———

The situation came to a head on a Saturday when Jody walked all the way from Al's farm into town, several miles on a gravel road. Her white patent leather shoes, meant for church, were all torn up by the time she got to the courthouse. She was looking for Miss Ella, but her office was closed, it being Saturday. I was down at the courthouse, waiting for Daddy to get back from a call on a couple of Saturday-morning drunks. Jody proceeded to tell me how Miss Sudie had come out to Al's over a week ago, and that Sudie and Al had harsh words. It was the first time she'd ever heard Al yell, Jody said. Ever since, Al sat at the kitchen table, not talking or eating and not even getting up to feed the chickens. Jody told me not to worry, because she and the hands had fed all the chickens every day and had gathered the eggs. She said she'd made sandwiches for Al, but he hadn't eaten a bite. She said she knew he wasn't sleeping because his eyes were open. Jody was worried that Al was mad at her, because he wouldn't say a word. She said she decided to make the trip into town when the dog, Al's blue heeler that took such pleasure in herding the chickens, started chewing on Al's foot, eating clear through his house shoes. Al, silent, didn't budge.

I knew something bad had happened to Al. Jody was slow but she knew, too. But what could she do? She was hoping Miss Ella could help. When Daddy showed up at the office, I told him the story, all in a rush like I always did when I was excited. Right away, he called Doc Skrivek to meet him out in front and piled Jody and me in the car. He tried to drop me off at the jail, but Jody was crying and holding on to me, so we drove fast as Daddy could manage out to Al's place. Daddy kept looking at me in his rearview mirror, worried I was going along to see something I shouldn't, and knowing full well Mama was going to throw a fit when she found out.

As we walked up to the house, the smell told us it was bad. I'd never smelled anything like it, not even when Bill and I had found a dead cow that had been missing out at the farm. Daddy right away told me to go and sit in the car with Jody. Jody smelled it, too, of course, but she said her daddy had taught her never to comment on the odor of another person.

Daddy and the Doc came out with handkerchiefs over their faces and stood beside the car, and through the window I heard Daddy say to Doc Skrivek that it was hard to see how a man "just kind of melts." Those were his exact words.

He knocked on the window and when I rolled it down, he said soft in my ear, "You and Jody take a walk down to the chicken house while we get Al out of here. I'll call you when we're done."

Jody was quiet as we walked through the crowded, dusty chicken house. She petted any chicken she got near, talking to them like they were children. I thought people probably had been talking to Jody like that all her life. It was cool in there, and the air-conditioning kept the smell down, but neither one of us could get Al and that smell out of our minds.

We didn't wait long enough before heading back up to the house, and that's when we saw them carrying Al on a stretcher across the yard to the funeral home van.

Al had not been a skinny man, but now he was swollen terribly, and his skin was greasy and liquid looking, with bloody looking gaps where it had split, letting a kind of ooze seep through. His clothes were wet with it and stretched tight. Daddy was right, a man melts when he's not tended to right away by the funeral home.

As Doc Skrivek turned the stretcher to fit Al into the back of the van, we saw, sticking out from Al's swollen puffed up greasy legs, the bones of his feet, stripped nearly clean of meat and blood, white showing through like blackboard chalk. I sat right down in the dust of the yard, ready to cry. Jody sat down with me, patting my arm, like I was one of her favorite chickens. That's when I realized she'd been seeing Al like this for days.

I'd never seen a dead person. I wasn't supposed to see this one, and I hoped I'd never see another. It sure wasn't like all the Westerns I'd seen at the Matsonian Theatre where shot people didn't bleed and old folks dropped off to sleep with a smile on their faces. I worried about how they'd ever get Al in a regular-sized coffin.

I collected myself and grabbed Jody by the arm, practically dragging her back down the hill into the chicken house. I didn't want Daddy to know I'd seen anything. Maybe he'd want to talk to me about it. Or even worse for him and me both, he'd have to tell Mama. If she didn't want me to see a drunk prisoner staggering into the jail, what would she think about me seeing a dead body chewed on by dogs?

———

Daddy left Jody and me at Miss Ella Darwin's house. It had taken some talking from Daddy and me to get Jody out of Al's house. She didn't want to go. At Miss Ella's, she hung onto me and Miss Ella. She was worried about those chickens, of course, and knew in spite of it all, that Al was gone.

After Jody fell asleep on the sofa with a patchwork quilt thrown over her, Miss Ella talked to me long into the night about death and dying. I figured Mama had put her on to me, like I was another of her social work cases, and that I'd get Mama's version of this same Big Talk soon as I got home. Miss Ella didn't treat me like a child. She told me what she thought about death, how scary it was, even for adults, even for her, but how it was a natural part of life. She said when she was a girl, people almost always died at home, had their funerals there too, and everybody, even children like me, would see the dead body and go on with their lives.

"Anything that lives, dies," she said. "The world keeps turning." She tucked an escaped gray curl back into the no-nonsense bun at the nape of her neck and went on to talk about how your body returns to the earth. "Might not be pretty," she said, "but it's a process of getting there. Like Al. He's on his way back to becoming earth. Dust to dust."

I liked the idea, and thought of how in a hundred years, wherever they buried Al, there'd be nothing but dirt. I pictured loamy, fertile topsoil with cotton growing tall out of it, and maybe a few chickens scratching around in the dust.

Miss Ella smiled when I told her this, and so did I, surprising both of us that we could. Miss Ella's death talk would stay with me, and help me in the years to come.

Sudie Ripper took the whole thing really hard. She took the blame for the whole thing, and there were plenty of folks who agreed. It seemed that Al had a heart attack, there at the dinner table after Miss Sudie preached at him, and died on the spot. Her husband preached Al's funeral, and Sudie got Jody into the Episcopal Home up in Waco, even though Jody was over the age limit. She had her own little cottage with chickens in the yard, and Jody's hens soon were laying enough eggs for the orphanage kitchen, so Miss Ella said. Miss Sudie was not through making up for what she'd done, though. She offered to take the little blue heeler to be her own dog.

This news so shocked my brother Bill that he could not quit talking about it for days on end. He reminded me, and anybody else who'd listen, how once a dog has killed a chicken, it's no good; from then on it'll kill chickens, getting a taste for it, he'd say. "Well," Bill went on, "Al's dog has got a taste for human blood and will be going after it again, sure as shooting."

It was a joke I couldn't participate in, and that was a great disappointment to Bill, since usually I'd be right in there with him on a gross one like that. When Miss Sudie came down to the jail to pick up the heeler, and it licked her in the face, nearly wiping out those penciled on eyebrows of hers, I didn't even laugh at Bill's own funny eyebrow wiggles.

After she left, Bill made fake gagging noises until Daddy made him stop it. Anytime he saw Sudie and the heeler around town, he'd act real scared like he was afraid the dog would turn on him and try to eat him alive. I still could see Al in my mind's eye, hear Miss Ella's words, and I was just plain unable to laugh. Bill thought I'd gotten way too serious.

I had to give Mama credit. She made a real effort to hide the worst stuff from us and had locked the coroner's pictures of Al in Daddy's desk drawer at his office in the courthouse. But my brothers and me were just as determined to seek out this kind of thing as she was to keep it from us, and after lots of sneaking and searching, Bill found the pictures.

They were bad, maybe somewhat short of the real thing, but certainly bad enough. Even Bill was swallowing hard while he looked at each one. His face paled.

The next week, he and I ran into Sudie and her heeler at the feed store. Daddy walked up behind us and warned Bill he didn't want to hear a word about the dog, muttering something about it being in bad taste.

Bill didn't laugh or make the obvious joke at what Daddy'd said about bad taste like he would have before he'd seen the pictures. He just said "Howdy," to Miss Sudie like a grown-up would, and leaned down and petted the heeler.

Seven

Moving Out

You might think a big happening got Mama to move us out to my grandma's house, like Bill getting shot, or me seeing Al Sorenson's dead body, but it wasn't like that at all. Things were quiet around the jail, the usual drunks, brawlers, and wife beaters. Things were quiet that weekend it happened.

Jimmy Dills, a newcomer to the jail, got falling down drunk at the beer joint up on the square, and after Bub Wallis brought him down to lock him up, he swore out his cell window for hours—which wasn't too unusual, it's just that Jimmy, who worked at the cattle auction barn as the auctioneer, had the loudest voice you ever heard, and never did get tired or hoarse. Then, two fellows from a road crew down at Lions got into a fight after work, and when Daddy locked them up on opposite sides of the jail, they yelled at each other out their cell windows, not so loud as Jimmy Dills, but lots madder. Finally, Daddy brought in Marvin Miller, a wife beater. His wife, CeCe Miller, wearing her usual mud-spattered boots, stood at the jail fence hollering at him, and though I'm not the best judge, she seemed to be the most colorful talker of the bunch. The Millers would be famous, or infamous my grandma said, years later when CeCe died and Marvin's secret side girlfriend, Jenny McHugh, brought a covered dish to the house for the family like people do for funerals. CeCe's daughter was so irate about Marvin's girlfriend bringing food to her mother's funeral that she took the dish, said to be a meatloaf, and threw it through Jenny's big plate glass front window. The window was covered with cardboard and duct tape for weeks for everybody to see. Daddy's only comment was that the CorningWare dish it was in had held up amazingly well and was not even chipped. He touted CorningWare for years afterward, and bought Mama a set for Christmas one year. He had returned the dish to CeCe's daughter, who never returned it to Jenny McHugh, and used it for years in her own kitchen.

But this kind of thing and the language we were hearing was so common that we thought things were relatively quiet. Bill, as usual out in the jail yard talking to the prisoners, was getting a kick out of Jimmy Dills swearing nonstop, auction-barn style. I was asking questions about what was going on and why, and that day I was quizzing Mama on CeCe Miller's colorful language. Walter was studying most of the time, writing papers, and living the most normal life of us all. Walter was a good student. Daddy, hardly ever home for supper, hadn't made it one day that week. Mama was up half of every night opening the jail doors and answering the radio. It was an ordinary life; the kind people have who live in the jailhouse.

I never heard Mama and Daddy's fights this time, which is a miracle in itself, alert as I usually was, but I noticed lots of looks with raised eyebrows and heard heavy sighs. So the very next weekend, when Mama, my brothers, and I started spending Saturday nights at my grandma's farm, I didn't think a thing of it. I gave a passing thought to who might be manning the jail doors, but that was it.

My grandma had silvery gray hair. Everybody said she had it since she was a girl. She had what my mama called a stout build, and she wore sensible shoes and tall rubber galoshes around the farm. There were half dozen pairs of matching rubber galoshes in varying sizes out by the back door for her grandkids. A strong and capable farmer, she farmed cotton and raised chickens, selling eggs every day to the markets in town. She was a loving and kind caretaker of her elderly husband, whom she always called Mr. Maddox. But she was also sarcastic, ironic, critical, and funny. Her running commentary on all people, but especially people she didn't care for, was legendary in our family. We all had our favorite quotes. My three-times married cousin always told the story of our grandma's toast at her last wedding, Grandma raising her glass with "we hope this is when that 'she's old enough to know better' thing is going to kick in." Grandma famously told everyone that Mr. Maddox complained that she didn't listen to him. And she would add with a little smile, "At least I think that's what he said." My own favorite was how she'd say every single morning, "I slept like a baby. Woke up every two hours and cried."

It was a kind of adventure, staying out at my grandma's farm. She didn't have central heat, and her indoor plumbing was unreliable and sometimes you had to go out to the outhouse, and her phone rang when anybody on her party line got a call. Her ring was two shorts and a long, but I'd pick up the phone on anybody's ring and listen for a minute, covering the mouthpiece like our grandma said to. We'd go down to the creek for crawfish with bacon from her stove, help my grandma with her chickens, and ride her horse, which Bill said had to be the oldest horse in the county. My brothers and me thought we were roughing it, going back to our mama's time. It was fun, like sleeping over at a friend's house, or staying at Camp Creek. Daddy would come out to Sunday dinner and we'd all go home together afterwards. Much stranger things had happened than this, especially since we'd been jail people, so we kids were oblivious.

The novelty wore off pretty quick, though, and when we didn't go home with Daddy one Sunday in February, I asked Mama what was going on, and would we have to ride the bus to school that next day, and what about television, and I missed my room, and who was making coffee for Daddy? She, usually the source of all information, the instigator of so many Big Talks—didn't answer me. But her look shut me up. It was an exact duplicate of the look I was giving her. Her face said that she wanted to know what was going on, what about television, and who was making coffee for Daddy, but she didn't have a clue. How could our family live here, and live there? It was confusing, and unsettling, though I had trouble putting a name to it.

We did take the bus that next day, and for the next two weeks. We went by the jail a couple of times a week, picking up and dropping off clothes, books, and whatever we'd forgotten. Usually, Daddy or one of his deputies was there, and everything was as normal as could be. Nobody was fighting. Nobody was giving anybody the silent treatment. Everybody seemed normal, smiling and acting like our living out at my grandma's was the most normal thing in the world.

I missed Daddy. When I'd see him, I'd laugh, smile, and joke, and feel like crying, and I noticed that Mama did the same thing, only her tears really would fall after we left. Daddy still came out to dinner every Sunday, and he'd sit on the gallery, like always, and he didn't look any sadder than usual, but he did stare after Mama, following her with his eyes from the sink to the kitchen table and back to the living room chair all afternoon.

Finally, the third Sunday of our "jail holiday," which is what my grandma was calling it, Daddy broke down and gave me the Big Talk about what was going on. Daddy's Big Talks were more the "don't worry, Dolly, it will all be fine" variety, rather than information like Mama's. He sat beside me on the porch steps, with his arm around my shoulder, giving me a squeeze every now and then. As usual, he was calm and seemed like he could accept just about anything that came his way and not get flustered.

"Your mother's not happy at the jail," he said, so soft I almost didn't hear. "She worries about you kids living there. We both do." He sighed. "But it'll all be fine. We'll work it out." He was what my grandma called a dyed-in-the-wool optimist. By now, he was smiling. He had talked himself into it, and I was right there with him. Daddy had a way about him, making people take comfort in every word he said. If you knew him, you knew he could turn your head.

I told him not to worry, that I'd talk to Mama and tell her how much I liked living at the jail. "She'll come around," I said, putting my arm around him, but my arm didn't even stretch halfway across his broad back. The very size of him was comforting. He laughed his little closed-mouth chuckle, down in his throat, and I felt good about this Big Talk. I still didn't know what was going on, but I felt like I might not be the only one.

Next thing I knew, Mama and Daddy had rented a house across the street from the high school. A frame house, white, with a green asphalt shingle roof. It had a huge kitchen, and a hallway down the middle like our old farmhouse. My bedroom, twice the size of my jail bedroom, felt cavernous and empty. Just looking at it, I hoped we wouldn't be there long, and Mama said it was just a trial. My grandma said no, it was a tribulation. I thought the street was noisy, even if the house was convenient, there by the school and only five blocks from the jail. Daddy wore a path, coming and going. Within a week, Mama was wearing the same path, cooking and shopping and helping Daddy like she always had done. Daddy tried hard to be at the rent house for supper every night, and he'd come in during the early morning hours to sleep sometimes, and he always was there for breakfast, if you got up early. Lots of times, we'd find him asleep at the table, his cigarette burned down to nothing in the ashtray in front of him, fully dressed in yesterday's suit, his tie still tied tight around his muscled neck, his head in his hands. Eventually Mama got him another reclining chair, just like the one at the jail, so he could sleep sitting up, dressed for calls. But unlike the jail after two or three in the morning, he hardly ever took off his suit to lie down in bed. This way of living was starting to show on him. After a week or so, there was talk of having the jail phone ring there at the rent house.

———

I went to the jail to practice piano a couple of times each week, and wound up staying longer and longer, and then riding to the rent house with Daddy for supper. I liked being there at home (the jail), and I hoped nobody would get the idea of moving the piano up to the rent house.

Bill still went down to the jail every afternoon to run errands for the prisoners. He made his spending money and liked talking to the guys. He told us their stories, probably embellished, over supper every night.

Walter had decided he could only study at the jail, in his own room, and he went there directly from school every afternoon, and would stay until his homework was done.

Mama came in and out of the jail, cooking, keeping the jail records, and while she was there, she'd answer the phone, talk on the radio, open the door for whatever lawman arrived, do the jail laundry, and then rush back to the rent house to make supper. One of the prisoners' favorite foods was Mama's famous Frito Chili Pies, which she claimed to have come up with one day when she didn't feel like doing dishes at the jail. She'd take a bag of Fritos, cut open the side, pour in her jailhouse chili and top it with onions and cheese. All you needed was a fork. Around the high school, word got out about this dish, and soon, Mama was selling them to high school kids across the street from the rent house, adding café cook to her list of jobs.

One day as I was practicing my piano, Bill brought tobacco and rolling papers to the prisoners, and hung around the kitchen, where Mama was making the inmates chicken and dumplings. Walter was studying in his bedroom. Daddy came in the back door after having locked up two drivers who'd started fighting after a fender bender down on the highway. He told us he intended to let them out in half an hour, and Mama said in that case, she'd wait to feed the prisoners after those two were released, so we all sat down to wait it out and eat our chicken and dumplings. As Bill sat down, he urged me to keep on playing the piano, since hearing me play was part of the punishment Burleson County set for each crime. Walter heard that and said if that was the case, he was paid up for crimes he could commit into the next decade. Daddy put his arm around Mama, and they both smiled.

"If anyone's being punished by my piano playing, it's me," I said.

Suddenly, Mama's face got serious. She looked at us all, one by one, and asked, "Who's at the rent house?"

Of course, nobody was there. And nobody was there more and more of the time. We had gradually, to one degree or another, moved ourselves back to the jail. Even Mama.

"I hope you didn't pay the rent on that house for more than a few months," Mama said to Daddy. It was the first time I knew somebody could want things one way, and then want them another way, just as bad. I breathed a sigh of relief. We were coming back home where we belonged. We never stayed another night at the rent house. Frito Chili Pies turned out to be the only good thing to come out of that move.

Mama made a few demands, probably just to save face, since the whole thing was her idea in the first place, and she seemed happiest back there at the jail. She made Daddy promise that we kids would be protected from the worst of jail's bad influences, and that he would be home for supper every single night unless it was an emergency. I didn't say it, but I thought it was always an emergency, wasn't it? Daddy would lock any loud, cussing prisoner in the one cell with the window that wouldn't open. Bill would do his homework before he went out into the jail yard.

I was pretty sure things were back to normal and would stay that way for the next fifteen years, although Mama would never have used the word *normal* for a family living in the jail.

Eight

Belle

I could see the girl sitting at our kitchen table, and she was pale, white as a sheet. She probably was colorless all the time, because she had red hair, and people with red hair can be really pale, but there wasn't a bit of color on this girl's face, unless maybe it was gray. And she talked in a low, dull voice, like she just woke up from a long sleep. She looked around the table, stopping with my daddy, who was shushing the other men in the kitchen, just like he did us kids when we were talking and shouldn't be.

"Tell us exactly what happened, Belle," he was saying in the quiet voice he used in awful situations, like he thought the weight of his voice might make the problem worse. I got the feeling, looking at Daddy's sad eyes and hurting expression, things were bad. The way he leaned across the table, nobody else in the room could see the girl, and Daddy could block your view. He was what my grandma called a heavyweight, tall and substantial; some might say he was too heavy, but he didn't look soft at all, and had really big arms with hard muscles that had to have his suit coats made special for them. He had a kind of sad face, as though his heart had just broken, and a soft voice and a gentle manner, even with the prisoners. He was especially gentle with kids. As his daughter, I knew that, and anybody could see this girl needed soothing now, tonight here in the jail kitchen. He gathered up her two little shaky hands in one of his big steady ones.

When this girl, Belle Crowell, and her parents had arrived at the jail earlier that night, her daddy was carrying on in a really scary way, yelling even at my mama. Belle was crying her eyes out. Mama talked to Daddy on the radio, but before he could get there, Mr. Crowell called every lawman in town, and they were all here now crowded around in our kitchen.

The police chief, Bo Davis, was pacing and looking antsy as could be. The highway patrolman, Henry Marley, leaned against the wall, his uniform pressed just so. New in town, he was the youngest highway patrolman we'd ever seen. He looked like he was about to explode with excitement. Granite Bailey, the part-time-constable, part-time-security guard, who even I knew only got called when nobody else was available, leaned his forearms on the table, grim and tight-lipped, staring at Belle through glasses he had taped up on one side with a Band-Aid. Even Daddy's office deputy, Bub Wallis, who usually only took care of the business end of things, sat hunched over in one of our kitchen chairs, holding his hat in his hands and turning it around and around, just like I'd seen cowboys do in Western movies. They looked like a posse in one of those films, and the girl just kept looking at one of them and then the other but wouldn't say a word. There at the head of the table, she looked like the guest of honor at some terrible banquet.

"You men move on into the other room while I talk to Belle," Daddy said, standing up suddenly, giving them all a start. Daddy's deputy and the constable slipped out, looking relieved to get out of there. Bub Wallis sighed, took out his pocketknife and started carving on a little round piece of wood, catching the shavings in his hat. Marley, the highway patrolman, who'd been leaning against the wall by the door, shifted himself onto the other side of the door. Bo Davis moved into the doorway, out of the girl's sight, but where he could still see and hear everything, and I don't think he looked any too happy even to make that much of a move. I myself was standing in my dark bedroom doorway, right down the hall, taking it all in, or as much as I could without anyone seeing I was doing it.

Mama was standing in the hallway, too, but had her back to me. She'd sent me to my room soon as Belle and her parents had arrived, and Mama was very serious about getting me out of this situation, more than I'd ever seen her. So, I knew there was more to it than Belle's daddy yelling at her, scary as that was, but people yelled around the jail all the time.

Belle's mama, a real thin woman in a wrinkled print dress that was way too big for her, stood right behind her daughter's chair. Even though she faced all these men, she kept glancing down or up and around, never looking anybody in the eyes. Jimmy Crowell, Belle's daddy, was skinny, too. He looked starved, like an old dog we had that had gotten lost in the woods that later showed up at the farm with a wild look in its eyes. Jimmy Crowell's eyes were all swollen from crying, but he had that same wild look. He was shaking in his chair, trembling like a leaf, not just his hands, but all over.

He jumped up from his chair now, scaring the life out of me. Even Bo Davis, there in the doorway, flinched back against the wall. I thought this whole group was jittery, and it showed. Jimmy Crowell shifted from foot to foot and yelled in a voice that was as shaky as he was, "We all know what happened, Sheriff. She's been raped! Now let's go get him." Probably from crying, his nose was dripping, all the way down over his lips. With every head shake, drips would fall onto our kitchen table.

It was almost too much. I turned my head away, but only for a second, and then looked right back. Though we'd been in the jail two years, I'd never seen anything like this, not with so many people involved and all of them this mad and fired up. You could feel the jangled energy all the way down the hall to where I stood. It was like seeing lightning and waiting to hear the crack of thunder. I didn't know what rape was, but I'd heard the word, and knew it was something terrible, like murder, but worse because it was shameful, not just mean. This rape had Mama and Daddy upset worse than I'd ever seen them be. Mama kept looking back down the hall to where I was supposed to be in my room, and I knew if she saw me, she might put me in the car and drive me over to my grandma's house. She'd done it before.

In his calmest voice ever, Daddy said, "Just let Belle tell me what happened. Sit down and let her tell it." Belle looked up at him with her blood-red eyes peering out of that colorless face. Like her mama and daddy, she was bony, but she didn't look gaunt and sickly like they did, maybe because she wasn't old like they were. She probably was a teenager, I guessed, maybe five years older than me.

She squeezed her eyes shut and started to talk.

"I worked my regular shift at the café, and then waited in the back for Mineola to finish up. I'd been driving her home. Every night. I've got my own car. Bought it with my own money." She opened her eyes and kept talking, kind of dreamy like now.

I knew she meant the Ranch Café, where Daddy and everybody else went for coffee, and I knew the big cook, Mineola, with the shiny black skin. She'd make me special blueberry pancakes on Saturday mornings. I always thought she looked like an African princess, so tall and straight backed, her hair slicked back into a knot on her neck. But in 1958, in Texas, even I knew, young as I was, nobody white thought of colored café cooks as queens or princesses, or as much of anything except cooks and maids and such as that. Most people didn't even come in contact with other races, but my family did. Here at the jail, we came in contact with every kind of person there was.

"I drove her down to the Flat, where she lives. You know where she lives, Sheriff?" Daddy nodded, and she went on. "She sat in the back seat, like always. She told me there was deep sand on both sides of her lane, so I was staying right in the ruts. She got out soon as I stopped the car and went inside. She never would stay and talk." Belle stopped and looked around, remembering where she was. When she began again, her voice was soft and weak. "I started back down and came up on a good-sized tree limb right in the middle of the lane. It wasn't there when I went in." She was looking up at the ceiling now, crying so hard her tears were making a puddle on the table.

"Just take your time, Belle," my daddy said, giving the men in the doorway a back off look. Marley, the highway patrolman, edged back into the living room. He was so young he was likely used to getting warning looks like that from his own daddy. But Bo Davis stuck right there in the door, watching, his eyes hard and shiny.

Belle wiped her eyes with her bare fingers, and right away my mama dashed over with a handkerchief. "I knew I couldn't pull off in the sand," she said, wiping her eyes. "One of the things my daddy has warned me about is getting sand stuck, so I got out to move the brush myself." Her shoulders shook and she dropped her head into her hands. "My daddy warned me." She looked up, tears running down her cheeks. "When I picked up the branch, I heard something behind me. I thought it was an armadillo or something. I wasn't scared," she said, looking through her tears right at her daddy. "Then something hit me here," she pointed at the back of her head. "I was out for a little while, I don't know how long. I must have fallen down, but I came to real fast, like no time had passed, and he was on me. I just started screaming, but . . . " She had been talking real fast, not even stopping to breathe, like she was trying to get it all out while she still could. Now she fell silent.

"Enough!" her daddy yelled, spraying spittle all over. "You've got enough. Get out there after him."

Daddy didn't stop focusing on the girl. "Who was it, Belle? Did you know him?"

"It was Harold, Mineola's boy."

I'd seen Harold, and knew him to be big and muscular, probably could lift a good-sized tree limb easily. He hadn't been in jail, but his mother had asked Daddy to talk to him when he wanted to quit school a year or so ago. I remember thinking he looked way too old to be in high school, even then, and turns out he really was.

"He could be in Mexico by now!" Belle's daddy hollered. Half the people in the room looked as if they'd been shot. Bo Davis pushed his way into the kitchen to stand right next to Belle's daddy.

"The boy doesn't even have a car," Daddy said. "I'm sure he's down in the Flat somewhere and will probably come in peaceable when we find him." He stood up, took a slow, deep breath, and faced the group of men in the doorway, where they'd clumped up. "So," Daddy said slowly, like he was talking to a group of kids. "Don't get carried away, and no guns!" He raised his voice on the last two words, and I knew that he meant business, even if these fellows didn't, but I hoped they did. "We have no reason to think the boy is armed." With that, the men rushed to the door.

Daddy smiled a little, and I knew he was thinking how he'd blocked their cars with his, so they'd just have to wait. He whispered to Mama, "Hopefully we can find him before they get too worked up. They're so damned excited, him being a Negro and all. I know most of the empty houses in the Flat, and I'll bet he's in one. I better try to cool these guys down some before we take off."

"Go on then," Mama said and kissed him real quick, and he was gone. I walked out into the hall.

"Aren't you supposed to be in bed?" Mama said. But she didn't sound mad. She hugged me, smoothing my hair back from my face. Then we went together to stand at the front window, watching as Daddy talked to the men, leaning in close to each one in turn, taking the longest time with Bo Davis, who stood with his hands on his hips, rubbing his right hand on the butt of his gun.

Even I could see this whole thing was worse because Harold was a Negro and Belle was a white girl, just about as white as they come. We didn't focus on race that much in our family, what with the criminals and the victims coming in all colors. I knew lots of people who did, though. I knew lots of people thought white people were the only good people. Living in the jail for any time at all put lie to that idea.

We watched them all drive away in a line, following Daddy's black Chevy with its radio antenna whipping in the wind, and then all of their antennas doing the same. The only time I'd ever seen so many police cars at one time was in the county fair parade. They weren't blaring their sirens and their red lights weren't on, but they got your attention, the lot of them, together all at once.

"Don't be scared," Mama said into my hair, and I told her I wasn't, but I thought she was talking to herself just as much as me. Then she started in on how Daddy could calm people down, bring them in without a struggle, and I said I knew that, but she kept on going, saying how he never even had his gun out of the holster in the whole time he'd been sheriff, and did I remember all the times he'd called people on the phone, talk to them a few minutes, and they'd come down to the jail on their own and turn themselves in?

"Sure," I said. I always tried to be in on everything that happened around the jail. Sometimes I'd hear Daddy saying to some hard-eyed criminal, "You don't want to let your mama down," and they'd cry and come in and promise to change their life. Or to find out something he needed to know, he might say to a mother, "I just want to help your boy," and she'd tell him anything he wanted to know. I knew Daddy was more likely to use family as a weapon than he was his gun, and I was glad of it, since it seemed safer. Even though I'd been watching how Daddy worked for two years, tonight was a different story.

Mama and I went back into the kitchen, where Belle was still sitting at the table with her mama. I looked at her, trying not to stare like the men had been doing, but wanting to get a good look at her all the same.

I had seen beat-up people before, more than Mama knew I had, and Belle didn't look that bad, nothing like last month when Mrs. Hinkel had sat right there at that same kitchen table after her husband had beat her up. She'd been a sight to see, with her lips swollen up, both eyes black and puffy, and a tooth gone. All the time she was talking to Daddy, she kept sticking her tongue through that hole where the tooth had been. One of her arms was just hanging there, but she kept saying, "He didn't break it," like that was a point in her husband's favor. My mama was worried about her ribs being broken and poking through her lungs, but Mrs. Hinkel kept saying over and over, she was okay, she was okay. There had not been any big posse of lawmen that night. The constable had brought her down to the jail, and when her sister wasn't home, she called her husband and he came to pick her up. Nobody had to search for him; he walked right up the driveway, carrying an icepack, and my mama asking over and over wasn't there someplace else she could go.

Now, I knew Belle was hurt and must be hurt bad, even if it didn't show on her like it did on Mrs. Hinkel. Belle and her mother got up to take Belle to the hospital to get checked out. My mama told them both things would look better in the morning, something she always told me, and usually she was right, but I wasn't too sure this time.

When they were gone, my mama put her arm around my shoulders, and sat me down in the same chair Belle had been sitting in for all that time. It wasn't even warm. Still holding on to my hands, Mama sat across from me and told me that this man Harold had hurt Belle in a terrible way.

"Do you mean rape?" I asked her.

"Well, yes," she said. "Do you know what that is?"

"Yes, I do," I lied. I didn't want Mama to have to tell me about it. I was embarrassed that she might try to. I thought it might have to do with kissing but mixed up with hitting or maybe worse. Something to do with a person's private parts. I knew what I had heard tonight: Harold had hit Belle in the head with something, and he was on her when she woke up, and that seemed to be the worst part. I had this inkling that it might be like cattle breeding but I couldn't figure out how that could be possible.

Mama kept looking at me, a puzzled expression on her face. She seemed more than a little worried about how much I knew, and how I knew it. I thought she might just dive right into a Big Talk about rape, but she didn't.

"We can just hope there's no baby," she said, and I didn't have the least idea what she meant.

They found Harold even before the dogs arrived from Grimes County to track him down. He had hidden in a vacant shack down in the Flat just like Daddy thought, not that far from his mama's house. They said later it was his favorite spot to hide from his mama. They fought often, to hear the neighbors tell it. They said Mineola expected a lot from people. Some of them thought she was too hard on him, and others thought he was a mean one and deserved every beating he got.

Harold must have heard one of the police radios through the window. He had crawled across the floor on his belly, gathering dust balls on his clothes and even in his hair and eyebrows, making him look gray-haired. He jumped out a back window, at a dead run, tried to bound over a barbed wire fence, heading for the woods at Copperas Hollow. The area got its name from the copperhead snakes that were everywhere in the area. Everybody knew that, but poisonous snakes didn't stop Harold from going that way, which showed just how desperate he was. Harold's pants, heavy old gabardines, caught on the fence and he went down. Bo Davis was on him in a rush, in spite of some confusion over the gray hair, and Harold's hands were cuffed in seconds flat.

It happened so fast that Harold didn't resist, simply lay on the ground, breathing in the dirt with every breath he took. Running out of the dark came Belle's daddy, waving a baseball bat over his head howling wild and loud. He scaled the fence in a crazy off-balanced leap, trying to pummel Harold, but fell on the ground himself. Bo Davis was stunned stiff, he said, for a second or two, then leapt on Mr. Crowell like lightning, pulling him off the prisoner, putting himself between the two, taking a few licks while he did it. Daddy finally wrapped up Belle's daddy in a bear hug, holding his arms at his sides while Bo Davis locked Harold into the patrol car.

"We got him. We got him," Daddy whispered into Jimmy Crowell's ear, trying to pacify him. That's when Daddy noticed Norton Duff, a layaround is what my grandma called him, standing beyond the fence, also holding a baseball bat and smiling right at Daddy, holding that bat up like he was offering it to anyone who might want to use it. Norton had been in our jail a couple of times, usually for fighting. Fights that he started himself. He'd also been arrested for nigger-knocking, a nasty business where a carload of what my grandma called no-goods would drive through Freemantown or the Flat and go after the coloreds with rocks, or bottles, or bats. Norton was the worst of them. Daddy said they were cowards of the worst kind who would always try to find one man alone, or even better, a boy.

Jimmy Crowell was crying, carrying on while Daddy held him tight. "I've got to kill him," he wailed. "I've got to be a man. I've got to kill him for touching my daughter."

"You know you can't do that, Jimmy," Daddy said, not loosening his grip. "I have to protect every prisoner, any prisoner, it's the law."

Finally Jimmy Crowell wore himself out. He told Daddy that Norton Duff had given him the bat, urging him to "kill that nigger" while he had the chance. Daddy was about to send Henry Marley out to search for Norton Duff, in case he tried to stir up more trouble, but Norton had disappeared.

———

Once they got back to the jail, all the lawmen sat in our kitchen, going over and over the details that night, so I got to hear everything, everybody's take on it.

"Good job protecting the prisoner out there," Daddy had said to Bo Davis, and they exchanged a look. "It's not always easy," Daddy added. Even I had heard that Bo Davis took no pity on prisoners, and he and Daddy had had their differences about their treatment. I heard Daddy telling Mama that tonight, Bo had done his duty and saved Harold's life, even if it was probably for nothing. "You think he'll get the chair?" Mama asked.

"Yes, I do," Daddy said. "More than likely. Way things are." I knew about the electric chair, and I pictured Harold in it. An involuntary shudder passed through me.

There had been a reporter at the jail that night, and he took pictures of all the policemen lined up against the jail yard fence. The article in the paper called it the crime of the century, and Mama said it was the first time they ever used the word "rape" in the local paper. In the picture, the lawmen looked tired and dusty, not at all proud, maybe even a little embarrassed instead. Bo Davis's eye was swelling up from Jimmy Crowell's baseball bat. Daddy stood off to the side, looking sad and out of place, not like a sheriff at all but more like a dairy farmer just helping out. And that's how he saw himself, even now.

Next morning, while Daddy was at the courthouse with Belle, her daddy and Norton Duff showed up at the jail. Norton banged hard on the door while Jimmy Crowell hung back. When Mama opened the door, he told her that he and Mr. Crowell wanted to talk to Harold, and she should let them into the jail. "Just talk," he sneered, making it clear that it was not what he really meant. Mama said, looking beyond Norton Duff and addressing Jimmy Crowell, "No, Mr. Crowell, only officers are allowed into the jail."

"Are you an officer?" Norton barked, moving in front of Jimmy Crowell and pressing up against the screen.

"Yes, I am, and you're not. No way in hell you're getting in there without the sheriff being here, and I doubt he'd let you in there anyway, Norton Duff, unless it was to lock you up!" She slammed the door and rushed to the phone to call Daddy.

From my usual place at the front window, I watched the two of them move out by the jail yard fence, Norton yelling and Jimmy Crowell follow-ing. They yelled at Harold's window, calling him every name in the book. Harold never showed his face. Norton Duff went to his car and got out his baseball bat and began to hit hard on the jail yard fence poles. Whap! Whap! I locked the door, including the dead bolt. Mama came in, checked the door, and nodded her approval at me.

Just then, Belle and Daddy drove up for the official identification. Still banging on the fence poles, Norton was shouting, "That girl's daddy's gonna kill you, boy. He's gonna kill you!"

Her thin red hair flying behind her, Belle jumped from the car before it even came to a complete stop. She grabbed her Daddy by the arm, jerking him around behind her.

"Shut up!" she yelled at Norton Duff. "You shut up and stay away from my daddy. He's not killing anybody." She stood straight, eye-to-eye with him. "Don't speak to my daddy ever again," she spat out.

Norton's eyes bulged and his mouth fell open, as Belle dragged her daddy off toward Daddy's car. After a second or two, he stuttered a little and then hollered, "Bitch. You nigger-loving bitch!"

Daddy charged around the car and just like that had Norton's bat in his hand. He raised it over Norton's head like he meant to bring it down hard. I gasped in air, but Daddy lowered the bat slowly. A big wet spot appeared on Norton's khaki pants.

"Get out of here right now, Duff, or I'll lock you up myself," Daddy growled, in a voice I'd never heard him use before. Norton Duff backed away and walked around the far side of our house to his car, staying as far away from Daddy as possible. I was thinking it could have been worse for Norton Duff if Daddy had known how Norton had talked to Mama.

It was the last we saw of Norton Duff. Mama said later of the confrontation, "It's not what you say, it's how you say it." Daddy said it helped if you had a baseball bat in your hand.

Harold pled not guilty and never made a statement about the rape. His sister Bertha came down to see him in the jail, but she was the only one. A cafeteria worker at Freeman High School, Bertha was tall and beautiful like her mother, who never did come to visit Harold. Bertha told Mama, "We weren't a happy family, even before this terrible thing happened."

Daddy put a double lock on Harold's cell, for his protection, and except for the trial he stayed there until the prison van from Huntsville came to get him. I only saw him a few times myself, but when I did, I always was startled at how ordinary he looked, with his downcast eyes, much like any other prisoner. It was plain to see you couldn't tell by looking what people might do. Most of them had a kind of stunned look, like they couldn't believe it themselves. Harold had that look.

Harold was found guilty, of course, what with Belle's testimony and all. She came to court with her parents. Her daddy had gained some weight and looked downright respectable in his black suit. Belle seemed even skinnier and had started to look for all the world like her mother, in just those few months. She didn't look a thing like the fierce girl who'd faced Norton Duff in the jail yard. I still didn't get it, but everybody kept on thanking God there hadn't been a baby.

Harold didn't make any appeals and was executed in the electric chair. They put a piece about it in the Caldwell paper. The night of the execution was one of the few times I saw Daddy drink whiskey. He sat at the kitchen table with the bottle and a jelly glass decorated with red and yellow apples. Mama took calls for him. He never said a thing about Harold or Belle or any of it, but he drank until he went to bed.

Norton Duff moved to Silsbee, Texas, over by Beaumont. Daddy knew where he was because he got himself arrested for assault, and the Silsbee sheriff wrote to check his record. Belle went back to work at the Ranch Café. Belle's daddy got a good job at Pepsi Cola. That rape had really reaped the whirlwind, my grandma said, and when I asked what that meant, she said it changed people's lives. But, except for Harold's, it was hard to tell.

Later that year at school, during the noon hour, sitting on the wall by the gym where the pittosporum hedges made a little covered area with flowers that smelled of grape candy, Patti Seymore, a year older than me, told a group of us girls what she called the facts of life. She gave us the unbelievable story of how a baby is made, with detailed descriptions of men's and women's private parts. She gave us more particulars when we asked questions, but there was lots of guessing and beating around the bush, as I recall, because she didn't know everything either. But it dawned on me, right then and there in a flash: I knew what the rape was all about. That's what happened to Belle, that's what Harold had done to her. I thought about how it had been done, out there on that sandy lane, with Belle knocked out and then screaming. It was bad enough to get everybody so worked up, ready to kill Harold with a baseball bat, enough to send him to the electric chair.

"It's rape," I whispered.

"It isn't always rape," Patti declared, in her most mature voice.

But for a long time, death and violence and sex tangled in my mind. The idea of a man and a woman together meant rape to me, always with the vague notion of somebody getting knocked in the head and raw images of people yelling and then somebody dying in the end, a horrible death, as punishment.

It was Mama's worst fear, about the kind of thing I might learn from living in the jail, come to pass. Even Patti Seymore said living in the jail was making me crazy, anybody could see that.

Nine

River Mansion

*E*very time we crossed the Brazos River on the big iron bridge, I'd look back over to where you could see the bell tower of the River Mansion and watch until it disappeared from sight. It seemed like a fairy-tale palace right here in our very own county. My mother couldn't tell me much about the River Mansion, except that a rich family from Italy had built it before World War II, hoping to grow grapes in the rich river-bottom soil. What happened to them and who lived there now remained a mystery. Once when some trees on the riverbank were cut down, I could see the big doors that opened onto the lawn that looked out over the river. I made Mama slow down, and I stared until the pickup truck behind us honked his horn, long and hard.

Adding to the mystique of the River Mansion were the liquor stores across the highway from it. Brazos County, on the other side of the river, was a dry county, and our county was wet. That meant that people living in Bryan and College Station would have to drive the ten miles or so to the river to buy liquor. This gave the river side area a sense of freedom and license to be wild, get drunk, or at the very least, have a good time.

The main attraction of the River Mansion was the river itself. The water all around gave it a palace-like feeling, as though it had a moat. The big Brazos de Dios river ran wide and fast right out in front of it. The river could run brown and muddy, and smell of dirt and sludge, but late in the evening when the sun was going down, it could shine red like fire. On a bright day, the water might reflect silver, like a mirror. There were times the river would overflow its banks, flooding the river bottom for miles around. The River Mansion, on a high point, never flooded.

Sometimes, the river made fog. We'd be driving along on a clear day, get near the river, and be enveloped in an eerie mist, and then a few miles on the other side of the bridge, the air would clear again. Though you could barely hear it from the bridge, the river ran loud, swirling and gurgling. And it was dangerous, very dangerous, with whirlpools and undercurrents and water moccasins. Whether swimming or falling in, people drowned. Daddy would be down there, dragging the river for the body. It was awful if they never found it, and sometimes even worse when they did.

———

After Christmas break, there was a new girl in my sixth-grade class. I'd gone to school with the same kids since kindergarten, so a new person promised something new and exciting. Her name was Carrie Pidgeon, and she was interesting from the get-go. The boys called her Carrier Pidgeon, and she laughed along with them. I sat by her in the lunchroom, and she brought the oddest foods I'd ever seen. Her steamed asparagus and black seedless grapes made me look at my Velveeta cheese sandwich and Sunkist orange in a different light.

When we talked about her name and the boys teasing her, she told me her real name was Carat, like the weight of a diamond, because she'd been so tiny when she was born. She was still little, and fragile looking, with long black hair, which I noticed all the more because I was a big, solid girl, with too much curly blond hair on my head. My grandma told me I was sturdy peasant stock, like it was a big compliment. I wasn't so sure about that. Carrie and I couldn't have been more different if we tried.

She told me that her father (and she called him *Father*) was a bookie. She had to explain to me that a bookie was a kind of gambler, and I told her my daddy was the sheriff, and we got a good laugh out of yet another big difference between us. She'd been to ten different schools in her life already, while I had hardly left the county. She said it might well have been a sheriff that caused some of their moves, and although that made me uneasy, I was too fascinated to worry.

We decided to have a sleepover that first weekend, at her house. Her mama, whom she called her *Mother*, came to pick us up in a beige (she said champagne!) Cadillac convertible. We headed out towards the river, and when we turned off right before the bridge, I felt faint from excitement. We were headed for the River Mansion! As we approached, I saw the huge yard stretched right down to the river, where a swing of wooden slats, big enough for two people to sit in, swayed from a broad live oak. You could hear the river from anywhere in the yard.

The front entrance was just as I'd imagined. Wonderful ivy-covered columns flanked the front door, and the entrance foyer (Carrie used that previously unknown word) was filled with actual statues of river gods. Carrie's sisters gave me the back stories of each one. I was as happy as I could remember, as I mentally took notes on Achelous, the Greek River God. The River Mansion had more rooms than I could count, distracted as I was by the sight of the river shining right outside the windows. Carrie and her sisters each had their own rooms, each with a bathroom all her own, and when I thought of Bill, Walter, and me all fighting to get into our one bathroom every morning, I had to smile. I knew this weekend wouldn't be long enough.

Later that night, when I talked to Daddy on the phone, he worried about me being so close to the river and warned me not to go swimming under any circumstances. He said to stay away from the bank so as to not fall in. Even though that sparkling, swirling water entranced me, I told Daddy it was January and I wasn't foolish. He sighed, like he thought I might be.

We, of course, didn't go in the river, but I sure watched it a lot. Carrie's mother thought it was funny how I couldn't take my eyes off the river. Mrs. Pidgeon was as glamorous a woman as I'd ever seen in real life. She wore silk clothes and high heeled shoes. Even when she took her shoes off, she still stood up on her tip-toes as though her high heels were still there.

The Pidgeons had lots of company that weekend, and during the day they sent Carrie and me out to the Carriage House, a big structure out by the garage where many cars were coming and going. The room was bigger than our whole house at the jail. It had a pool table, and a juke box that you didn't have to put money in to work. Best of all, it had my favorite song from the late-night Nashville radio station the prisoners listened to: "Yes, it's me and I'm in Love Again," by Fats Domino. I played it until Carrie said she'd be sick if she heard it again. Mirrors covered the walls, and we danced in front of those mirrors all day long.

At night, Carrie's parents and their company met in the Carriage House until very late. The phone rang over and over. I couldn't sleep for listening to the river right outside my window. Cars came and went long into the night.

Sunday afternoon, just before Daddy came to pick me up, out in the parking lot among the fancy cars, I saw him: Audie Murphy, the movie star. I would say big as life, but he wasn't big at all. In fact, he was probably not more than a few inches taller than me. Even if I was a big girl for my age, his being shorter than even my brother Bill was a letdown. With a salt and pepper beard and bloodshot eyes, he looked like he'd had a hard night. After three years in the jail, I knew what a hard night looked like. Even rumpled, he was as handsome as could be, and had the whitest, straightest teeth I'd ever seen, giving him such a smile. Carrie's sister called his smile dazzling, and I had to agree. My grandma said later that it was probably the work of a Hollywood dentist.

Walter had seen every showing of *To Hell and Back*, starring Audie Murphy, at the Matsonian Theatre. If Walter told me once, he told me a thousand times that Murphy was the most decorated soldier in World War II. Walter was so taken with the movie he read the book, and more miraculous, Bill read it too. Audie Murphy was a hero around our house, and here he was, standing right beside Carrie's father, who everybody was calling Bird, when my daddy drove up.

"Hey!" said Carrie's dad. "We should get a picture of the two sheriffs in town—the movie star one and the real one!" Daddy, always a little diffident, tried to beg off, but after some shifting around on the stairs so Audie wouldn't look so small next to Daddy, everyone who had a camera snapped shots.

When we got home, my brother Walter could not believe that he had missed seeing his hero. While he paced up and down, holding the book with pictures of Audie in the army, he wondered if Daddy could find a reason to go back out to the river. "He's a real hero, not just a movie hero." In the pictures, when Audie was just a young man, and before people thought to put him on stairs, you could see he was short. Walter thought Audie's stature was a point in his favor.

"He's just a regular guy," he said. "Not even a big guy, but brave, and he saved the lives of his buddies. Size doesn't matter." I could see Walter was thinking anybody could be a hero, maybe even him.

One of the pictures of Daddy with Audie and Carrie's daddy taken that Sunday came out in the Bryan paper the next week. I was so proud. I thought Daddy looked more like a sheriff, a hero, than Audie did. Daddy didn't say a word about it, but I heard Mama ask if he thought anything would come of those pictures. I wondered if she thought someone would ask Daddy to be in a movie. But his response surprised me.

"Don't worry, Honey."

Worry? Why would she worry? But I could see by the way the little line deepened between her eyes that she did.

Electioneering had already begun for next fall's election. Even though in January it was still cold, people held rallies with candidates appearing at church socials and community meetings all over the county. The kickoff rally this year took place at the Cooks Point Lutheran Church. Mama had to tear me away from the kolache table to listen to Daddy's speech. A gooey, filled Czech pastry that Burleson County is famous for, kolaches were the only good thing about an election rally, and Arlene Morak's storied poppyseed kolaches were almost gone. But Mama liked us kids to applaud when Daddy finished his speech, probably so nobody could hear his sighs of relief. Daddy was really good at rallies face to face, asking each person for their vote, but he was hesitant and shy about giving a speech. Mama hated this political stuff more than even the jail stuff, but politicking aside, she enjoyed a church social, even if she had to be nice to people she didn't like.

All the politicians stood on the church steps, and when it was Daddy's turn, he moved up to the top step and started his usual speech.

"You all know me. I've lived all my life in Burleson County. I've tried to do a good job for the people of this county, and I will do my best to protect people and give each and every person a fair shake from the law. I appreciate your support in the campaign and your vote on election day."

His was always the shortest speech, and the end caught the crowd by surprise. Mama elbowed me so I'd start clapping and I did. Walter, having taken speech in high school, had tried to get Daddy to practice and "articulate," but Mama said he did just fine.

Jake Pickard, Daddy's opponent this election, moved up the stairs to speak. A hulking, tough-looking man with a droopy mustache, he had been the sheriff when Daddy was elected four years before. Mama said he and his wife, Edith, a bulky woman who looked like she could take Jake, tough as he looked, in a fight, had run a dirty campaign in that election. They'd campaigned asking how Daddy could make people obey the law when he couldn't even force people pay their milk bills. Mama herself used to lecture Daddy about being too soft, letting people "postpone" payment and still giving them milk. But she sure didn't want Jake and Edith Pickard talking about it. Still, Daddy had won. And the Pickards were none too happy about that, even now, four years later.

I could see Jake Pickard held some kind of placard in his hand. When he held the thing up, displayed before everyone's eyes was a blown-up picture of Daddy with Bird Pidgeon and Audie Murphy.

"Who wants a sheriff that carouses with known gamblers?" he bellowed. "And did you know the sheriff of this county lets his very own daughter spend weekends at this Brazos River Gambler's Den?"

My face burned red, and I nearly choked on my kolache. This was a new low for Jake Pickard, going negative at a church social, and even involving a child of his opponent. I looked at Daddy, hoping he'd get up there and tell how that picture had happened, how I'd spent the night with a school friend and he didn't even know her daddy, much less Audie Murphy, and Audie Murphy was a war hero besides. But Daddy and Mama kept their election year smiles pasted on and went about shaking hands.

That night, as we sat around the kitchen table, Daddy told me not to worry, that people at the Cooks Point Lutheran knew he wasn't a gambler. "And they darn sure know you're not." He chuckled. "Besides, there's no evidence that Mr. Pidgeon has done anything wrong." He said that people were probably right now wondering what kind of man Jake Pickard was, not able to talk about what kind of sheriff he'd be, but rather talking about the daughter of his opponent.

Walter agreed that it was good Daddy didn't respond. "If Daddy went on talking about it, people would say, *Methinks thou dost protest too much*."

Even though Daddy, Walter, and Shakespeare agreed, Mama didn't like it. "Even if we're in the public eye," she said, "we needed to defend ourselves."

"I'll never go to the River Mansion again," I said, "if it hurts you in the election." It wasn't an easy promise, because I'd been hoping against hope for another visit.

"Don't worry about this, Dolly," said Daddy, tapping his ashes into the star-shaped ash tray on the kitchen table. "You go about your business like you otherwise would. I'll worry about this election."

But I did worry. I didn't go to the River Mansion all that spring, and I didn't see Audie Murphy again except in the pictures Jake Pickard carried around with him. As a compromise between new best friends, Carrie Pidgeon spent the night at the jail a couple of times, and she was as fascinated by the jail as I was by the River Mansion, if you can believe that.

Daddy never mentioned Jake or Edith at the rallies, although he added a line to his standard speech about how he was dedicated to protecting his family and all of Burleson County. I thought that statement was vague, but it was as close to answering the Pickards as he would come. At a picnic rally at Deanville Hall on July 4, he got a loud cheer and standing ovation from a stranger in a bowtie. I asked Mama who he was, and she answered he was a gambler from Lyons, and beneath her election year smile, even she looked worried.

I worried, too, for Carrie. All those visitors at the River Mansion, cars coming and going, her family's frequent moves. And I knew about gambling. I'd heard about it my whole life, even before we lived in the jail. Just last year, Walter's friend, Julie Ventura, who lived in a big fancy brick house on Buck Street, woke up one morning to find her mother packing everything they owned. They moved that very day into a small frame house down by the high school. Julie's father, known to be a sometimes gambler, had lost their house in a card game. Just like that, and most everybody in town knew about it. But most gambling around wasn't that dramatic. Tables full of old men played Shoot the Moon for money up by the courthouse square, and nobody seemed to care a thing about it. There was bingo at church halls. My own mother might win five dollars in a domino game with the Chief of Police's wife and her friends, and that couldn't be illegal, could it? The slot machine that Daddy and the Texas Rangers brought into the jail from a nightclub out at Clay Station was the only illegal gambling I had ever heard of. My brothers and I played it with the same four quarters for days until the Rangers hauled it to Bryan as evidence, but even that didn't seem so bad.

Were Bird Pidgeon's visitors, including the hero Audie Murphy, breaking the law out in the Carriage house of the River Mansion? I needed to know.

Daddy didn't hem-haw. "Yes, bookmaking is illegal. People betting more than they can lose causes all kinds of problems, and not just financial. It hurts their families. But here in the county, there are lots of laws being broken every day, lots of people getting hurt every day. We do the best we can, set priorities. Try to keep people from hurting one another, stealing from one another, driving when they're drunk. We try to look out for children and women who can't look out for themselves." That wish-I-was-back-on-the-farm look washed over his face, followed by the I-wish-I-didn't-have-to-have-this-talk expression. "So, if a man wants to gamble with his money, I have more urgent problems to attend to. Besides, proving that type of thing would take a bigger operation than me and Bub could ever muster." He even smiled a little at that thought.

I understood. He didn't enforce all the laws, simple as that. He couldn't. But whatever the case, he was not investigating Bird and Audie Murphy, and I, for one, was glad about it, even if I did feel a little bit like a criminal myself. I looked hard at my daddy, and wondered if he did, too.

Knowing that the Pickards probably had the letter of the law on their side, I was truly worried when election day came that fall. The returns were being chalked on a huge board out on the courthouse lawn in the evening after the polls closed. Lights were strung up in the trees. Entertainment and games were set up, including my favorite, the cake walk, in the street in front of the farm credit office. I was so nervous that I didn't try for the huge coconut layer cake that usually would have had me walking round that painted circle all night. Instead, I congregated with the grownups, watching the chalk board. The early returns showed bad for Daddy, good for Jake.

"Those are from Jake's home precinct," Mama said. "Don't worry, not yet."

But, of course, I did worry. I worried that we'd be moving back to the dairy, and Daddy would not collect the milk bills like Jake and Edith said. We'd go hungry, or only have milk to drink, and it was all my fault for wanting to stay at the River Mansion. I worried the night away, going from smiles when Daddy took a precinct, to near tears when Jake won one. I blamed everybody I could think of, from me, to Audie Murphy, to my brother Walter, who still idolized him.

But in the end, it wasn't even close. Daddy won big, and I floated around the courthouse square with the guilt lifted, laughing and smiling my own version of the election-year smile.

Jake and Edith retired out to their ranch in Black Jack, that first precinct Daddy had lost election night. I saw them a year later in the county fair parade. They rode two big black horses and wore identical brown serge Western suits, except that Edith's was bigger in the butt, my grandma said.

The next summer, Bird Pidgeon disappeared. Carrie's mother came down to the jail and told Daddy that Bird had been gone for over a week. She said he'd never done anything like that before, family man and loving father that he was. She was in tears at our kitchen table, like so many people had been, but when she stood to go, Daddy put his arm around her shoulders and stood her up tall. When he took his arm away, she stayed that way.

They contacted all Bird's friends, including Audie Murphy, who was making a movie in Montana. They called all the hospitals in the area, and finally brought in the FBI Missing Persons people. Carrie didn't come to school anymore. I was heartbroken for her, and sad I couldn't tell her so.

Worst of all, they dragged the river for miles, up and down from the River Mansion. One of the big silver hooks they used, kind of a giant fishhook with sharp prongs going out in all directions, sat in the back seat of Daddy's car, its heavy coiled rope mud stained and looped onto the floor. The sight of a body getting snagged by those sharpened hooks was one I hoped

I'd never see. The thought of Carrie's Daddy caught there was just too much to even consider. I was glad Daddy didn't let me go with him dragging the river when I asked. He agreed, though, to take me to see Carrie. Driving out, Daddy drove slow, and we didn't talk much. He was troubled, I could tell, because I was too. He looked over my head, out towards the river and said, "Maybe I should have done more when I could." He said it more to himself than to me.

"Nobody was happier than me that you let Bird be," I said. He reached over and patted my hand, his eyes still looking out toward the shining Brazos River.

When he left me at the River Mansion, Carrie and I sat in the wooden two-seater swing and stared at the river, not saying a word. She held my hand real tight and cried a little.

"I miss my father," she said. My throat got tight, like I couldn't swallow if I wanted to. "I hope he's not in the river."

The river shone bright, clear and silver. We sat in silence, our hands gripping one another's. A shower blew up, the drops making rain rings on the water as far as we could see. The river was so beautiful. I hoped to heaven he wasn't in there either.

If he was, they never found him. Bird was gone for good. The family was moving away, leaving the River Mansion empty.

At the memorial service for Bird in Bryan, the priest prayed to Saint Adjutor, patron saint of drowning victims who could calm whirlpools by throwing Holy water into the river. The thought comforted me. I pictured the river's churning waters being calmed by Saint Adjutor right out front of the River Mansion, and peace prevailing on the Brazos.

Ten

I Swear Club

*O*t was bad luck that we held the I Swear Club meeting the same week Jane Ann Dewar's mother disappeared. You'd think we would have called it off, or that Jane Ann's daddy would have suggested we move it to one of the other girls' houses. But Jane Ann said he insisted she go ahead like normal, despite her mother's being gone three days, in the middle of the week, without a word to anyone.

People were saying she'd run off, or even maybe she was dead, and Jane Ann surely had heard that talk by now. Dougie Dewar had come down to the jail to talk to Daddy after Aileen hadn't come home that very first night. Aileen Dewar had never gone anywhere without him, Dougie said, and her whole family lived right here in Caldwell, and none of them had the least idea of where she was. Dougie's father, Old Mister Dewar, everybody called him, was in our kitchen every single day after that, worrying out loud about poor Aileen. That's what people called her, *poor Aileen*, except for Dougie. He called her "the little woman," or "my bride," or "the missus," and every time he'd do it, I'd see my mama's lips go thin.

Dougie was home more than most daddies because the Dewars were rich. He would approach a bunch of us girls in front of the school, telling us to come on over to play with Jane Ann, and Jane Ann, sitting there in their big black Lincoln Continental, would wince like somebody pinched her, but then she'd smile a put-on smile, and say, "Sure, y'all come on over." Sometimes we did, but mostly we didn't, until the I Swear Club brought us to her house regularly. Her daddy always hung around when we were there, cracking jokes, getting involved in any game we were playing, bringing us Cokes and big bags of chips. Peggy Worsek, my best friend and daughter of a county commissioner, said he asked her to sit on his lap one time, and we both thought that was weird for anybody's father to ask a visiting kid, but we were not alarmed. The only lap I'd ever sat on besides my own daddy's was Santa at the Sears Store in Bryan. Tall with curly hair, Dougie wore colored suits; a flashy dresser, my grandma called him. He had a mossy green one on the day the I Swear Club met at his house, and when he'd come in all the girls looked at one another with eyebrows raised, if Jane Ann wasn't looking. Nobody even mentioned her mother.

Dougie worked for his own father, who owned the lumberyard and was very rich, but people said Old Mister Dewar was stingy with his money. Except for the big house he built for Dougie and Aileen—the biggest, most modern place in town—my grandma said he still had the first nickel he ever earned.

Jane Ann was a shy kind of girl, especially for being rich. In elementary school, she had gone to a Galveston boarding school, but came back even shyer than before she left. My mama had thought sending a young girl off away from home to school was terribly cruel and had said so more than once.

Jane Ann was an average-looking girl who wouldn't stand out in any crowd. She had long, thin legs and arms, like her daddy, and a rounded middle. Her hair was light brown and curly from a permanent wave she got down at the beauty shop on the square, making her look like a small version of her own mother, Aileen, who had the exact same hairdo. They dressed alike, too, in pastel shirtwaist dresses, with wide belts that matched, cinched up tight around their thick waists. Jane Ann said the mother-daughter dresses were her daddy's idea. She favored lime green and lemon yellow, while her mother wore peach and pale blue. Jane Ann talked just like her mother, kind of a coo, that odd voice some women use to talk to little girls.

People said Dougie was breaking Mr. Dewar, running the lumberyard into the ground, showing up down there in his colored suits, yelling at the workmen if he got any sawdust on him. But over at Jane Ann's house, you wouldn't know Dougie had a care in the world. He told us kids to call him Dougie, but Mama told me not to dare do it.

I'd joined the I Swear Club about six months before, and had just barely gotten in. It was a girls' club sworn to secrecy. We also had to swear to get in, really curse. We had to say five different cuss words during the initiation, out loud, in front of everyone. Peggy Worsek told me that the whole group was looking forward to my initiation, since living around the jail and having two brothers, I was sure to know some first-rate swear words; real criminal cussing, Peggy called it. As it turned out, I was a real disappointment to the club, and barely squeaked in, having to use both the words "fart" and "fartblossom" to make my five words. Unfortunately, I hadn't heard enough criminal cussing, or much of any other kind either, around the jail. If a prisoner began cussing where I could hear, Mama would hustle me out of there in a hurry, to go for a drive or over to my grandma's house. And home was a total bust. My daddy's favorite expression was "Me, oh my," and Mama never cussed. My own grandma wouldn't even say the words, "I swear," instead saying "I swan," as a kind of weak substitute. I had tried to use the word *hermaphrodite*, something I'd heard my brothers say. But the club, in secret committee, refused to allow it, deciding it was too medical. Peggy told me when Jane Ann had joined right before I had, she had shocked the rest of the girls, cooing out "cunt" in her little woman's voice. We'd never heard the word, but it sounded shocking. She had also used the F-word, which we'd never in a million years heard said out loud. Most of our mothers didn't even know what the I Swear Club was all about, and we all tried to keep it that way. When Peggy Worsek asked her mother the meaning of "cunt," we all knew trouble was brewing for the I Swear Club.

The club met at each member's house, rotating every month. What terrible luck that we gathered at Jane Ann's house the week her mother disappeared. We were all careful not to mention anything at all about her mother, or our own mothers either for that matter, so she wouldn't be reminded of it. Dougie stood in the doorway, looming in his strange green suit, keeping a close eye on us. He watched Jane Ann even more closely. We were all a little tense. Nobody's mother had ever disappeared before. My fingers tickled like they did before I went to the dentist, a sure sign that things were amiss. I guess we were all a little relieved when Dougie rushed in and offered to drive us home. He was breathless and red in the face, and as we crowded into their black Lincoln, he lit a big cigar that choked every one of us. We were hardly out of the driveway, when he told Jane Ann, right there with all of us in the car, that her mother's car had been found, down by the river, and that there was blood in it. Jane Ann, who was hard to read at the best of times, seemed to shut down entirely. No questions, no words, no emotion on her round face. Everyone's eyes were watering so from Dougie's cigar, I didn't know if she cried or not.

When they dropped me off at the jail, Mama, who knew about the bloody car, came out and put her hand through the car window to touch Jane Ann's cheek. When Jane Ann said that her daddy had explained about her mother's car on the way over, Mama gave Dougie a look that should have frozen him on the spot. They drove off with Mama staring after them.

Parked by the river, Aileen's car was "blood soaked," as the *Burleson County Citizen* put it, and according to my brother Walter, who saw the car after it was towed into the yard by the highway patrol, that was the God's honest truth. He said it looked like the hanging area where we butchered cows and pigs at the farm. The crime lab from Austin came in to check out the car in the secure lot, and that very day, everybody in town knew that bloody fingerprints were all over the car. Whose they were was the topic all over town, in the cafés, the barbershop, and even in the jail. The current group of prisoners had their ideas about crime in Caldwell, this one in particular, and Mama thought they were probably right, thinking like she was. Even at school there was talk. The talk was whispered in the halls, out of Jane Ann's earshot, but most everyone thought Dougie had killed Aileen. It's always the husband, everybody said.

Dougie came through with an alibi, accounting for his time with a series of witnesses, detailing exact times of where he was and when and with whom. My mother thought this was a little too cut-and-dried and made her point by asking us to account for our time over one day, not an entire week like Dougie had. Mama said the only reason Dougie could be innocent was that he'd never want to get blood on his shiny shoes.

Mama was more interested in this case than usual and enjoyed it, as much as a person can enjoy a murder case. She talked about it constantly, even to us kids, and she kept a little notebook like Daddy's where she wrote down every new fact as it came to light. It was the first time she'd gotten so involved in a case, and it seemed to keep her mind off living in the jail with her kids. As facts came out, Mama said it was like peeling an onion. "Sometimes it doesn't smell so good, and sometimes it makes you cry."

"Nothing like a murder mystery to make you into a detective, is there?" Daddy kidded her when she asked him for details.

Of course, it was deadly serious. No body had been found, even though Daddy spent days with the recovery divers dragging the river. Dougie never turned up at the river to watch, but his father was there every single day, walking up and down the banks, his mouth a straight red line across his face, his thin gray hair blowing wild in the wind. Mama even went down there a few times when she could get away, to take Daddy and the others sandwiches and coffee. One day she'd be hoping they would find the body, and the next she'd pray they wouldn't.

The blood type for all that blood in the car matched, just like everybody predicted it would, Aileen's. But the bloody fingerprints were not Dougie's. He had insisted that he be fingerprinted to prove his innocence. Mama and even the prisoners thought he should have been a little more upset by people thinking those fingerprints might be his—such a slur on his character—but he walked around town with his usual crisp clothes and smile on his face and his posters asking for information about who might have reason to kill his wife and offering a reward. And Daddy investigated insurance policies on Aileen. She was insured, but not for much more than a burial would cost if they ever got to bury her.

Much as folks wanted to blame Dougie, it looked like he was confident about his innocence. Mama told Daddy he ought to be looking at Dougie's friends, if he had had any. It was one of the first Dougie jokes Mama made, but not the last.

Jane Ann couldn't be read. She pasted on a smile and behaved like a woman of fifty would whose mother has died, after a long illness, sitting in class taking notes and eating dinner at all the local cafés with her daddy. I wondered how Jane Ann had gotten so good at hiding what she must surely be feeling.

It took a couple of months before the Rangers and FBI finally identified the fingerprints as belonging to one Lyndon Newman, a career criminal from Houston. His record of violent crimes was long and terrible, and he'd served years in the penitentiary. He'd been released only the year before on a technicality and had disappeared. Everyone thought he'd run off into Mexico. It looked like he was the *culprit*, the *perpetrator*—words we were learning, just so we could attach them to Lyndon Newman. These words were words better suited to the I Swear Club, my grandma pointed out to me.

So, who'd surely done it had been discovered, but why was still a mystery. Far as anybody knew, Lyndon Newman had never even been to Caldwell, and didn't have any connections here. Nobody had ever heard of him. All of his crimes had taken place in Houston. He was a big city criminal. Of course, there was still some doubt about what had happened, since no body had been found, just lots of blood. The search for Lyndon Newman began. The Texas Rangers assigned to the case came and went from the jail, and the search went on for months. Mama would make snacks for the update meetings the Rangers would hold in our kitchen, hanging on every word. When Dougie came to these meetings, she'd hold back on the cookies and coffee until he was long gone.

Meanwhile, Dougie began to make a show of his grieving. He held a big memorial service for his wife at the country club. Jane Ann wore a black shirtwaist that had belonged to her mother. Dougie wore a black suit, and black shoes, a departure noticed by one and all.

A couple of weeks later, the I Swear Club met again, this time at Peggy Worsek's house out in the country. The club had expanded, and we were doing each other's hair now. Peggy and I were using platinum rinses on our blonde hair, turning it kind of purple, and we were trying to get Jane Ann to go purple, too. Peggy thought it might cheer her up. Right there in Peggy's kitchen, with purple rinse running down her neck onto her mint green shirtwaist, Jane Ann started to talk about her daddy.

"Daddy has a girlfriend," Jane Ann said, her face frozen and unreadable. "Her name's Donna. I think she's young. She seems young. Maybe nineteen?

She's a dancer from Houston, beautiful with big beehive hair like Priscilla Presley. Nobody's supposed to know, especially not Grandpa Dewar, so don't say a word."

We promised, and she smiled one of those fake adult smiles we knew so well. But then her face crumpled as though all her muscles had gone slack. I worried she might be going to fall down. But she only began to cry.

"He said it would just be the two of us now," she wailed as she slid down on the floor in front of Peggy Worsek's sink. I knelt down next to her, getting purple dye on my best sweater. She let me hold her hand for a moment and then she shook it off. She looked up and you could just see her face fix itself, like she had put on a mask. I couldn't see her face well now, but I thought she was smiling as she stood up, sticking her head into the sink to rinse off the purple stains.

"Daddy needed comfort wherever he can find it, what with Aileen murdered and all." She seemed to be calling her mama Aileen now.

Old Mister Dewar came to the jail many nights after the lumberyard closed, so concerned and upset about Aileen's death, talking it through with Daddy. Mama took his visits to heart, worrying about the old man. With us, she constantly theorized, discussing the case at the supper table, in the car. She said it sometimes seemed like the old man was in love with Aileen himself. My grandma said Mama was kind of a romantic.

After a statewide manhunt, Lyndon, the perpetrator, was finally apprehended in a South Main bar in Houston. Tall and handsome, he looked like a soldier, dressed neat as a pin. He had silver-gray hair, and a little trimmed mustache, and was tanned and fit. He would say later on the stand that he got his tan on the golf course. He was not your ordinary thug, even if he was a repeat offender, violent even and none too good at staying out of jail.

He had enough experience in the criminal justice system to know that he ought to make a plea deal. After all, he had no reason to kill Aileen Dewar. "I am just the hireling here," Lyndon pronounced clearly on the witness stand, in his fancy Northern accent. "I am a Soldier of Fortune."

As a result of his deal, he got to stay in a federal prison in Bastrop, instead of our jail. Daddy said at Bastrop he thought they had a small golf course. We heard later that Lyndon complained bitterly when it was only a putting green in the prison yard.

Donna, the girlfriend, also turned state's evidence. The courthouse regulars were calling her Donnorhea by this time, a name that mystified Peggy Worsek and me. My brothers would only tell us that we ought to take it up with the I Swear Club, but even the club's slang dictionary handed down by Peggy Worsek's older sister was no help. Donna had connections on South Main, too, it turns out, and one of those connections was Lyndon Newman. He was her father. It all came together: the motive, the connections, everything.

About this time, talking to Daddy in the jail kitchen over a cup of coffee and cigarettes, Old Mister Dewar finally revealed what he'd done. Several years before, as a way of reining in his wayward son, Old Mister Dewar had worked with a fancy lawyer from Dallas to put everything in Aileen's name: the big modern house, the shares in the lumberyard, stocks and bonds, even the Lincoln. He liked her; he respected her, thought she was smart and responsible, and that she was Dougie's best hope of ever amounting to a hill of beans. They had talked all the time about what they could do to help Dougie, whom they both loved more than he deserved. They hoped they could reform him. Mr. Dewar never, ever, thought he was putting Aileen in any danger. He hadn't imagined his son would do Aileen any harm.

Holding his head in his hands, he said, "Aileen thought having control of the money would give her control over Dougie, and I thought it might put us in a better inheritance tax situation." His eyes filmed with tears. "I was actually thinking about taxes." Jane Ann wouldn't listen any of the talk about her father, right up until the trial. She told everybody at school that she was taking care of her daddy, that he needed her more than ever. She did her hair up big and teased just like Donna's, which was just like Priscilla Presley's beehive, and was wearing Donna's blue eye shadow, and nobody our age wore eye makeup like that.

Aileen's body never turned up, and that hurt the state of Texas's case. But the state did have Lyndon, who was such a colorful character that he made a popular witness, despite being an admitted murderer, up there on the stand talking like a professor, cracking jokes in his fancy accent about how quaint Caldwell was and all. My mama was scandalized, called him the Professor of Death, and some other things when she didn't think us kids could hear.

Though out on bail herself, Donna never came to see Dougie in jail. There was a big controversy about him not being able to smoke his cigars in his cell. The other prisoners hated the spoiled rich wife-murderer and intended to make his life miserable by holding firm on no cigars, and by holding back my mom's good cooking until it was cold and greasy. They made sure there was no hot water when it was shower time for Dougie. Dougie couldn't believe his own daddy was letting him sit there in our jail being cussed at by common criminals instead of going his bond, big as it was, but the old man told him, the one and only day he came around, that Jane Ann owned everything now, and he couldn't afford it. Dougie finally bought some chewing tobacco from my brother Bill; He would spit through the bars of the jail window all day long when the trial was in recess, with a hangdog look about him.

Jane Ann was his only visitor. Before the trial began, she had come every single day. Mama even let them visit at the jail kitchen table on Sundays, as a favor to Jane Ann. It was all I ever saw of Jane Ann, what with the I Swear Club breaking up like it had. We had just run out of swear words, and besides that, cussing didn't seem so exciting anymore anyway. Then, after sitting in on just that first day of the trial, Jane Ann quit coming to visit her daddy, and never looked at him again in the courtroom. Mama said she finally saw her daddy for what he was.

Mama was in court the day the judge handed down the death penalty, and she said Dougie was the only one who cried. He laid his head on the table, and finally had to be lifted up to get cuffed and escorted out of the courtroom. All the rest of the spectators just kind of gasped and sat still. Mama said Jane Ann gave one of those winces, like she used to when Dougie would embarrass her in front of her friends, but her eyes stayed dry. Lyndon got life, and Donna got ten years.

That night, Mama enthused as to how the case had been like a real-life puzzle, with all the pieces finally fitting together. Jane Ann inherited everything, but wouldn't spend a penny on Dougie's appeal. She transferred to a private school for rich kids in Austin.

Even Old Mister Dewar had to get Jane Ann's permission when he wanted to buy a new pickup a year or so later, but it didn't seem to bother him too much. When she came in from Austin to sign the papers, Jane Ann looked entirely different, not at all like Donna anymore, and certainly nothing like her most likely dead mother. Her long straight hair, dyed black, swept down her back. Her solid body looked smooth covered in a black skirt and sweater, and she had black lines drawn on the top and bottom of her eyelids. Her lips were frosty beige. This was surprisingly a good look for her. As if she finally had on her own clothes. Her own identity.

When I asked her how the new private school in Austin was treating her, she answered in a strong, deep voice, "Cool." Then the corners of those frosted lips turned up, looking for all the world like a real smile.

Eleven

Hostage Situation

$\mathcal{T}$hings had settled after the sensational murder case, and I began to think, once again, that everything in Caldwell was ordinary. The crimes were especially mundane by anybody's reckoning, not worthy of my mama's newly developed crime-solving skills or my interest. So many domestics. Daddy called them family squabbles, and Mama called it wife beating, and took an especially tough view of those prisoners. A man couldn't hit his wife and hope to get fed any good prisoner food at our jail.

There were also lots of drunk-and-disorderlies and many cases of disturbing the peace. Those two were hard to tell apart, in my view. Drunks would disturb the peace, and many people disturbing the peace were drunk and disorderly. It was a close call that only Daddy could make. If Mama were filling in the jail register, she didn't care enough to find out and would put both offenses by the prisoner's name. The other big item was fighting, a catchall for all sorts of scraps. There were a few real fights, or fisticuffs as Daddy's deputy Bub Wallis liked to call it. But hostage taking was never even heard of in Caldwell before 1961, when it happened and got Daddy's picture in the big city papers, even the *Houston Chronicle*, whose funny papers I read every day. To have my daddy in the same paper with *Dogpatch* and *Dagwood* was more than I ever expected out of life.

School was pretty ordinary, too, I can assure you. I went, though, every day, like clockwork, even if it was half against my will. I knew by now there wasn't even a small chance I'd be going off to a fancy boarding school in Austin or anywhere else, much as I'd fantasized about life in the big city after Jane Ann Dewars went to one. I'd be lucky if I got to go out to my grandma's and fish for crawfish in her creek. To create at least a little bit of excitement, my friend Peggy Worsek and I would get to school early and exchange clothes. Then, at noon, we'd change back. We imagined that it was confusing to people—like Superman putting on glasses and becoming Clark Kent. We felt clever. Our hijinks were pretty conventional, but we were making an effort.

That day in 1961, when we learned what a hostage was, everything in our county became extra-ordinary for a change. It happened in a small community called Rita at the one-room schoolhouse there, a little white frame building standing alone out in a grassy clearing, down from the church. About twenty colored kids of all ages went to school there when the weather was good, and when there was no cotton to be chopped. Miss Willie Mae Jones, the only teacher at Rita School (and the principal, too) later told my daddy they were doing an English lesson when in comes a man with a gun. "Lord knows how he ever happened onto the place," she declared. He stood at the door, waving the gun around. Miss Willie Mae said the gun seemed to look bigger and bigger as the day wore on. The kids, scared out of their wits, started crying, especially the younger ones. The gunman rushed to the front of the classroom, holding the gun up to Miss Willie Mae's head. "Quiet those kids down!" he shouted. Miss Willie Mae saw right then that the gunman himself was agitated and crying some himself. After calming her students, she tried to talk to him like she did scared kids on their first day of school when she'd hunker down low to their level so as not to scare them with her bulk and hug them to her huge bosom. Now this fellow, she told Daddy, had that same scared look about him, but she wasn't about to try and hold him up close, not with that gun in those shaking hands.

"What's happened?" she asked. "Are you okay?" "What can we do?" But every question seemed to agitate him more.

He made all the kids line up against the blackboard in the front of the room, little ones in front, and it looked so much like a firing squad that Miss Willie Mae, near panic herself, kept asking questions, trying to keep him talking, and he didn't try to stop her. He finally told her he was just trying to put them where he could see them all at one time. He assured her he wasn't a child murderer, and the way he said it set off alarm bells for Miss Willie Mae, like maybe he had done horrible things, just not child murder. But except for the kids being hot and scared half to death, and then getting tired from standing in the front of the classroom not moving for an hour or more, nobody had gotten hurt yet. Some of the younger kids continued to cry, and the gunman was getting more and more antsy all the time. It got so loud he finally moved the kids out on the porch, all but two older girls. Quiet girls, Miss Willie Mae said. A couple of kids sneaked off into the woods and ran home. There were no phones out there, so it took a while before word got to the jail. But finally one of the kids and his grandma made their way to a dairy farm with a phone and called the sheriff.

Daddy tore over to the school with a new highway patrolman named Don Chaplan. Don was quiet, capable, and hard-working, and Daddy liked him, and probably thought he'd be an asset in a crisis. He was young and could take a joke about his height, which barely passed the highway patrol standard.

Don and Daddy approached the school cautiously, trying to calm the crying children on the porch. "Hello, in there," Daddy called. "Come out, let's talk. No need for the guns," he urged. The gunman sent Miss Willie Mae out, holding the two young girls at gunpoint, and demanding Daddy lay his gun down. For a time, he refused to talk directly to Daddy, keeping the law outside and just using Miss Willie Mae as a messenger. Daddy tried to get as much information from Miss Willie Mae as he could about the gunman, but the standoff seemed to be at a standstill. Communicating in this round-about way made everybody more and more anxious, including the gunman. Miss Willie Mae weighed about 250 pounds, just about my daddy's size, my grandma said later, and was breathing hard in the heat. She had tried to comfort both the girls, who were sweating profusely and crying, as were the gunman, and even Daddy. Miss Willie Mae was getting shorter of breath with every trip out onto the porch. Daddy worried what might happen if they lost their contact, if Miss Willie Mae went down.

Daddy offered to exchange himself for the two girls. The gun-wielding man did the smart thing, and took my Daddy, in his starched white shirt, looking fresh and healthy, and sent those sweaty, crying girls on their way. The gunman searched Daddy thoroughly for a weapon, and settled him down at Miss Willie Mae's desk, standing behind him with the gun pointed directly at him and Miss Willie Mae, right at their heads. Outside, after a few questions, Don Chaplan let those poor girls go home, where I pictured them taking a cool bath when I heard the story later.

Once inside, alone with the gunman and Miss Willie Mae, Daddy got to talking with him, like he could do with anyone. He gradually got the whole sad story. The man admitted he'd killed his wife and daughter. He'd planned to kill himself, too, but lost his nerve. Miss Willie Mae later said he was a child murderer after all, and a liar to boot for denying it. Worse, he was a dangerous man with nothing to lose. By the time the Rangers arrived on the scene, he was pacing and shouting, making Miss Willie Mae walk with him to and fro, keeping the gun pressed to her back. Several times, he'd place the gun to his own temple, or to Daddy's. His eyes were wild, but tired, Daddy said later. Even his voice was tiring out. As time went on, Daddy's calming influence and soft voice were having some effect.

My mama, home by the phone like always, said her blood was running cold. Over the police radio, she heard about Daddy exchanging himself for the two girls and decided to drive out there in her own car. She couldn't wait at home when half the lawmen in the county and the newspaper reporters from all over the state were out there. She said she gave the Rangers hell when she got there, for letting Daddy and Miss Willie Mae stay in the school with an obviously crazy man, a murderer, no less, who had killed his own wife and child. Mama paced up and down in front of the schoolhouse, ranting about how the Rangers weren't doing a thing to save their lives. They told her she'd have to leave the scene if she didn't get behind the barricades. The gunman himself sent Miss Willie Mae out onto the porch to tell whoever was creating such a ruckus to stop it, so Mama had to go sit in her car.

Me, I just walked home from school like always, ate my bag of Fritos and drank my 7UP like every day, and watched *The Mickey Mouse Club* on TV. I didn't know a thing about what was going on in Rita as I watched Annette, my favorite Mouseketeer, sing and dance.

The gunman, Joe McCullough, as they knew his name to be by then, had demanded food, so Daddy sent Don Chaplan to Curley's Drive In down on Highway 36 North, to retrieve half a dozen burgers with everything, knowing that two of Curley's hamburgers could put a healthy young football player down for the count; heavy food to say the least. The Rangers ordered a dozen for themselves, and pretty soon Don had taken orders from most of the reporters and the crowd that had gathered. Mama included an order for the prisoners, since she wouldn't be there to cook. When he got back, Don was real proud that he'd stuck the Rangers with the bill for the entire order. When Daddy came out to get the food and heard who paid, he said, "Good police work, Don."

Alone in her car, Mama ate a burger. Calming down and getting a little sleepy herself, she told us all later that right then, she had smiled. She knew, with her sharpened criminologist instincts and the effects of those burgers on her, that it would all be over soon. She could see Daddy's plan.

After McCullough devoured two hamburgers and greasy French-fried potatoes, he started looking very tired and low, talking about his family, crying and hating himself, wanting to turn the gun on his own head, but being a coward and crying some more about that. It was very late, and it had been a long day. His head nodded a couple of times before he went down, sound asleep, the gun falling to the floor, where Miss Willie Mae grabbed it quick as a flash, and Daddy seized Joe McCullough in a bear hug, shouting for the Rangers to get in there. They rushed in and had Joe McCullough on the floor and handcuffed before he was wide awake. A couple of Rangers and more than a few reporters had to be shaken awake once the whole thing was over, being under the influence of Curley's burgers themselves.

McCullough came out in handcuffs, and it was all over before midnight. The crowd of onlookers, mostly reporters and Rita school kids along with Miss Willie Mae's family, clapped their hands, and somebody gave a shrill whistle. The two girl hostages hugged Daddy and thanked him for exchanging himself for them, and that's what got their pictures in the *Houston Chronicle*. The picture came out in all the local papers. And the whole time I'd been home, watching TV, wondering where everybody was.

My daddy told us late that night how Curley's hamburgers were the newest crime-fighting weapon, and my brother Bill kept saying how "murdering your family could really make you hungry and tire you out."

My mama forgave the Rangers and had them in for coffee at the jail, where I heard the whole story, secondhand, and in great detail. Daddy said Mama was getting to be a real softy, forgiving the Rangers so quickly. I was so upset about missing everything that I started hanging around the kitchen every day after school, listening to the two-way radio up on the refrigerator, answering every single phone call, hoping to high heaven I wouldn't miss the next big thing.

Twelve

Playing Detective

The two Texas Rangers looked at me hard. I didn't know either one of them well, and they were trying to decide if I had good sense, or maybe if I had any sense at all. They knew already, before they got around to me, that they had a case, but they weren't sure yet if I had anything that might help them, or if I was just some silly thirteen-year-old talking about a teacher she didn't like.

The older ranger, with the shiny silver hair and the John Wayne walk, said, "What did you see yourself, with your own eyes?"

He must have been asking witnesses that question for a lot of years, in his lets-get-down-to-brass-tacks-and-don't-tell-me-what-you-*think* detective voice. I wondered if he worked at his John Wayne drawl. His partner, much younger with a high school English teacher air about him, added, "Don't be scared. Just tell us everything." I'd seen him a few times and heard he was smart. He'd worked with Daddy last year when Mrs. Holland, maybe the richest person in Caldwell, had her safe stolen. But both of them were acting like I might not have a brain in my head, probably because I was just a kid they'd been seeing around the jail for years.

Way before these guys showed up, I had been doing my own investigation, along with a few other kids from school. Who wouldn't want to know what was going on, even if we didn't know what we were onto when it first started? We thought it was just a really serious case of teacher's pet.

I even thought it could be my bias, since there was no love lost between Coach Bobby Bengud and me, ever since he sent me to the principal's office when he caught me reading *Belle Boyd, Confederate Spy* in study hall. The book had been left behind by one of the prisoners—but in his defense, a smart prisoner, a professor, in fact, from Texas A&M who happened to have a drinking problem. Even if it had some sexy chapters, it was, when you got right down to it, a history book. Coach Bengud, who I doubted had ever read a novel, wasn't impressed by any of this, and insisted that Mr. Black, the principal, call my mother to let her know "what type of smut I was reading."

While I sat in the dusty principal's office waiting for Mama to arrive, Mr. Black read some of the book, stroking his chin with its famous mole. I knew Mama wouldn't be mad, since she knew I took it from the trustee cell. Mr. Black and I talked about the Civil War. He was amazed at how much I knew, for an eighth grader, and when I claimed it all came from *Belle Boyd*, he was on my side, too, I could tell. I didn't mention I'd been studying up on the Civil War ever since our babysitter told me when I was in first grade that the North had won. Since I only knew I lived in the South, I worried about it, not understanding one thing about slavery or states' rights, and started at that early age trying to get it all straight. Anyway, Coach Bengud thought I got off easy, and the trouble between us had begun.

Coach Bengud was a big man, looked like one of his own high school football players if you didn't see his face. He wore those black high top basketball shoes all the time, which let him move around fast and perhaps even gracefully. What he really did was kind of prance around, as though he were the star of his own show. He wasn't a handsome man, by any means. He must have been about forty, with dark hair, long and wavy, and slicked back. All the other coaches had flat tops, crisp and clean, usually blond. Coach Bengud wore thick glasses with old-fashioned clear frames that sat up on his most prominent feature, a big nose shaped just like Miss Ada Palmer's green parrot Porky's beak, only three or four times the size. It looked good on Porky. Not so much on Coach Bengud. And he had trouble with his nose. Maybe it had gotten broken in football when he was younger, but he struggled to breathe in, and he snorted little snorts every time he breathed out. Nose hairs stuck out and fluttered with every snort. Except for the basketball shoes, he dressed like the other coaches, even wore that key chain they all hooked to their belts. But Coach Bengud's key chain was outsized, with more keys on it than our school had doors. He made a racket when he walked down the hall, like Tinker Bell turned into a maintenance man. With those keys and his breathing problem, I don't see how he ever snuck up and caught me reading *Belle Boyd*.

In Coach Bengud's classes, we did lots of reading in class, copying questions and answers at the end of each chapter. He rarely talked. For the last fifteen minutes of a class, he had us put our heads down. To raise your head for whatever reason made him irate. I thought maybe he took this tactic because he'd run out of steam like teachers do and that he couldn't deal with kids. I kind of felt sorry for him at first. Boy, was I wrong.

Coach Bengud's class monitor, Sandra Snowden, was a smart, cheerful girl. Sandra was popular, pretty except for needing braces. It was as though she had too many teeth in her mouth. She played clarinet in the band and was good at it, beating out high school girls for first chair. I played clarinet, too, but sat way in the back beyond where they numbered the chairs. I thought she must practice at home, like the band director said we ought to. Sandra had developed early, and by this time, had a good figure, as my brothers had repeatedly pointed out to me. Even in her band uniform, you could see she was curvy. I was envious, I've got to admit. At first, I thought that might be coloring my judgment.

Sandra did all of Coach Bengud's paperwork, keeping his attendance record and his gradebook up to date. When I got my report card, I recognized her handwriting on the A-, the minus probably because of *Belle Boyd*. He moved her desk next to his and stood there when we were reading aloud. The day I looked up when we were supposed to have our heads on our desks and saw him rubbing her neck, I thought I might be seeing things. I told myself she must have a sore neck, and him being a coach, he knew about muscles and was administering therapy. But I started peeking up more often after that, and saw them talking softly and once, shockingly, holding hands as he stood beside her desk. It was so weird, far beyond anything I'd seen or heard of or even imagined, that I doubted my own eyes.

When I told my friend Peggy Worsek about it, she laughed at me and said, "That's absurd!"—her new favorite word that she applied to everything. Peggy sat in the front row too and couldn't see Sandra's desk without twisting and turning, so she never did glimpse the goings-on. Then, during the lunch hour one Monday after Columbus Day vacation, Peggy looked through the classroom window and saw Coach Bengud with his hand under Sandra's sweater, rubbing her back then shifting around into the front. When Peggy found me out by the bike rack, she grabbed me by the arm, dragging me along, talking so fast I couldn't make out her words at first.

"Coach Bengud is petting Sandra Snowden!" she sort of whispered, but loud enough for anybody within ten feet to hear.

"Everybody knows she's the teacher's pet," I said.

"No!" she hissed. "I mean they're *petting*. You know what I mean. Come and look! You can see them through the window."

We started to run. Peggy's description sounded innocent, but I got the idea. When we reached the window, we saw them talking by the desk, but nobody was touching anybody. When a few other girls gathered around, Peggy told us what she'd seen and everybody but me thought she was crazy. If I hadn't been looking up from my desk during rest periods, I would have thought the same thing.

Though only in eighth grade, many of us played in the high school band, including Peggy and me and Sandra Snowden. Every morning at ten, we practiced upstairs behind the gymnasium. The band director, a young man just out of college named Stanley Piwolski, had lost control of the band. Seventy-five kids with musical instruments, even if generally the good kids, made such a racket that keeping command was a tall order for the toughest of teachers. Stan the Band Man, as everyone called him right to his face, didn't stand a chance. The older kids were always sneaking out of the band hall, wandering around the gym, or out to the tennis courts for a smoke. The young kids usually stayed put. I was so focused on the struggle with my clarinet, that I never considered ducking out.

Peggy noticed that Sandra left almost every day, sometimes asking permission from Stan the Band Man to go to the restroom. Once, when she disappeared for most of an hour's practice, Stan remarked on her absence. With all the shenanigans going on in that band hall, it was amazing he noticed. He asked Dianne See, a senior flute player, to go to the restroom to be sure Sandra was okay. When Diane returned, she announced that Sandra was not in the restroom at all. He said he'd check on her later, but with all his problems, I was sure he'd forget all about it, and that nothing would come of it.

Peggy and I didn't forget. Later we heard from kids in Coach Bengud's class that he would leave the class about that same time every day when the students had their heads down. Since they were cutting up and having a good time in the teacher-less room, none of them cared where he was or how long he stayed away. Peggy and I began putting two and two together but felt creeped out, maybe even scared, and didn't know what to do.

The next Wednesday, we headed for the band hall, but veered off up the steps to the stage, where we hid behind the heavy purple curtain. From up there, we had a view of the whole gymnasium, all the stairs leading in and out, down to the locker rooms. We were hoping Stan the Band Man would not get around to calling roll that day. Before we told anybody, we had to see something. And if we saw it together, we might stop doubting ourselves. We needed proof.

Coach Bengud came in through the gym's side door, holding his key chain so that it wouldn't rattle. He walked directly to the locker room stairs, glancing now and then over one shoulder then the other. Peggy and I held our breaths. I was terrified of what he'd do if he caught us spying. But we were hidden in the folds of the purple velvet, and after he hurried down the stairs, when Peggy and I could breathe again, I said, "I hope and pray Sandra Snowden doesn't come out of the band hall."

"I never wanted anything so much," Peggy whispered back.

We saw her as soon as she made the top of the band hall stairs, looking all around just like Coach Bengud had. My heart felt like a heavy stone in my chest. Playing detective wasn't fun anymore.

During the time they disappeared into the locker room, we didn't say a word. Finally, Sandra came out, looking innocent in her blue dress with her blonde hair in a high ponytail. But she had changed in my eyes, and when I looked over at Peggy, I knew she felt the same. Then Coach Bengud came out, smiling. I never liked him, but that smile was the last straw. Now, I hated him.

"Let's go see what's down there," Peggy said.

We tiptoed down the stairs, looking all around over our shoulders like they both had done. I guess sneaking around looks the same on everybody.

Entering the forbidden territory of the boy's locker room made the back of my neck prickle. Once inside, my anxious breath sucked in the smell of sweat, reminding me of my brothers' clothes hamper. One by one, we tried the doors that lined the back wall—all locked, until finally, behind the showers Peggy turned a knob, ever so slowly. On the floor lay a bare mattress, gray and white stripes, like the jail mattresses. Crumpled on top were tangled bedclothes and pillows with no pillowcases. Braver than me, Peggy stepped inside and placed her hand on the head-shaped hollow in one of the pillows.

"It's still warm," she breathed. And then she started to cry.

I stared at the stained pillow. "I don't believe it," I said. And I didn't, because I didn't want to.

For the rest of the day, in and out of class, we talked about what to do.

"Do we tell?" Peggy asked.

"Who do we tell?" I asked.

"Could we be wrong?" we both asked. "It could be nothing," we said, wishing we thought so.

Even if we decided who to tell, we couldn't imagine what we'd say. We didn't have the words. How could we explain this to a grown-up? Certainly not with Mr. Black, the principal. I didn't think I could with my daddy. And then, we weren't sure, were we? We knew if we told anybody about our suspicions, they would have trouble believing it.

This kind of thing did not happen. It never had, had it?

Peggy and I sat by Sandra on the band bus to the Navasota football game that Friday. We talked about nothing. Peggy could talk longer and harder about nothing than anybody I knew, so I had a chance to study Sandra. I'd been thinking about her all that week, wondering how this good little girl who always did exactly what was expected of her got into such a mess. When Peggy took a breath, Sandra, looking calm and ordinary as always, with a smile, began to talk about her clarinet practice schedule.

"Coach Bengud gave me this. It's called *How to Make First Chair.*" She handed a creased booklet to me. "It's where I learned what it takes, practicing one hour on weekdays and two hours on Saturday and Sunday."

I realized she was still doing exactly what was expected of her. I myself had done some things I didn't want to, like dusting erasers or doing projects after class, to get a teacher's approval, to get that A+. I knew the pressure a good little girl was under. But I had learned from my brothers how to say no without getting hurt too badly, and that you can't please everybody all the time (or your brothers ever). Sandra didn't have brothers.

As we sat there in our orange wool band uniforms, Sandra's protruding and curving in places where mine was flat, on that heated bus full of rowdy kids squawking on their instruments, I felt so sorry for her. I wanted to tell her so. The words began to form in my mouth, but I couldn't imagine what I would say.

I didn't say a thing. I handed her back the worn-out booklet and said, "I don't think I could play so much myself," feeling like a chicken-livered coward. She probably needed a friend, and it could have been me.

The next day, I knew Peggy and I weren't going to do anything at all. We weren't going to tell anybody. We weren't going to be Sandra's friends. We let it go, hoping somebody else would do something. I thought they'd get caught on account of how blatant Coach Bengud was, and Sandra, too. If I could look up from my desk, couldn't anyone in the class? If Peggy and I could watch them meet in the boy's locker room during band practice, why not Mr. Black, or even Stan the Band Man? If Coach Bengud was going to slide his hand under Sandra's sweater right in front of an open window during recess where Peggy Worsek could see, couldn't Mrs. Lewis turn her head from the dodgeball game right then and see it too? Peggy thought the coach and Sandra were crazy, said they had lost their marbles, but I thought he was brazen. He just assumed nobody would believe such a thing would go on, so he believed he could get away with anything. It was like a magic trick. Hard to believe your own eyes. After all Peggy and I had seen, didn't we still wonder if we could be wrong?

Over Thanksgiving weekend, Barbara Sevesek, a seventh grader, and her family moved into the old Mosmann house. It was the oldest house in Caldwell, with three stories and a big round room on top of the front porch. When they moved in, they got a new telephone number and realized quickly that they were on a party line, even though theirs was supposed to be private. Barbara thought her family's connection to the party line might soon disappear, so she stayed on the phone all day on Thanksgiving, listening in on calls and trying to guess who she was hearing. The first time she heard the two people talking lovey-dovey, she called it, she hoped the telephone man would take his time getting the lines cleared up. She got a little more than she bargained for, though. She told Peggy Worsek all about it that Sunday when they sat in the same pew at church. By that time, Barbara knew who was talking about love and kissing on the phone. She easily recognized the snorting breathing of Coach Bengud. She'd never heard a single rumor, but she knew Sandra Snowden's voice on the other end.

Sunday afternoon, Peggy called me from Barbara Sevesek's house. They expected the phone to be fixed the next day, so if we were going to eavesdrop on Coach Bengud's calls to Sandra, it had to be today. When I got there, Barbara and Peggy were sitting on the floor in the round room over the porch, painting each other's fingernails Punch Pink. A celebratory feeling hung in the air. We picked up the phone every minute or so and did not feel the least bit guilty about listening to mystery people plan Sunday dinner at their mama's or tell each other how they hated Sunday dinner at their mama's worse than anything.

When Barbara picked up the phone and her eyes got big, showing all the white around the blue part, we knew what she was hearing. She held out the phone and the three of us crowded around, trying to be quiet while she covered the mouthpiece with her hand. I heard the snorting right off the bat. It was Coach Bengud all right

"Snowbird, snowbird, can't wait to see you," he said. And we heard Sandra Snowden's voice, calm and cool as anything, on the other end, "Oh Bobbin, will it be tonight?" He told her how much he missed her. "Do you miss me?" he asked. She laughed her answer, and she didn't sound scared at all. When he started talking about kissing her, we didn't giggle, or anything. Barbara carefully hung up the phone. We sat on the floor in her round room, looking out the big windows at the street below.

"I'm going to tell my mama about this tonight," she said.

Peggy and I looked at one another, packed up Peggy's nail polish and headed down the stairs. We left the job of revealing the truth to Barbara, a seventh grader, despite knowing what we knew weighing down on us like a ton of bricks.

It turned out not to matter that Peggy and I were a couple of cowards, or that Barbara told her mother about the phone call. The very next day, Sandra Snowden's father came to the jail and pressed charges against Coach Bobby Bengud. Sandra was pregnant, no denying it, and when her mama and Doc Skrivek forced the truth out of her, she admitted Coach Bengud was the father. She said he'd been coming in through her bedroom window since the third week of school. Sandra insisted they were in love and going to get married, even if she surely did know that Coach Bengud was already married and had a house full of kids older than she was.

"In my own house, Sheriff!" Stuart Snowden shouted. "In my own house with my daughter!"

Mama said Daddy put Mr. Snowden in a chair, grasping his shoulder with both hands. He was trying to calm the man, while gritting his own teeth in anger. He knew Sandra was my age, was in my class.

I knew that Coach Bengud had been foolhardy, swaggering around at school, thinking nobody would notice, but him going into her house through the window, under her parents' noses, was so reckless, so crazy, I couldn't think of a boy my own age who'd take a gamble like that. But I guess Coach Bengud thought he could do anything.

That night, Daddy said Bobby Bengud denied it all. Daddy looked tired and sad while he told us about the interview. He said Bobby Bengud claimed Sandra was lying. He told Daddy she had been after him, trying to get him to meet her after school and he had refused. He said the baby probably belonged to Greg Phillips. If it weren't so despicable and villainous of the coach to blame him, the idea that Greg Phillips could have fathered a child would have been funny. He was the wimpiest, smallest, most immature and frightened kid in eighth grade. He had taken Sandra Snowden to a church banquet the year before, probably the closest thing either of them had been to a date, and the idea that they had made this baby was laughable. Daddy said they would have to check it out, follow all leads. Even as he dialed Greg Phillips's parents phone number, he sighed what I thought could be the heaviest sigh ever.

"Under the law," Daddy said, "he's innocent until proven guilty."

I was so mad about Coach Bengud trying to blame Greg Phillips, and Daddy thinking that that horrible man might still be innocent, that I told

Daddy what I knew, what I'd seen at school and heard on the phone at Barbara Sevesek's house.

While I spoke, he stayed silent but gave me such a look of disappointment, I thought he might break down in tears himself. I couldn't have felt any lower. It was hard to hold back my own tears.

"When did you first suspect this?" he asked, running his hand through his hair with another heavy breath.

"Almost the whole school year."

Then, he sighed out loud. "If only we'd known then, it might have been stopped before things came to grief like this."

I knew he was right; Peggy and I might have made a difference. I had never felt more ashamed of myself than I did at that moment. I pictured Sandra Snowden on the band bus, and regret flooded through me.

"I can see how you'd be afraid to say something. But to me? To your mother?" He reached over and smoothed my hair gently with a big hand. "Dolly, you can come to us."

I couldn't force a word out, but I promised myself that I'd be brave next time. I never wanted my daddy to look at me like that again.

The next day, Sandra Snowden's desk was empty and we had a substitute teacher, Miss Kiel, who hardly looked old enough to be out of high school herself. She moved Sandra's desk back into the regular rows and told us we could sit anywhere we liked. Still, no one sat at her desk. All day long, the boys kept up a singsong, "Coach Bengud been BAD! Coach Bengud been BAD!"

Peggy Worsek told me that day that she thought Mr. Turkelson, the shop teacher, was looking at her funny. I knew things would never be the same.

The Texas Rangers were called in by the school district, and they talked to everyone. It came out that Stan the Band Man had reported Sandra's absences to Mr. Black and had told him Coach Bengud might be influencing her, a warning Mr. Black had found hard to believe and had done nothing about. Stanley Piwolski, Stan the Band Man, turned out to be the bravest and most honorable person in the whole mess. He had even talked to Sandra, offering his help in any way she needed, but she'd turned him down.

Peggy and I had to tell the Rangers what we'd seen with our own eyes, and yet had remained silent about. We told them how right up to the end we hoped it wasn't true. We didn't want to believe it. Barbara Sevesek had to admit to listening in on party lines, which the old Ranger told her, sounding strict, was against Texas law. The younger Ranger told each of us that Coach Bengud was going to prison for a long time. If they treated us like we weren't too bright, maybe it was because we had seen so much and had done so little about it.

The Rangers talked to Sandra in our kitchen, right there at the kitchen table. When they told her that Coach Bengud had said that Greg Phillips was probably the father of her baby, she laughed. It was a terrible laugh that could be heard out in the carport where we stood. The laugh dissolved into choking sobs, that made all us witnesses afraid to look at one another. Peggy pressed her lips together until they disappeared, and I kept biting my lower lip, hard. The Rangers let Sandra's mama take her home, and we couldn't look at her either as they walked out of the kitchen, passing us, thankfully, without making eye contact with anyone. They interviewed her later that day at her own house; she showed them the window Coach Bengud had crawled through. The young Ranger told Daddy Sandra never cried again.

Sandra didn't come back to school, and the Snowdens moved to Bryan. I saw her once while she was pregnant, leaving the Weingarten's store in Bryan. She didn't see me, and I didn't chase her down. Pregnant women, even adult women I didn't know, frightened me—and Sandra Snowden, pregnant and looking like a much older woman, scared the living daylights out of me. I couldn't look at her and never became her friend. I never knew if she'd wanted a friend. Mama said when the baby came, she gave it to a family that couldn't have children of their own.

I knew everything about the case now, whether I wanted to or not. I'd heard Daddy, the Rangers, even Sandra and Coach Bengud tell their stories. I knew every little horrible detail from start to finish, and I hated knowing them. I heard Coach Bengud's denials, his excuses to his wife, and finally his negotiating for a lesser sentence, throwing Sandra under the bus. I heard

Sandra's sad hopes that things might someday work out for her and Bobby Bengud. I wished, maybe not for the first time, that I lived in a regular house, where people didn't bring their troubles. Right then, I wanted a house where people didn't tell every bad thing they'd done, not where I could hear it. I wanted to be like Peggy Worsek, who would not allow anyone to tell her any of what she called the "gory" details of the case. She didn't hear one more thing, wouldn't let herself hear, after that day in the carport with the Rangers, and there were plenty of times I wished I hadn't either.

Coach Bobby Bengud went to prison, but only for a short time, less than a year, because of some technicality. It was the first time I'd heard of such a thing, where meanness goes unpunished because a clerk or lawyer made a mistake. Still another thing I wished I didn't know about.

I ran into Coach Bengud at the courthouse a year or so later. He was dressed in a suit, with regular dress shoes on, and without the keys, of course. I heard his snorting breathing behind me before I saw him. By this time, he had become in my mind a symbol of everything bad in the grown-up world, and I would have recognized him a mile away. Feeling his awful presence, my skin crawled and hairs stood up on my arms.

With penetrating eyes, he looked at me and I looked right back at him hard as I could, trying to finally show some nerve. I hoped he would see in my eyes that he never had fooled me, not for a minute, even if it wasn't true. I wanted him to think that even a coward like me would be ready for the likes of him next time; I wouldn't be so slow to recognize a bad person like him. Except for the eyes, he looked like an ordinary grown-up, and I kept staring, feeling brave.

Then he smiled the meanest smile I'd ever seen, right at me. Trying hard not to, I looked away.

Thirteen

Jail Christmas

*I*f one more person said "Have a Merry Christmas," I swore I'd spit in his eye. Based on what I'd gathered from my friends and, even more so, what I saw on TV, our Christmases just were not nearly as nice. Even our Christmases out at the farm had been better. We'd cut our own tree and decorate it together, and nobody had to rush out to arrest people. Even those memories had me feeling down during the season.

Father Knows Best and *Ozzie and Harriet*'s Christmases could break your heart and make you cry, with the families sitting around the tree, handing out presents, singing carols. At the jail on Christmas Eve, Daddy had dozens of calls early in the evening while people got drunk and celebrated, then later on in the night he'd get dozens more when some of those same people got depressed and fought with one another or stole one another's presents. Christmas morning was filled with lawyers and families trying to get those very same hell-raisers out of jail in time for Christmas dinner. It had been next to impossible for us to have a real family Christmas in the years we'd been in the jail, so somewhere along the line, our family had just given up. Even Mama had become holiday shy.

For Christmas dinner, we went to my grandma's. She was my grandma, but she was Mama to me, at least within the family. I never tried to explain to outsiders that I had two "Mamas" in my life. In fact, she was Mama to her own four kids and all eleven of her grandkids. When her whole family got together, like we did every few weeks, there'd be five women called Mama there. You'd think it would be impossible, but there was hardly any confusion. We all learned from the time we were little babies to add to the word "Mama." We'd say "my mama," "your mama," "Mama's mama," "Your

daddy's mama." We'd just throw it into our conversation easily and naturally. Anyway, these family get-togethers at my grandma's house were fun,
but they were worlds away from the one-family-in-their-own-house-giving-
gifts ideal I was dreaming of.

Another problem with our Christmases was that we opened presents
throughout the Christmas season, pretty much as they arrived. This was
partly because of all the business going on around the jail on the actual day,
but a big part of it was Mama. She could not tolerate an unopened present.
She was as bad, or worse, than my brother Bill, who didn't have the patience
God gave babies. I'd given them both a talking-to about how much fun waiting could be. They got a good laugh out of that, so I knew I had my work
cut out for me with my Christmas scheme. If I told them I was planning
a gathering to exchange presents, with the TV turned off, where we'd all
express our love for one another, Bill would be rolling on the kitchen floor.
I'd have to be discreet, or truthfully, I'd have to be downright sneaky.

I knew the present exchange couldn't happen at dinner, not when Mama
had a jail full of prisoners to feed. It couldn't happen Christmas morning,
when the jail would be Grand Central Station from daylight on. So I homed
in on Christmas Eve, but early, before too many people in the county had a
chance to get drunk or crazy.

I approached my brothers first, starting at the bottom of the food chain.

"Mama is sad we don't have a real Christmas," I told Walter. To Bill I said,
"Walter and I are planning a Christmas party for Mama." To them both, I
said, "I've bought you a great present," laughing so they'd know it was a joke,
but hoping they'd wonder. I knew I had to get them in on it, and I also knew I
had no influence whatsoever with them, so I'd have to be at my manipulative
best, and even at fourteen years old, I was good.

It was surprisingly easy; maybe they'd been watching what the TV families did, too. They agreed to six to eight p.m. Christmas Eve, after the college
football games on TV were over and before they went on their dates.

Mama was next.

"I think Daddy is missing the way Christmas used to be at the farm," I
said, a little catch in my voice. "And I know I do. Remember how we'd get up
early and sit around the fire?"

"I do," she said, and she looked a little pensive.

Clearly she felt sorry for me, poor little deprived child I was pretending to be. The fact that I was just proposing cookies and punch, nothing fancy, probably helped get her to go along, but she said "Sure, we'll do it."

Even Daddy agreed that the time period was the least likely for a call. He got to talking about Christmases when he was a little boy out on the dairy, even before I brought them up. Before TV, presents he got, Christmas trees he and his sisters had chopped down in the Pavlas's pasture. He was going for it in a big way. I loved those memories and hoped he'd share them again during our celebration. They were just what I was hoping we'd make more of.

We got a big Christmas tree from down at the grocery store, and even if my efforts to get the whole family to decorate it failed, Mama and me used every decoration we could drag out of the closet. That tree was so weighted down, it kind of leaned against the living room wall. But there in the jail living room, it created the right atmosphere of Christmas cheer and family tradition. I stared at the lights for hours on end. I'd turn them on first thing in the morning and leave them on all day. That we avoided a visit from the Caldwell Volunteer Fire Department is just one of those Christmas miracles you hear about. It gave me hope for another one or two.

I talked about gifts with everybody in the family, telling them I could help out with getting them. That year started an annual tradition where I bought Mama's gift from Daddy, a new robe, same gift each and every year. She was always having to get up in the middle of the night to open the jail, take in a prisoner or let a prisoner out, so she needed a good bathrobe. It was either that or sleep in her clothes, which she did plenty of times. Daddy gave me the money, said "Get her a pretty robe," and he would look at it before I wrapped it so he wouldn't seem surprised when she opened it. This year, so that there would be more presents to open, I even kept the grab-bag gifts I got at school and at the Methodist Youth Fellowship party. I was sure Bill had already opened and re-wrapped all of his presents, and I kind of suspected my mama had, too, but they were there, stacked up under the tree. It looked just like I pictured.

My grandma had brought us cookies early on Christmas Eve. She smelled everything before she'd eat it, even her own cookies. These were big soft oatmeal-raisin, made in the shape of stars, and turns out they did smell great. I was glad to not have to make cookies, a risky undertaking I had been dreading. Our Aunt Sissy, Mama's sister, had brought white divinity candy, wrapped in tissue paper in a silver foil box, almost a week before, and I'd hidden it, which was tricky with Bill and Walter in the house. They could sniff out anything edible quicker than you'd believe. Mama made eggnog, drinking a cup or two as she went, and was singing carols in the kitchen while she made punch for us kids. I hoped we'd all sing carols together later, but I put a Christmas record on the record player just in case family caroling was dreaming the impossible Christmas dream.

As six o'clock approached, I paced the living room, nervous as a cat. Every two minutes I pulled back the curtain, because Daddy hadn't made it home yet. Mama said he was trying to get Jessie Pollack's wife out of their car where she'd locked herself after breakfast that morning when Jessie told her he was going out with his brothers on Christmas Eve, whether she liked it or not. It seemed to me this family Christmas thing was throwing people for a loop all over the county; it wasn't just me. My brothers were fidgeting and antsy. I worried they might bolt any second. They were ready to get out there with their girlfriends. What were those girls' families doing for Christmas Eve? I wondered, obsessed like I was with the idea of family Christmases. I turned the tree lights off and then on again and picked up tinsel that had fallen on the floor.

Finally, at 6:15, Daddy drove in, screeching his tires on the concrete carport. It did my heart good to know he was hurrying. I rushed out to the carport as he opened his door.

"Anything wrong?" he asked. A worried frown played at the corners of his mouth. I must have looked as anxious as I felt.

"No, not a thing," I said brightly. We walked in arm in arm into the kitchen. Sipping a cup of eggnog, he told us how Jessie Pollack was going to stay home with his wife, after all—and had promised to go to midnight mass with her up at St. Mary's.

"Another miracle of Christmas," he laughed, since Jessie Pollack probably hadn't been to mass since he was baptized.

We were sitting down in the living room, all five of us, laughing. The TV was off, and the Christmas tree lights sparkled up the room. We talked and ate Mama's cookies. I thought it was too good to be true and, sure enough, it was.

The phone rang; Mama took it and said, "It's teenagers doing wheelies under the Christmas lights up on the courthouse square."

Daddy stood up, went to the phone, talked quickly, and hung up. Before I could say "Oh, Lordy," out loud, he called the chief of police right then and there, where we could all hear, and asked him to handle it.

"We're having our Christmas," he said into the phone, smiling at me.

I exhaled.

As soon as he hung up, I acted like the hostess. "Merry Christmas, everybody," I said, picking up the first gift to give to Daddy, but suddenly gifts began to move, not one at a time like I planned, but in a mad rush.

"Open this one." "Do you like it?" "Hand me another one!"

Paper tore, ribbons flew, and it was over in ten minutes, tops. I was happy. I was sad.

After more eggnog and divinity candy, my brother Bill slipped out the kitchen door.

In the kitchen getting more punch, I could hear "I Saw Mommy Kissing Santa Claus" by Brenda Lee playing on my record player, and I knew Mama and Daddy were dancing a slow dance. Then I heard Mama start to cry. In a panic, I ran to them, afraid of what I might find. But Mama was hugging Daddy and smiling and laughing and crying all at the same time.

"What's wrong?" I asked, hoping for the best, but fearing the worst.

Through her tears, Mama squeezed out the words, "A house. We're building a new house, out at the farm." She was pretty near beside herself with joy. I was happy for her, knowing how much she wanted a real house, but I couldn't help wondering if it was a house we'd move into now, or someday, when we didn't live in the jail anymore, or what? Whatever the answers, it was making Mama's Christmas tonight, and ought to give her some hope for a normal life, like she was always talking about.

Like jolting us back to reality from a fairytale, the phone rang with news of a break-in at Doc Fetzer's office down by the ice house. I knew Daddy would have to go, and he did.

Mama and I cleared away the wrappings and we went outside to listen to the Negro choir from the Church of Jesus sing Christmas carols to the prisoners out by the jail yard fence.

"It was our best Christmas, honey," Mama said, wrapping her arm around me. I leaned into her, knowing she was on Cloud Nine from the news about the new house.

It was seven o'clock. We had managed to get in forty-five minutes of hard-earned Christmas out of it.

———

Hard to believe, but Daddy was home by ten that night and didn't get another call. Even Bill and Walter came in early. We sat around the kitchen table, all five of us again (the second Christmas miracle) and talked about what a quiet night it had been. The TV was on, but at least it was in the other room. We talked about our presents, and everybody was thrilled by at least one thing. Even Walter, who was hard to buy for, liked his new corduroy jacket. Mama and Daddy drew little house plans on notebook paper, dreaming about the house at the farm.

Six o'clock Christmas Eve would become a tradition, we all promised.

But the next year, Daddy was gone all night when a plane crashed on Christmas Eve out by Dime Box, killing everybody aboard. The year after that, the LaMontes created a firestorm, literally, up on Alligator Street. Mr. LaMonte asked all his neighbors to watch their front windows where a candle-lit tree would be coming on Christmas Eve, copied after his Old World dreams of Christmas past. When he lit the very first candle, the entire tree, flocked in beautiful and flammable pink snow, immediately erupted in flames. It was beautiful, everybody said, but almost destroyed the LaMonte home, the flocked tree acting like a beautiful pink fire bomb. The LaMonte brothers were ever after famous for their gruesomely melted model airplanes.

Walter—about to be married—spent the next several Christmases at his in-laws. One year Bill was off in New Mexico, working for the railroad.

There was the Christmas Eve murder in 1966, and one year there was a fire in the jail.

We weren't like other families, much as I wanted us to be, much as I tried.

Six o'clock Christmas Eve jail Christmas didn't really make it as a tradition: only as a memory of that one good year.

Fourteen

Sister Ocean

I could hear him singing when I turned the corner by the feed store. "Cheer up, my brother," he boomed, sending his voice soaring out of every jail cell window, even the one that wouldn't open, to float across the used car lot up on Harvey Street.

The Reverend Jerome Johnson came every Sunday, without fail. He showed up early, too early to hear the hungover drunks out in the jail tell it, to preach to sinners in the county jail before he went to his own church out at Hix, Texas, to preach to the good folks in the Hix Church of Jesus congregation. He preached loud and with lots of feeling, nothing like the somber Methodist ministers I was used to. Sometimes he'd bust out in a hymn, right in the middle of his sermon. I would sit out in the backyard straining my ears for the part when he'd approach each cell and talk to each prisoner in turn. I never could hear much of that, but I knew it had to be his best stuff. My father, in his official sheriff's voice, said I should not, under any circumstances, listen in; it wasn't polite. But Reverend Jerome made Sunday mornings an event, not to be missed, and I hardly ever did.

But this was Saturday afternoon, and the jail was mostly empty, waiting for the Saturday night rush. Something must be up, I thought, as I hurried down the hill.

My brother Walter was sitting at the kitchen table, doing his calculus homework. He was taking the class for the second, or maybe third time, at Blinn College down the road in Brenham. Seeing Walter study was a fact of life around the jail.

"Why's the preacher here on Saturday?" I asked as I walked in the door.

"It's practice," he said. "They're going to have a jailhouse revival tomorrow. There's singers that came in from Houston, and they're in there checking out the echoes in the jail, or something like that." Trying to concentrate, Walter frowned at my interruption. Reverend Jerome seemed to be making his attempts at studying worse. So I went out to the carport to see what I could hear for myself.

Now I heard a woman singing. If the reverend could boom and shake the jail doors with his big baritone voice, this woman could pierce steel with hers. She was singing "Shall We Gather at the River," and I was ready to go to any river she directed me to, right then and there. I thought if anyone could hear her, they'd do the same.

I walked into the jail yard where the dogs were usually sleeping, and even their ears were pricked up, a feat for bloodhounds. For these lazy old hounds, named Bones and Cleo, it was short of a holy miracle. I got close to a cell window towards the back and looked in to see a short, dark brown woman with her white hair cut as short as a man's, which showed off her big, white, dangly earrings shaped like shells.

Her eyes shut tight and her head thrown back, she sang, "Gather with the saints at the river, that flows by the throne of God."

I'd heard that song all my life, but I'd never heard it like this. I felt something rise inside, and wondered if I was being saved, right there in the jail yard, with Bones's and Cleo's big heads spread out over my feet. I'd never had this feeling in the Methodist Church, sitting in Daddy's favorite pew like we always did, near the back where he could sneak out if he had to. I never got it at the tent revivals out at the fairgrounds either, where the preachers were loud and real emotional, and almost comical, as far as I was concerned. This felt like something special, but I couldn't tell what. I admired the reverend, but this was something special.

They were finishing up, so I went out into the carport to say hello to Reverend Johnson and to get a close-up look at the woman with the voice. The reverend was a big linebacker kind of man, and Daddy said that's exactly what he was when he played football for Prairieview A&M a few years back. His big bald head gleamed in the afternoon sunshine. I always wondered if he had hair and shaved it off, or if he was truly bald. He dwarfed the little woman with the white hair, and me, too, for that matter. He introduced us, said her name was Sister Ocean. I wanted to ask them about my feelings, but I worried how they'd react if I just came out with "Am I saved, or not? And how do you know if you are?"

She said "Hello," to me, sounding like anybody would, and I told her how much I'd liked her singing.

"Just the voice God gave me," she said in her normal sounding voice, and they walked away, leaving me to ponder salvation on my own.

After they left though, try as I might, I couldn't call up that feeling I had while she was singing, couldn't recreate it. Even closing my eyes and covering my ears and humming the songs she sang didn't help. The thing was gone. I guessed I wasn't saved after all, but I was looking forward to the revival the next day to maybe clarify things for me. If Daddy okayed it, I'd skip Sunday school to hear the whole service with Reverend Jerome and Sister Ocean right there in the jail. If he could save me, I was all for it.

Reverend Jerome brought the whole Church of Jesus with him. Daddy let them line up in the jail hallway and they were packed in tight. I asked if I could go in there, too, and I only had to say "Please, please, please" a few times before he agreed, like I knew he would sooner or later. I didn't tell him it might be my soul on the line.

Every cell was filled, even the two with the double bunks, and there must have been at least twenty Church of Jesus people, along with reverend, Sister Ocean, who had even bigger shells on her ears today, and me. When they started singing, I knew they'd been practicing. The whole Church of Jesus congregation was backing up Sister Ocean like an angel's choir. During the first hymn, "Farther Along," that feeling filled me—light and floaty, heaven-filled. As Sister Ocean sang "We'll understand why," it seemed I understood everything.

Again I wondered if this was salvation. I could see how a person might think it was, even if it wasn't. The prisoners stayed quiet as they could be, most of them with their heads stuck right in front of the little barred windows in the cell doors, looking righteous and saved, like me.

During Reverend Jerome's sermon, I heard Daddy's car drive out of the carport and take off down the hill to the highway, but other than a quick thought that he'd gotten a hurry-up call (not unusual for the sheriff on a Sunday morning), my head was filled with the songs of the service. All too soon, Sister Ocean and the congregation reached a fever pitch with a fast, almost rocking, version of "Just As I Am." The Church of Jesus people were clapping their hands to the rhythm, the prisoners tapping their cups against the bars. I'd even gotten to clapping my hands and shaking my head like what I might have called a holy roller before this. The music over, Reverend Jerome started speaking to each prisoner individually, and I finally got to hear his personal touch.

He put his shining head right up against the bars and gave advice, offered help when he could, answered questions, and seemed to reach every one of those prisoners, whatever their race, even the ones with the worst of hangovers. Nobody threw up the whole time, which just goes to show how affected they all were by the service.

He was just about finished with the last two prisoners, the Barley brothers, who had been in jail all week long after threatening to kill one another over a fence Fred Barley erected over the property line between their two properties. Reverend Johnson was dispensing wisdom about brotherly love, everyone looked in the direction of a commotion in the jail kitchen. We couldn't hear well, but something was definitely going on.

Mama, who was supposed to open the jail doors and let us all out at eleven o'clock, was running late. I knocked on the door, and the Reverend yelled a few times, before Sister Ocean said, "how about another hymn?" Everyone shouted "Yes!"

After a couple of more songs, and a round robin of salvation stories, I tried yelling through the door to get my mother's attention. I wasn't scared, but I was worried.

It was almost noon by this time, and by now I'd heard some cars come and go, engines racing and gravel crunching. The long-time prisoners started sharing their candy bars and Fritos, passing them through the bars. Naturally Reverend Jerome was reminded of the loaves and fishes at the Sermon on the Mount and preached on that. He told us that God saw what we needed and provided it. How our sharing would provide what the world needed.

It was the best sermon on sharing any of us had ever heard, and we said so. Sister Ocean began to sing, making up the words and the tune. It was more beautiful than any hymn I'd ever heard. . . . I could hardly believe we were locked up and couldn't get out and were feeling so good about it.

After a while, the congregation was getting a little restless, and I had to go to the bathroom. Sister Ocean had lost her voice, right in the middle of "Swing Low Sweet Chariot," which one of the Barley brothers had requested. Only Reverend Jerome was still going strong, talking to each prisoner again and again until he knew their stories every which way and could preach whatever lesson they needed to hear. I couldn't get over how Reverend Jerome could come up with something for every last one of them, always saying, "That calls to mind a scripture." He was amazing. We'd been in there for a couple of hours, and everybody began to quiet down. Not a scary quiet, or a mad quiet, more like still and downright peaceful for such a big group— especially with so many criminals.

"The peace that passes all understanding," Reverend Jerome called it, and I felt calm even though I was wondering what was keeping Mama. But as the singing had been winding down, so had my sense of so-called salvation. The feeling seemed more like the pews near the back at the Methodist Church, just nice and peaceful like that.

Finally, my mama, looking frazzled, her eyes red and swollen, opened the big jail door. Fresh air rushed down the hallway, startling me and finally waking the old baritone who'd eaten one of Fred Barley's moon-pies and fallen right off to sleep, snoring as deep and resonant as he sang. He kept calling me Little Deputy. We all perked up, stood up stiffly, and came streaming out into the bright sunshine, squinting like the gophers in my grandma's garden.

"What happened?" I asked Mama. "Did you forget we were in there?"

"Well," she started, her voice kind of trembly. "Yes I did. With all the goings-on. After the MPs came and took him." She trailed off.

"What MPs? Took who? What happened?" I asked.

She began her story with the whole congregation gathered around there in the carport, as if she were the preacher now, the sun shining on her face. That Sunday, everything had a religious look to it, but from the goosebumps I could see all up and down her arms, she needed the sun to shine on her.

She told us about a young GI from Fort Hood who had shot his lieutenant in the head, and then took off on a car chase across Central Texas, with the law in a dozen counties out chasing after him. That had been Daddy's call right after the revival started. Well, this GI, armed and dangerous, made his way to Caldwell and had stopped down at Pierce's Store and asked directions to the police station. Mr. Pierce, knowing like we all do that Caldwell doesn't have any police station, directed him to the jail.

The soldier drove up to the jail and walked in the kitchen door, carrying his gun out in front of him, and met my mother who was wearing only her slip, getting dressed for church. With his gun pointed right at her, she yelled out, thinking for sure he was going to shoot her right where she stood. They stared at each other for a few endless seconds. And then he broke down and cried, and so did she.

They sat down together on the floor of the hallway, him still holding the gun. He wasn't directing it at her but held it with his whole hand, like he was about to hand it over—which is exactly what he did, even if it was about an hour later. By the time she took the gun and got her dress on, the GI was telling her about his lieutenant and how he didn't mean to do it, and on and on, tears streaming down his face. She called Daddy right away on the radio, which alerted the Military Police, who were only a few miles down Highway 36, and screeched up to the jail in minutes.

The congregation had started peeling off now, heading for their cars, leaving just the reverend, Mama and me, and Sister Ocean. Sister Ocean was hoarse and looking tired, but she stayed by the reverend until he finished one last sermon for my mama, all about courage. Of course, Sister Ocean couldn't sing, but she nodded a lot. I was glad Reverend Jerome was there to work his magic on Mama. She told him that it was the first time she had feared for her own life in our years in the jail. She said she'd been afraid for Daddy, just about every day, and even for her kids, but never before for herself.

Maybe the reverend had helped, or maybe she could more easily recover from fear for her own life than for ours, but it wasn't long before Mama went inside to fix a late lunch for the prisoners, like nothing had happened. Minutes later, Daddy drove in the carport, fast and reckless enough to give us a scare and sending Sister Ocean hurrying to her car. Mama and Daddy were famous for their long hugs, but as he lifted the tray of prisoners' food from her hands there in the carport and set it on top of his car and gathered her up in his arms, I knew this one might be a record setter.

I walked out with Reverend Jerome to his car. He told me Sister Ocean had some record albums and said he'd bring me his copies the next week when he came to preach, and he did just that.

One was *Sister Ocean Sings Spirituals,* and the other, a real surprise, was *Sister Ocean Sings the Blues.* I held the albums in my hands, looking at Sister Ocean on the covers. On the spirituals, she had her head thrown back and her eyes closed, looking as saved as I'd hoped to be when I heard her sing. On the blues album, she looked out right at me, sad eyes open and haunted, looking as ready to cry as I did. It gave me a big lump in my throat, just looking at her picture. Even from my little record player, with the speaker in the lid, I could get the feeling from Sister Ocean whenever I wanted.

When I played the record for Mama, she'd try to cover it up, but I could see her tears. Just like I knew Sister Ocean had to have been feeling the blues to sing like that, my mama's crying meant she had felt the blues. I wondered if she'd been that sad before we lived in the jail, but I couldn't remember.

Reverend Jerome let me keep Sister Ocean's records until I could get my own.   y Sunday when I returned his copies. I walked out to his car by   fence with him. "I don't think it's salvation I feel when Sister   I said sadly, almost apologetically. He said right away, "Don't worry. If it's not salvation, it's the next best thing. It's joy! And that's a gift from God." He smiled at me and looked so happy I could feel it inside me, too. I knew right then that Reverend Jerome was a great preacher, capable of reaching even someone like me, who wasn't even saved. "Joy is about as hard to come by as salvation." "Be grateful!" he cried out.

I knew from watching my mama that joy was surely hard to come by, and I was grateful. But it was complicated, just like my so-called salvation had been, because I felt my gratitude not to God, but to Sister Ocean.

Fifteen

Bevo

*A*dog is better than a cow. Ask anybody. If you've spent much time with cows, like my family has, then you know they're dull animals. Except for a short time when they're calves, when you can ride them for fun, spending time with cows will get you nothing except milk, or maybe flies, and of course, steaks.

Cows don't care about you, not like dogs who are happy to see you coming, licking your face and all. A cow might lick your face if it were coated with molasses. My brother Bill has done it. But the whole idea is too disgusting to consider, especially if you've ever felt of a cow's tongue, or eaten one, which lots of people swear by as a delicacy. My daddy says cows can care about you. He says he had a milk cow that he's sure loved him and she knew he loved her, too, and I take his word for it.

But in Texas cows held a place of reverence for some, including my own father and his favorite milk cow. Dogs were also treated special in Texas. Mr. Jim Hultz, a bachelor farmer friend of my grandma's from out at Second Creek, was a good example. When his beloved blond Pomeranian, Sissy, died, he kept her in the chest freezer for six months before he could bear to part with her. Then he buried her in the side yard beside his vegetable garden with a granite tombstone the size of a small refrigerator.

The discussion of dogs versus cows became important every fall and could be heard all over Texas when the Aggies played the Longhorns, and Caldwell was no different. The old codgers playing dominos at the National Bank building, kids at school, men drinking coffee at the Ranch Café, and women hanging their laundry in the yard all talked about the mascots (the dog, Reveille, and the longhorn steer, Bevo), the team colors, and even sometimes the teams themselves.

College football was like a religion in our part of Texas, only more important. Certainly more people went to football games than to church. People were either fans of the Texas A&M Aggies, or the University of Texas Longhorns. There was no middle ground, even for children. Babies wore either Aggie maroon, or UT orange. Even if you didn't care about football (and you'd never admit such a thing), you chose up sides.

That decision was a kind of life choice. The down-to-earth Aggies were farmers, as they proclaimed that in their school songs and yells sung by men in military uniforms. They graduated the best veterinarians and engineers in the world. Farmers were right there in the name. The Aggies were urged to "gig 'em." The Longhorns were tea-sippers, pampered or cultured, whichever way you saw it. Their showband featured baton twirlers in teeny sequined tights, and the biggest bass drum in the country, named Big Bertha. They graduated world-class doctors and lawyers and poets. Their cry was "hook 'em."

Because Caldwell was so close, twenty-five miles from College Station, home of A&M, most folks were Aggie fans, but there were enough UT alumni and people who liked Austin, home of UT, to make the rivalry the topic of conversation. The big grudge game was played around Thanksgiving since the 1800s, and every year the rivalry worked up to a fever pitch.

———

"Reveille's been kidnapped!" my brother Bill yelled across the kitchen as he ran in the door. The Aggie mascot, Reveille, was a little collie dog that wore a maroon kerchief tied around her neck and ran around the field during games. She was cute but revered and trained to bark at anybody trying to get onto the football field.

"You mean dognapped, Bill," said Walter, barely looking up from his studies.

"Those dirty tea-sippers took her during the night. They better not hurt her." Bill was an Aggie fan; he loved dogs and seemed sincerely worried about the little collie. Bill never missed a *Lassie* episode when we were kids.

He took up for old Mr. Hultz when people were saying he was crazy with that dog in his freezer. Just the year before, the Longhorn cheerleaders had taken Reveille up onto the state capitol dome in a portable kennel cage and left her hanging there most of a day before the Texas Railroad Commissioner, an Aggie alumnus, noticed her as he walked to his office in the capitol office building. He tried to get a special resolution passed that day in the legislature censuring the University of Texas for cruelty to animals. Whenever he'd talk about how wonderful dogs are, Bill would quote my grandma's story. He'd say, "Lock your girlfriend and your dog in the trunk of your car, wait an hour, and see which one is glad to see you," and he'd laugh uproariously.

The Aggies were not total innocents, by any means. They had taken Bevo, a longhorn steer that roamed UT's sidelines, on long rides throughout the state, and last year, when the game was played in Austin, the Aggies had cut a big A and a big M into the grass of the football field and had thrown the grass clippings in Bevo's pen. People talked about the symbolism of Bevo eating the grass, but I didn't get it, and if truth be known, I think the Aggies involved probably didn't know either, if it meant anything at all. "Bevo Eats A&M" probably isn't what they were thinking. The university had resodded the field, but the A and M were a brighter green, and showed up prominently.

Bill kept me updated on the Reveille situation all week long. She was still missing on Wednesday night, when the Aggies were having their bonfire. Every year, Mama and Daddy drove me over to College Station to see the bonfire, and this year, with Reveille dognapped, even Walter and Bill went along. Walter pointed out how no ransom note had appeared, and tempers were running high. In the field beside the fire, Aggies, standing and reduced to tears, called Reveille's name over and over. Bill was choked up himself and fell quiet all the way home to Caldwell. I was sure he was thinking of all the awful things that could be done to poor little Reveille.

Thursday morning early, the news broke that Bevo went missing. That the Aggies were getting their revenge perked up Bill considerably. He wasn't worried about Bevo, since Bevo was a steer, even if he was a now somewhat rare longhorn steer. You didn't see those around much anymore. Cows, even if you loved them like a pet, were made to slaughter, made to become steaks and hamburgers. If Bevo had become a steak during the night, it would be sad for the tea-sippers, Bill said, but not a tragedy. Nothing like a dead dog.

"We better not see a dead dog!" Bill snarled.

The University of Texas band always stopped in Caldwell on the morning of the games to practice their halftime show on our high school football field. There was a big crowd every year, and Daddy, engaging in some real low-level sheriff duties, helped with the parking and such. I was about to leave to walk up to the field myself, when the phone rang. When I picked up, I heard, in a thick German accent, "I have a purple cow in my front pasture." If not for the serious adult voice, I would have thought the call a joke, you know, the nursery rhyme, "I've never seen a purple cow . . ." But I took down all the information, like a good sheriff's daughter: a purple cow in Emil Heil's pasture on Farm-to-Market Road 62, two miles from the Dime Box cutoff. I wrote it down in my best printing.

I told Bill I would be looking for Daddy to give him the message about the purple cow, and if he saw him first, to do it himself. "Emil Heil, FM 62, Two miles, Dime Box Cutoff," Bill repeated, and shot out the door.

Later that morning, when I found Daddy at the high school, surrounded by University of Texas people, I asked, "Did Bill give you the message about Emil Heil?"

"Yes," Daddy said, and I went off to watch the band. I could already hear *Texas Fight* starting and stopping in the distance, as the band practiced stepping off.

———

Later that day, sitting in our freezing living room, where the air conditioner was blasting in spite of it being November, I watched the big game with Daddy and my brothers. We'd already gorged on turkey and dressing, and now Mama worked on fixing big trays of it for the prisoners. Mama was not a football fan, and not afraid to say so. For her, it was just another day in the jail.

The Aggies were losing, and Bill was getting surly. But then, between plays, the announcer said excitedly, "Reveille is back! She's patrolling the field!" A camera panned down to the field where the little collie romped, barking up a storm. Bill looked like he might bust out crying, he was so happy. He jumped up from the couch and danced around the room. The announcer went on to say it was sad that Bevo was still missing, and an appeal went out to anyone who might know of her whereabouts. This reminded me of the purple cow.

"Daddy" I said, reaching into the bowl of popcorn, before Bill turned the whole bowl over with his shenanigans., "What happened to the purple cow in Emil Heil's pasture?"

"What purple cow?" Daddy said.

His eyes down, Bill got up and slinked toward the door, looking guilty as sin. Walter started to smile, like he knew something, too.

"I thought Bill told you," I said. "Emil Heil called about a purple cow he found in his front pasture this morning, and Bill was going to tell you about it."

"Well," Daddy said watching Bill go out the door, "Bill said Emil Heil was bringing a cow out to our farm for me to take a look at this weekend. Said it turned up in his pasture and wasn't his."

Daddy stood up and walked out to the carport, and I followed. Bill sat in Daddy's patrol car, looking like he was ready to drive right off in it. "Is the cow Emil Heil brought to the farm purple?"

"Well, Daddy, it's more like maroon," Bill said. "I called Emil and asked him if he could bring it over to the farm so you could have a look, then Walter and I drove out to the farm to check it out. He's a sight to see." Bill was laughing some by now but was watching Daddy for any signs of trouble. Sometimes it was hard to tell with Daddy, but, of us all, Bill was probably the expert at the signs.

"Is it Bevo?" Daddy asked, not quite smiling but looking like he might. Daddy went to Baylor himself, played on the football team, but when it came to Aggies versus Longhorns, he was an Aggie fan, probably due to proximity, but he admired the veterinary school as well.

"It's a maroon longhorn," Bill said. "That's all I can say. Now, Bevo, who is a brown longhorn, is missing, but this is a maroon longhorn. I just couldn't say if it was Bevo, although I guess you could make a case for it." Bill was good at this kind of talk. I admired his skill.

Daddy went into the kitchen and said to mama, "I've got to run out to the farm to look at a cow." For Mama, Thanksgiving was just another abnormal holiday at the jail, and she never expected we would spend it as a family. However, she surprised us, "Oh, I'll come too." All five of us piled in Daddy's car, always an unusual event.

On the ride out, Daddy said in the most somber tone he could muster, "All my calls are serious, kids, even if you think they're funny. Even if I think they're funny."

"Daddy, soon as the game's over, I was going to tell you about what's most likely Bevo. I didn't think anybody would come out during the game to get Bevo." He was really sorry, and groveling now, and swearing to be a better kid in the future.

"Well, I suppose it's been out there only a couple of hours," Daddy said. I could see him giving Mama a little smile as I leaned forward from the back seat.

Mama giggled. That got us kids laughing.

Daddy mustered up a frown, and said again, "Sheriff's business is serious business." We were all smart enough to be quiet for the rest of the ride, even though Mama giggled now and then.

We crossed the cattle guard and drove down the lane, past the pecan trees, already starting to lose their leaves, and approached the half-finished house nestled under three big live oaks, just up from the barn. Started last spring, the construction was slow going. Daddy bought materials and hired help as extra money would allow. At this point, you could see the frame, and where the rooms would eventually be, and the big front porch stretching all the way across the front. Even slow as it was going, Mama seemed satisfied to see it going up, and Daddy looked pleased with every new board nailed on. Every couple of days, Mama came out and walked through the framed rooms, or she'd sit on the front porch, the only finished part, even after all this time. Daddy stopped right in front; Mama got out and walked up the steps without a look back at us.

We drove on down the lane, and there in the holding pen in front of our barn stood a massive longhorn. A cow purple as a Grapette soda. The massive horns were purple, too.

When Daddy got out and grabbed the hose to wash it down, purple dye ran down onto the sandy floor of the pen, making a big violet puddle. I sat perched up on the top fence rail, laughing, trying not to fall into the pen and get purple feet for my trouble.

When Bevo was brown again, except for those amazing horns, Bill laughed at how Bevo looked like something out of a kid's coloring book, colored all wrong.

"They might have to get themselves a new Bevo," Bill croaked.

From his patrol car, Daddy called the Brazos County Sheriff's Office.

"We've got a longhorn here, brought in by a local farmer. Found in his pasture. It's brown but has long maroon horns. Probably Bevo," Daddy radioed. We could hear the deputies laughing in the background. Aggie fans, I guess.

We left Bevo, safe and secure in our barn holding pen, with plenty of hay. The longhorn looked happy enough, if a little bit funny, with those purple horns somehow long and stately, despite the color. Bevo was impressive.

We found Mama sitting in her rocker on the front porch of the half-done house. She ran down the steps and plopped in the car without a look back. I could sense she had to buck herself up to go from her house dreamworld, with privacy and a porch to sit on, back to the real world of the jail.

When we got back, the game was just finishing up. The Aggies were three points behind. We heard the announcer, "We just got word, Bevo has been found. Unhurt!" The crowd roared. The Aggies may be losing, but knowing both animals were safe was reason enough for an Aggie crowd to cheer. All of us but Mama were glued to the TV to see if Daddy was mentioned. He wasn't. Mama had out her kitchen drawings for the new house and, after the game was over, kept Daddy at the kitchen table for an hour going over the plans.

When the tea-sipper cowboys, as Bill called them, arrived at our farm just about sunset to get Bevo, Bill laughed at their orange silky shirts with white fringe.

"Those wouldn't last a minute on a real cowboy," he jibed. "And those have to be the whitest hats you ever saw. And take a look at those white tennis shoes. Not even real boots!"

It took three of them to get Bevo in the trailer, having slung ropes around the head and horns, while one other fellow stood by with an electric cattle prod. "Emil Heil had brought her over with one little halter, by himself, without a bit of trouble," Bill said.

"Emil is a heck of a cattleman," Daddy said.

Bill smiled. "He must be an Aggie."

The cowboys were just sick about the color of Bevo's horns, swearing retribution on whoever did this to their beloved mascot. Daddy suggested they try bleaching them, since that worked to remove the red ear medicine he used on his own cows.

"Got some bleach water in the barn, if you want to try it," he said kindly.

It did work, even if took the orange out of one of the cowboy's silk shirts, leaving Bevo with blond streaks around the head and neck. In the end, Bevo looked like a nearly normal brown longhorn steer with blond highlights. If you looked close, you could see a purple tint to those impressive horns.

Everybody except Bill looked satisfied with the outcome. He'd been hoping the horns would remain purple forever. He'd decided these cowboy dudes right here were the dognappers, and anybody who'd mess with somebody's little dog deserved a cow with purple horns.

Sixteen

Running the Box

$\mathcal{I}$ remember laughing so hard, I could hardly stay upright, as we sprinted across the open field under a shining moon.

"Shut up!" one of the boys had yelled. "He's still after us!"

It was true. A big and scary truck driver was lumbering toward us, in hot pursuit of eight tittering teens across the Sikorski's pasture. I had thought he wouldn't catch us, but then I never thought anything bad could happen to me. I know now that lots of young people think that, and bad things happen to them all the time. Still, taking chances was part of being young. I was definitely taking a risk that night, running the box, but I'm pretty sure I'd never had so much fun, unless you count that time we stole watermelons out on Poor Farm Road and the farmer shot at us. We all thought later that he probably pointed his gun up in the air, but I had liked thinking he was aiming right at us, because it made for a better story down at the Dairy King, where we told it for at least a year afterward.

Now I could hear my brother Bill chortling and cussing as he loped through fresh cow manure. Following his voice and the smell, I rushed on through the night.

"He was pretty mad," Bill said when I caught up, "and maybe drunk. Probably thinks there's something serious going on here."

Serious was not what running the box was about. It was the boys' new favorite thing to do that summer, hoping for fun and excitement in small-town Caldwell. We would be so bored when we got together in the evenings, our collective tedium would reach a critical mass and send us off to do something stupid. Even though boredom was the clear reason for doing these things, it didn't serve as an excuse if you got caught. We tried hard not to get caught, especially Bill and me, since as the sheriff's kids we'd be in double trouble. Our older brother, Walter, made it through high school without getting into trouble of any kind, and though you had to admire that kind of thing, I didn't have such perfection in me. Bill, of course, didn't have a prayer, as someone in trouble a big part of the time till he was a grown man. Mama used to say if he wasn't getting in trouble, he was breaking a bone. So, with boredom running rampant around the Dairy King, one of the boys came up with running the box.

Nobody knew if the idea was original or if kids were running the box all around central Texas in the summer of 1963. This activity might have been a natural for a town like Caldwell, right at the junction of two state highways, with two-lanes running out of town in all four directions. Ray Don Dilger claimed he'd concocted the plan. A real good-looking boy, he had soft blue eyes the girls called Jesus eyes. Unfortunately, he was conceited, wanted the spotlight on him, and taking credit for running the box was no different. With those eyes, he need not have bothered. But whoever thought it up, some of the boys had been doing it for about a week or so before Peggy Worsek and I joined in.

It worked like this. You take a suitcase, or a toolbox, something that looks like it's worth something. In fact, it has to be something that would merit turning around on the highway and going back for. You put it out on the highway, right in the road, or maybe off to the side a little bit. The guys engaged in hot debate about placement, and since most of your time running the box is spent waiting around for a car to come, hot debate is half the experience. Anyway, you tie a rope around the target and wait for a car to come by. Once the car has passed, and the driver has taken a look at the box, gotten interested and starts turning around, you pull the box off the road into the bushes or wherever you're hiding, then watch some poor person search all over for the thing, yelling back at his wife in the car, "But I did see a suitcase out here."

The more they look and drive up and down searching, the more we'd laugh like idiots. It sounds completely dumb now, so I guess you had to be there, but we would laugh ourselves silly by the side of the highway.

That's what got us caught.

At least that's what Bill said. "Girls laughing got us caught, and girls should never have been allowed running the box."

Peggy Worsek did have a funny and loud laugh. In fact Bill had made the hyena comparison more than once. And when she'd get tickled, she could not stop. That crazy cackling is part of what made hanging around with her so good. She enjoyed things so loudly and so apparently, nobody ever wondered to themselves, "Is Peggy having a good time?" You could just tell, and when you're a teenager, not everything is that sure about people, but there was Peggy, sure as can be, having a good time.

But that night out in the bushes, when the truck driver laboriously backed his eighteen-wheeler down the road to look for the suitcase, Peggy was having a blast, and so was I. The case, a pretty yellow Samsonite, belonged to Honey Hudson, Bobby Hudson's mother, who would have been irate if she knew its whereabouts that night. The truck driver, hanging out the cab window, was cussing and carrying on with words I'd maybe heard in the jail yard, but never ever said. He was really mad! The perfect target for running the box. But I changed my tune when he jumped out of his cab and started to search the bushes, yelling the whole time.

Peggy, even with my hand over her mouth, had the giggles. The boys, all six of them, crowded around us, trying to shut her up and trying to be quiet about it.

Then suddenly, everything changed.

The trucker killed his motor, and Highway 36 North fell quiet as a grave, except for the crickets chirping, and, of course, except for Peggy, who was on the ground rolling by this time. This sort of laughter is catching, I guess, or maybe I got caught up in the excitement of the moment, making me laugh out loud, too.

By the cab lights we could now see the driver. He was big and burley and missing a couple of teeth. Clearly, he'd heard us and stormed our way at a dead run. The boys sailed over the barbed wire fence in a flash, and even though all country kids know how to jump a barbed wire fence, Peggy and I, laughing like we were, got tangled and had to rip her blouse half off her to get going, just as the truck driver came so close we could smell the whisky on him. That dreaded scent propelled us out across the pasture. It felt like the time of my life, kicking up my heels, running from a drunk truck driver through cow manure in the dark of night, laughing so hard my stomach clenched. Just no telling what's going to be fun when you're young, until you get there.

Fortunately, the truck driver was fat, so his sprinting petered out. We were young and could have run all night. He turned back, crawled through the fence, went back to his truck, got his flashlight, and started searching the bushes where we'd been hiding. He found Honey Hudson's yellow suitcase, and even though it was empty, he carried it up to his rig. We saw his cab lights come on. The engine roared to life, airbrakes screeching a time or two—and then he stood out on his running board and yelled out at the pasture, "Take that, you little pissants!" Then he fired a pistol a couple of times and drove off in a cloud of dust, just like in the movies.

Well, that gunfire pulled us up short. We got quiet for a minute or two, spread out in the dark listening to the crickets chirp. Peggy said she might throw up. Even though they postured all manly, the boys probably felt like me inside. Scared and shaky, and unsure. I wondered, just for a second, if I really might die someday.

Gradually, we gathered ourselves back through the pasture with nervous chuckles and straggled through the fence, back to the highway, walking down to our cars parked in Sikorski's lane, out of sight.

Then we all got to talking nonstop, everybody giving Peggy a hard time. A couple of the boys thought it could have turned bad, the truck driver armed probably with a pistol and drunk and all. We agreed he was scarier than any of the local farmers with a shotgun. Bobby Hudson worried, of course, about what he'd say when his mother got ready to go someplace and started looking for that suitcase. He decided on a complete and total denial of any knowledge, and we all agreed on that as being the best idea.

As we got into our cars, I could feel it, the coming-down feeling. I just wasn't ready to call it a night, not with my heart still pumping, so I started in on the group to go sneak into the swimming pool for a midnight swim. I had to promise Bobby Hudson to keep my clothes on to sell the idea. Then, I promised Ray Don Dilger I'd take them off.

In no time, we vaulted over the fence and into the pool and were barely wet when, wouldn't you know it, the chief of police pulled his car up, his red light flashing. His spotlight landed on half a dozen teenagers, by this time strung out over the pool fence like prisoners in the movies making a break for it. Somehow, we sprang over the fence and into our cars. But the police chief and the constable materialized, shining their flashlights in our eyes. Wet-headed and soaking, clothes and all, we reeked of chlorine. We were in for it now. Parents would be called: the whole deal. Bill had been in lots of trouble before, but not so much me. I was really sorry I had come up with this idea. Even the memory of running across the cow pasture had lost its glow as we sat there, soaking the car seats, shivering from the cold and fright. The police chief, Bo Davis, knew us all, me and Bill especially, seeing us down at the jail almost about every day like he did.

Bo Davis hadn't really liked me ever since that time on July 4 when a bunch of us kids were popping firecrackers just up from the jail on Harvey Street. When somebody called the police on us, Bo had driven up with his lights flashing. Most of the kids had scattered, but I bravely went up to his car, and leaned into the window. "No," I said confidently, "I haven't heard any firecrackers." Right then, a big cherry bomb, the loudest of all the fireworks we had, exploded right under Bo Davis's car. And I laughed. I couldn't help it. I think that laugh is what put me on Bo Davis's list. I still laughed any time I thought about it.

"Well, kids," he drawled, sticking his head in Bobby Hudson's car window. "You could be in some big trouble if you been swimming in that pool there after hours."

Nobody said a word. Then, to my horror, he looked directly at me, shined his flashlight right in my face and said, "You, young lady." I was about to cry, being singled out like that, like he knew the swimming pool was my idea. "Your daddy said for you to get yourself home right now."

I hadn't expected those words, but they soothed me a bit since it sounded like I was getting to go home without any more trouble. I hadn't had time to think it through yet.

"Let's go, then," I said. Bo Davis stepped back and let us drive off.

Everybody exhaled. We were sure glad to get off so easy. Who knew it could feel so good to get shot at, almost arrested, and then, to be heading home, safe and sound, and not in trouble. Being the sheriff's daughter had paid off big time. I felt quite special.

The other kids all were really happy to drive off after letting me and Bill out of the car at the jail, so they said later, since they knew they were off scot-free; their parents wouldn't know or anything, and mine would, already did, in fact, which was starting to dawn on me. As Bobby's car made the corner, Peggy's cackling laugh erupted in the dark.

I had to face Daddy, and he'd be disappointed in me. His sad face worked on me every time I did something I shouldn't. His eyes would look like they were about to well up with tears, and I'd be done for. When I was out late, he'd say, "Been out all night with the dry stock?" Dairy kids like us knew, of course, that dry stock cows didn't give milk, and therefore were worthless, eating good cattle feed and drinking up tank water. I hated upsetting him, but I couldn't seem to help doing a few bad things.

I lagged back, letting Bill go in first to face the music. Hearing voices from the kitchen, I hoped my father was busy with a call. That way I could relax and sneak off to bed. But Bill stood in the kitchen door, shooting me crazy, eye-rolling looks, his head tilting toward the kitchen. When I looked around the doorway, oh Lordy, I couldn't believe my eyes. Honey Hudson's yellow suitcase, big as day, lay like a bomb . . . on the floor. If that wasn't enough to give Bill and me both heart failure, there at the kitchen table, ranting about what a night he'd been through, sat the truck driver. In the bright lights of our very own kitchen, he looked bigger and uglier than I'd imagined. A pirate tattoo glowered on his arm. His presence seemed to be the last nail in our coffins.

Maybe it wasn't so great being the sheriff's daughter after all. The mighty had fallen. I suddenly knew firsthand what people mean by a double-edged sword. Being the sheriff's daughter and the culprit both might be a dilemma.

"It was a robbery attempt, Sheriff," the truck driver exclaimed. "They got me to stop, and then tried to rob me." The truck driver was describing the group of teenagers he'd had his run-in with, making us sound like criminals or worse. "If I hadn't had my gun, they'd have taken me," he was almost shouting now. As I listened, I wondered how he'd gotten such a convoluted idea of what had happened to him.

All the while, Daddy frowned at us from the corner of his eye. Obviously he suspected who the culprits were—and we were standing in his kitchen. I knew I'd get the dry stock comparison tonight, or worse.

Daddy calmed the trucker down, took his statement, promised an investigation and a complete report, and sent him on his way. Bill and I kept fidgeting, and sweating, and eyeing each other the whole time. When the trucker had barely stepped out the back door, carrying Honey Hudson's suitcase with him, Daddy turned on us.

"Okay, what's going on? Whose yellow suitcase is that? Why was it on the highway?"

Bill sucked on his lip and didn't say a word. I stood still and stared at Daddy for a full minute, and then it all came out. "We were running the box," I blurted. "We hid on the side of Highway 36 and put the suitcase in the road, and then hid it in the bushes." I was almost in tears. "When the truck driver saw it, we pulled it off the road and ran across the pasture, and Peggy was laughing, and he shot at us, and then we went and jumped in the swimming pool, and it was a big group of us, and I don't want to say who, and I'm sorry, Daddy."

Bill watched my confession with a look of disbelief, his eyes getting bigger as I went along, telling everything. I knew it would be a long time before he took me along on any mischief he was up to.

Sure enough, Daddy told us we couldn't go out of the house for a month. We had to promise to seriously consider "how dangerous your actions were," he went on in his don't-let-me-down-now voice. Of course, we promised never, ever, under any circumstances to run the box again.

That month went by, uneventful, and it was my last grounding, ever. My last punishment. Daddy had come upon the most precious commodity for a small-town Texas teen, and sprang it on me, and it worked. It worked so well. He bought me a car. A car that I wanted and loved more than anything in my young life, a car that I would be the best daughter in the world to keep and have at my disposal. It was, for a frivolous teen, almost as important as disappointing my beloved Daddy. He knew me, loved me, wanted to control me during these dangerous years, wanted to please me, and to keep me safe. And that car did all that.

It was a 1960 Studebaker Lark. Not the exquisite VW Beetle I was praying for, but a compact in that time. Seated six comfortably, often way more. And according to my Uncle Merrill, who picked it out for Daddy, it was safe. That turned out to be true. No accidents during my entire high school career, despite driving many thousands of miles, taking friends wherever they needed to go, being the "Bus" for so many, always safely. After I was in college in another car Daddy picked out for me and the Studebaker had been sold, Daddy arrested a couple of cattle rustlers in my old Studebaker, two calves in the back seat. It was an all-around wonderful car.

As I went through high school, I worked with Daddy. Made a deal with him. I'd be the kid he wanted, and he'd take care of me, keep me in the car. It was a simple arrangement, but very adult and very important. Not something I'd ever risk for something stupid like running the box.

Seventeen

LoBoy

*L*oBoy was a regular at the jail, had been ever since we'd been living there. He was an alcoholic, and not just that; he got crazier than most when he drank. He'd blackout, wake up in jail, and not remember a thing about the night before, sometimes the whole day before. We had other drinkers, and other crazy drunks, and other drunks that would blackout, but nobody could match LoBoy.

LoBoy Logan was a short colored man, I guess that's why they called him LoBoy, as in low to the ground. He worked down at the used car lot, detailing cars, and everybody there said he was the best worker they'd ever had. He loved a clean car.

Short as he was and with a broad face, he wasn't much to look at, but LoBoy was popular with the ladies. Maybe his charm came from his smooth brown skin that glowed like my grandma's leather wing chair when she'd oiled it up, shiny and rich. He might have been twenty-five, or thirty-five, or maybe even forty-five, I could not tell. Without a line on his face, it was an impossible call, though I could have checked the jail record book, where his birthday was entered each time he got locked up.

Miss Ella, the social worker up at the courthouse, told my mama that LoBoy had kids spread all over the county. The absent father, Miss Ella called him, but of course she'd never say which kids were his, except to Daddy, what with confidentiality and all. Daddy said the women liked him because he spent his time in the bars, talking, just talking, on and on, smooth and cool. LoBoy was a talker for sure. Even here at the jail, we knew that. LoBoy's wife, who was broad as a barn, my grandma would say, would make him pay a price when she found out about another woman. Mrs. Logan looked like she could do some damage, too, strong and forceful as she was. But LoBoy kept on risking his wife's fury, on many a Saturday night.

One time, after an awful night when he was sleeping it off on his couch, one of his lady friends came right up to the Logan house, telling Mrs. Logan that she and LoBoy were in love.

"You'll just have to step aside and not stand in the way of love," she was rumored to have said.

Mrs. Logan, frying up bacon at the time, plucked the bacon out to drain, and calm as you please, walked over to the couch and poured the hot bacon grease into LoBoy's upturned ear. As you might imagine, it woke him up, but after the hospital, LoBoy didn't see how he could file charges against her, her being his wife and simply jealous as she was. It was almost as though he was proud of her for caring so much. Becoming deaf in that ear didn't change his ways at all.

When LoBoy's wife was pregnant, well into her seventh month, he'd gotten in a drunken brawl at a beer joint down in the Flat, joining in the fighting just for the fun of it, he said. He and his wife were not getting along around that time, her being with child and him still running around with other women. Daddy had had to go down to break up their fights over the past several few weeks. For a day or two, LoBoy'd sober up and they'd be as happy as they could be.

Daddy thought they really did love each other; it was just the whiskey. He had gotten LoBoy into AA meetings down at the jail on Sunday mornings since he was often locked up on Sunday mornings anyway. LoBoy would turn over a new leaf—but it never lasted.

One Sunday morning, LoBoy, hungover and sick, focused his eyes to see where he was—and right there in the bed beside him lay his wife in a puddle of blood, having bled out. The baby, soon to be born, probably dead inside her. LoBoy walked right up to the jail in his bloody clothes and took my daddy down there to his house, crying and sobbing the whole way. He didn't remember a thing but admitted he probably had done it himself. Even though there were no fingerprints on the knife, her blood was all over him, they fought all the time, and he was a blackout drunk, and everybody in town knew it. Nobody had any doubt, not even LoBoy, that he had killed his pregnant wife, whether he knew it or not.

———

That first day in the jail, locked in his cell, he asked my mama for cleaning supplies. She worried that he might be going to try something crazy, suffering the way he was over what he'd done. So she waited for Daddy to get home. Daddy gave him the Ajax and Pine-Sol and Clorox, and by the next morning when Mama took breakfast in there, he'd scrubbed his cell from top to bottom, even washed the windows through the bars, and she thought that alone probably took him hours. Daddy let him clean the hallway the next day, then all the empty cells over the next week, and what with moving the few prisoners around some, he got the whole jail clean and shiny, smelling like a hospital. When a drunk threw up in his cell, LoBoy would be upset, and couldn't wait to get in there to clean it up. Mama sure didn't miss that part of jail life, even though she understood. She also might clean extra hard when worried or upset, just like LoBoy. After a few weeks, LoBoy became the trustee.

That gave my brother Walter, who'd had college English by now, a chance to tell us about truster and trustee, that the trustee receives the trust that the truster gives. Bill got the idea and proceeded to show me puncher and punchee, like the old days, and he and Walter demonstrated tickler and ticklee, with me yelling I was too old for this kind of child's play, which egged them on. The concept occupied us for a few days, with Bill coming to the breakfast table, hands on his hips: "I am the eater; where are my eatees?"

So, LoBoy was trusted by Daddy, and became the Trustee. He was the trustee of all trustees. Taking the position to heart, he got to thinking of the jail as his own place. He not only cleaned but painted the whole inside of the place, even the floors, and then he painted the metal bedsteads. After a month, he started collecting things for his cell. The preacher brought him a rug, and Mama let him use an old rocker. His cell was looking really homey. Daddy drew the line at curtains on the window.

About this time, up in Cameron, the district court judge died on the bench, so things slowed down in the courts, leaving LoBoy, even if his case was open and shut like everybody said, to sit in the county jail while awaiting trial. His wait stretched on for months, and he became a part of our jail life.

LoBoy washed and waxed our cars and did a great job of it, since that was his old profession, like he told me and anybody he could get to listen. He liked being outside, even if only in the carport between the jail and the house. So he'd take most of the day on one car, but nobody minded unless he'd endlessly chatter, which he'd do sometimes. He'd tell Daddy and me about his life out on the Holland plantation where he'd been a farm hand, how happy he'd been before they brought in the big cotton picking machines. He showed us where the cotton bolls had scarred his fingers.

"I never had any trouble out there in the river bottom," he said. "I didn't drink then. That started after I moved into town. Sometimes I wish we could turn back the clock."

"I know what you mean," Daddy said, and I knew he did, what with his reminiscing like he did about the peace and quiet of the farm most every single day. Then we fell quiet for a while, thinking back on the farms we had all three grown up on, where we'd all been happy. My favorite place came to mind, a dark cavernous corner of the barn I'd practically lived in as a kid. I could almost see the sunlight shafting in through the nail holes in the walls. Before I knew it, I had said out loud, "Me, I miss the barn."

I was a little embarrassed, but Daddy agreed, "It's a good barn."

LoBoy always talked to me about Rome. His grandfather had been named Caesar and had told him stories about the Roman Empire and Julius Caesar. I found a picture book about ancient Rome at the school library and gave it to him to have a look at. He lit up with smiles and asked to keep the book a few days. When I told him a couple of weeks later it was overdue, he looked so heartbroken, I told him to keep it. Daddy gave me the money to pay the fine when Miss Arla Sampson, my school librarian, called me in. LoBoy memorized that book. Mama noticed he wore a bedsheet wrapped around him, and when she asked him about it, he said it wasn't a bedsheet, it was a toga.

When he would start talking about Rome, Bill would try to sneak off without being seen. Bill loved to talk to the prisoners, getting an education, he'd say, just to get Mama to react, but I don't think Roman history was what Bill had in mind. And LoBoy could go on.

One time, Mama had to go to her sister's house for a few days, and LoBoy wound up doing the prisoners' laundry, hanging it on the line in the back-yard. When she came home, he begged her to let him keep on doing it, and she agreed. He even came inside to the kitchen a few times to wash the dishes when Daddy was home and could keep an eye on him, as if he needed an eye on him, which by this time, nobody thought he did, what with his earning the trustee title many times over the months.

The height of his trustee duties came during an unexpected emergency situation, when he looked after my cousin's kids in the backyard while Mama had a meeting inside the jail for a couple of hours, without incident, as we all expected.

My grandma was the only one who thought a thing of all this, asking my mama on the phone, "What's the murderer doing today?" When she'd come over, she'd ask "Where's the murderer? Do I need to keep looking over my shoulder?" She'd say, "I'll probably come over and find you all dead in your beds, that murderer running around loose." We'd laugh at such a thought, even Daddy. LoBoy was Trustee, in the full meaning of the word.

LoBoy was seriously into AA by now, with the Sunday morning jail meet-ings becoming the high point of his week. He talked AA to all the regular drunks coming in and out of the jail and had made a few converts. Some of them asked Daddy to force LoBoy to let them sleep off their hangovers in peace, but LoBoy wasn't giving up on a single drunk, whether it was a regular at the jail or a one-nighter just passing through Caldwell charged with DWI. But LoBoy was going strong and had found his religion, felt it strongly, like the converted can, seeing the error of their ways. LoBoy saw his errors more clearly than most anyone ever did, even if he didn't remember most of them.

Once when the jail was full, Daddy allowed the AA meeting to be held in the backyard, under the wide branches of the fig tree, right outside the kitchen window, where I could stand at the sink and pretend to do dishes and watch everything. As each man stood to give his name and talk, they shared their own personal stories, how they'd reached rock bottom on alcohol. LoBoy went last, and his rock-bottom story was by far the saddest, the meanest, and surely the most horrifying. As he told how his wife's dried blood had felt crusty and smelled like pennies on his skin for two days after he'd killed her, there wasn't a dry eye in the yard, and not one at the kitchen sink either. I suddenly appreciated his love of Clorox and Pine-Sol during his early days in the jail. LoBoy looked around the group, happy and satisfied like a preacher who might have just saved a church full of sinners from following in his errant footsteps.

When LoBoy'd been dry for months, Daddy and a rich ex-drinker from Houston took him to a big meeting in Rockdale, driving him up there in a big Rolls Royce convertible, and they had a cake for him, with candles for each month he'd been abstaining. Except for being in jail, facing trial for murdering his wife, LoBoy was enjoying life.

———

His trial finally did come up on the calendar and, quick as could be, he was convicted and sentenced to twelve to twenty-five years. He took it well, Daddy said, but on his way back down to the jail, said he hoped he could serve as much of his time as possible right there in the county jail. Daddy knew that was wishful thinking, of course, but he did tell him he'd wait for the prison van to come through instead of taking him off to Huntsville himself. So LoBoy stayed for some weeks more.

When the prison van arrived, LoBoy came out in shackles. He'd never even had on handcuffs before. Tucked under his arm was the Rome book. We all stood out in the yard, waving as he drove away, knowing we'd miss him, Mama and Daddy most of all. He'd become our friend. Daddy said he'd never have another trustee like LoBoy. LoBoy sent Mama a leather wallet from prison, one he made himself in the prison workshop, all engraved and hand tooled, and he wrote Daddy a letter or two, thanking him for the good treatment, and the AA meetings.

After a couple of years, we heard that he'd gotten to be a trustee up at the prison farm in Sugarland and had an AA group going there. When that news came, Mama said it was rehabilitation, pure and simple. Daddy said it was the reason we were here, and Mama almost looked convinced.

Eighteen

The Great Train Robbery

*T*here's nothing like a train wreck. Especially in small-town Texas, and Chriesman is as small-town Texas as you get. And to teenagers who live there, a train wreck is an answer to a prayer. Yes, nothing like it—except for maybe a train robbery.

It all started when two Santa Fe Railroad track repairmen, working off a handcar just before quitting time on a 105-degree summer afternoon, took a break from the heat to head into MacGregor's beer joint in Chriesman. Chriesman is six miles up the tracks from Caldwell, and maybe more if you go by the highway. The repairmen left their handcar right there on the track in downtown, which consists of Hagar's store, with a sign out front advertising refrigerated air (which meant a wheezing old window unit in the back), and MacGregor's across the street, which had a window fan and a sign out front advertising cold beer. One beer at McGregor's led to two, and so on until the 6:15 freight train came rumbling in from Milano. The railroad men heard it coming and shot out of McGregor's at a dead run. But it was too late to get that handcar moving and onto a sidetrack. The locomotive, deafening brakes screeching, smashed into the handcar with a terrible crash, knocking it into Hagar's gas pumps, which luckily had no gas and hadn't had for more than fifteen years. It whizzed right on past the south side windows where Mrs. Hagar watched from her stool by the big pickle jar. The locomotive's efforts to save downtown Chriesman from a flying handcar led to a pileup of freight cars jackknifing off the track, and into the gullies all the way back to Otto Roskey's farm half mile up the tracks.

Mac McGregor said except for the locomotive brakes and the crash into the handcar, the whole thing was way quieter than you might expect. The freight cars just creaked a little and rolled right off the tracks. A big pipe clanked noisily off a flat car, and a few cars opened up with a giant can opener sort of noise, but Mac was plain disappointed in the noise level, according to the *Burleson County Tribune* that week.

"I really expected more," a let-down Mac was quoted as saying. "But the wreck has been awfully good for business."

By the time Daddy was called and the Santa Fe people were massing in Chriesman, word was already out that nobody was hurt, except for one of the two repairmen who'd left the handcar on the tracks. After the impact, the two men ran around checking for casualties, and finding none, headed back to MacGregor's, called their bosses, and proceeded to get falling-down drunk, literally. One fell down in MacGregor's bathroom stall and hit his head on the toilet seat, becoming the one injury resulting from the Chriesman train wreck. The Santa Fe employee who'd been in the caboose, which somehow stayed on the tracks, also got roaring drunk at MacGregor's, and suffered a terrible hangover that reportedly lasted several days, but you couldn't quite call that a casualty, not officially.

So no one was hurt, and there were freight cars piled up all along the tracks, and people were coming from all over the county to look. It was perfect. For the teens at the Dairy King, me included, this disaster was a godsend on a summer Friday night. We got there as soon as humanly possible, considering the obstacles, like deciding on whose car to take and how to get gas money and Cokes to go, and letting everybody go to the bathroom who had to. Getting out of town was a logistical nightmare worthy of wartime, but our first train wreck motivated the heck out of us.

We arrived to find flares, railroad lanterns, and headlights lighting up Chriesman and the tracks as far north as you could see. The Santa Fe had procured cars and trucks to pull off in the fields along the tracks to shine their lights on the wrecked railroad cars. People were milling all around, everywhere you looked. I saw Daddy and the railroad detectives on the front porch of Hagar's, looking pretty serious, and I knew they wished all us people, especially the kids, would go home. Fat chance of that. Peggy Worsek and I looked in each and every boxcar, walking farther than we had all summer, and we were not impressed. Everything seemed to still be in boxes.

There were no animals running free. Nothing was on fire. We headed back to the Dairy King before 10:00 p.m.

My brother Bill's friend, Donald D. Duff, known to all as Duffy, was living at home alone that summer. He was, after all, eighteen years old, and his daddy worked for the railroad, which meant he had to travel, sometimes taking Duffy's mom with him, so Duffy was on his own. Bill had spent as many nights at Duffy's that summer as he had at home, and having Bill out on his own, with nobody knowing when he came or went, eighteen-years-old or not, was cause for concern for everybody who knew about it, especially our mother. Bill had a new girlfriend, Neta Plots, from what Daddy called an unconventional family. My grandma said that was a nice way to say they were crazy as loons. The Plots liked to have Bill stay overnight, which made things tough on Mama that summer. She almost never knew where the heck Bill was. It was bad enough for her when she did know.

Walter, still the good kid, had been living in a dorm at College Station, going to Texas A&M, where he still got good grades and never caused any trouble. He came home for the summer, commuting for a couple of courses, and working part-time at the campus cafeteria. Nights, he studied at the jail. Summer nights! Bill and I could hardly believe it. Bill was always after Walter, usually without success, to go out with Bill's bunch of wild friends. Finally, though, even Walter couldn't pass up a train wreck, so he took off with Bill and Duffy and a kid my age who ran with them named Pinhead. Pinhead was a strange kid, wild as anybody, but eerily quiet about it. He kept his hair clipped so short as to look almost bald. He got his name from his small head that was nearly pointed on the top.

When they dropped me off at the Dairy King that night, I was happy to see Walter out with the dry stock, as we called the trouble-causing kids, for a change. Even Peggy Worsek asked, with disbelief spread all over her face, "Was that your brother Walter in the back seat with Pinhead?"

Daddy stayed out at the wreck until dawn on Saturday morning. Mama stayed up handling the jail traffic that night, and I was the only one to get any sleep. Neither Walter nor Bill came home, but what with the train wreck and Bill's spending the night here and there throughout the summer,

Mama didn't worry, not too much. When Daddy came home, he looked tired, but somehow, as usual, with clothes fresh looking and unwrinkled, his white shirt still crisp. We all wondered how he did it. It was a family joke that Daddy always told Bill he looked like a train wreck, or his room looked like a train wreck, or he and his friends were like a train wreck, and lots of the time, Daddy was right. So, right away, Mama said to Daddy as how he didn't look a bit like a train wreck, even though he'd been at one, which reminded them both of Bill. Daddy looked my way, a little funny, I thought, and the two of them went off into the bedroom to talk. It was getting harder and harder to eavesdrop as I got older, but I did hear a few words about the train, something about stolen property, and a mention of Donald Duff's car. Then I quit listening and started to worry. I hoped Bill wasn't in any trouble.

To clear it all up, I thought I'd call Duffy's house to make sure he and Bill hadn't gotten into anything. I hoped not. They had Walter with them, for goodness sake. I picked up my new princess phone in my room (my fifteenth birthday gift—an extension, not the private line I'd been hoping for), and I heard my daddy's voice.

"Donald Duff?" Nobody calls him Donald, I thought.

"Yes, Sir." Wow, Duffy was being polite.

"This is the sheriff," Daddy said, quiet but a little scary if you didn't know him.

"Yes, Sir," Duffy said, just as softly.

"Is Bill there?" Daddy asked.

"No, Sir."

"Did he stay there last night?"

"No, Sir."

"Were you out at the Santa Fe train wreck last night?"

"No, Sir," Duffy answered. I knew he was lying now. But I didn't know about what, or why.

"Somebody saw your car out there by Otto Roskey's place. That true?"

"No, Sir." Duffy was on a roll with the "no, sirs." I swallowed a giggle.

"Somebody stole some tuna fish out of a wrecked railroad car. Was that y'all?"

"No, Sir."

"Somebody stole thirty-seven cases of tuna fish. Not y'all?"

"No, Sir!" Duffy said emphatically. "We took only one case." Then he sighed. He knew he'd confessed more than he intended, but kept on going, "But Bill really isn't here. He went home with Neta, before we ever went out to the wreck."

I was relieved, but tried not to sigh in Daddy's ear, though I did worry about Walter. Where the heck was he?

"Well, Donald, you take that case of tuna fish down to the Santa Fe Railroad office and return it to the detectives there, and that'll be the end of it. You'll do that?"

"Yes, Sir."

Daddy hung up, and I did, too, quietly as I could. Then I picked up the phone quick as you please and dialed Duffy's house.

"Hello?" He must have thought Daddy was calling back to tell him to bring himself down to the jail to get locked up like the common train robber he was.

"Hey, train robber," I laughed. "Are my brothers really there or not?"

"Your daddy told you?" he asked horrified.

"No, get real. They tell me nothing around here, I just happened to pick up the phone and heard the whole thing."

"Oooh," he groaned, "and you'll tell everybody in the world about it?"

I wondered what he thought I'd been doing around the jail all these years, if not learning a little discretion. A person had to learn to hold his tongue, but I didn't want to get into that with him.

"Of course not, Jesse James. Is Bill really at Neta's?"

"He is. They were going to drive out to the wreck with her crazy parents. That's who probably took those other thirty-six cases of tuna fish."

"How 'bout Walter? Is he there?" I asked carefully, watching my bedroom door, and listening for any telltale clicks indicating someone picking up the other phone.

"He is, sleeping like a baby. Full up on tuna fish salad sandwiches. That boy can sure eat!"

"Walter stole tuna fish?" I gasped. Walter had never stolen anything in his life, not even a chicken leg off Bill's or my plate at the dinner table when we weren't looking, which most anybody else in the family might do.

"Carried the case himself," Duffy said. "It just took a little egging on by Pinhead and me, and he was off and running. But don't tell your daddy after he's trusting me to take it back. I don't want Walter to get in trouble when we're the ones that talked him into it." He laughed, and I liked Duffy more than I ever had.

I heard later from Walter that they had to go to Mr. Pierce's store, Polansky's market, and out to Hagar's in Chriesman to get enough cans of tuna fish to replace what they'd eaten that night when they got home. In the end, they bought an off brand and hid it underneath and in the middle of the case of Chicken of the Sea in order to bring the case up to the right case number.

At the Santa Fe office, Duffy went in alone, bless his heart, but had to almost fight Walter to keep him away. He told the railroad detective, "I think you're looking for a case of tuna fish, and there's one out there in my car." The statement was about as vague as he could get, steering clear of any kind of confession, like he possibly might not know how it got into his car in the first place.

The detective looked him up and down and said with a sneer, "Well, boy, it ain't doing me any good out there, is it?"

All the detectives and railroad hangers on laughed long and hard as Duffy walked out to the car. They watched him get the case and carry it in, setting it on the detective's desk. As he counted the cans in the box, the detective got right up in Duffy's face.

"That ain't tuna fish I smell on you, is it, boy?"

Again, the men laughed. Duffy walked out to the car, feeling so humiliated, as he told me later, that he hadn't gotten off quite as scot-free as he thought he had, after all. I thought again that Daddy knew what he was doing.

"Well, it sure as heck rehabilitated me. No more train robbery." Duffy smiled.

Daddy was always asking kids to do the right thing, especially if it was the first time they'd gotten into trouble, and then leaving it to them alone to do it. This was another instance of his not enforcing all the laws all the time, something that had worried me when I was younger. This tactic usually worked, though, and he probably figured he'd hear about it somehow if they didn't do what he'd asked them to do. Lots of times I'd hear stories at school, how Daddy had caught an underage kid drinking, taken them home, had a deputy drive their car, and had a big talk with them and didn't tell their parents. His method straightened some of them out, some not, but I think Daddy always thought it was worth the try.

Once Daddy caught carloads of boys Walter's age drag-racing their parents' cars on an open stretch of highway down in the river bottom. He told them he'd let them go home if they'd drive thirty miles an hour all the way, and he'd be following them to make sure. He turned off after a mile or two, but word around school was that they went thirty the whole way and were glad they had the chance. Usually, I'd hear the stories second- or third-hand, but occasionally somebody would corner me to tell me how my daddy had changed his life. I was proud, but sort of embarrassed, too. This time, with Duffy, I was proud. And happy for Walter that he didn't get caught.

But wouldn't you know it. Walter wouldn't let it go. He went to Daddy and confessed; even said he ate more of the tuna fish than anyone else. He wanted to admit his guilt to the railroad detectives, too, but Mama wouldn't have it. She knew, as Daddy did, that that one case of tuna fish was the least of the railroad's worries, especially today, with wrecked freight cars strewn all up and down the tracks. She also knew Daddy had told them "a young boy" would be bringing in stolen property he'd recovered. He hadn't identified Duffy yesterday, and he would not be identifying Walter today. But to Walter, finally getting into trouble after all these years, it was Train Robbery, pure and simple, and had to be owned up to. Me calling him and Duffy "Jesse James" every chance I got probably didn't help. I would have called Pinhead the same if I ever spoke to him, but I never had, and wasn't going to start now.

Mama didn't know how to act about the whole thing. She'd worried about Bill and me, and Daddy especially all our years in the jail, but Walter had hardly given her a moment's concern. He didn't associate with the prisoners like Bill did, didn't seem interested in the goings-on like me, and was hardly in any danger like Daddy. Now, Walter wanted to go to the Santa Fe

Railroad and confess to train theft. Mama kept correcting us, telling us that it was train theft, not robbery, which required a weapon, and try as I might to convince her that Pinhead was deadly as any weapon, she didn't see the humor in it. She was just disconcerted by Walter having done wrong, and even more so by his hard-headed attempts to make it right. She was proud of him, but wanted to kick his butt, which my grandma told me was a common predicament for parents.

In the end, Daddy had Walter write out his "confession" and make "restitution" for the price of four cans of tuna fish. Daddy put it all in an official evidence bag, and when Walter went back to school a few weeks later, the bag went in the bottom drawer of Daddy's desk at the courthouse and no farther. He gave Walter the same chance he'd give any kid.

Bill, who couldn't believe he'd missed all the excitement, took his cue from me and started calling Walter the Train Robber, and knowing Bill, he would probably keep it up for the rest of Walter's natural life. Daddy said that was punishment enough, might even be cruel and unusual.

Nineteen

Bill and the Whores

here was a famous brothel in LaGrange, one county over from us—the oldest whorehouse in Texas since back before Texas was a state. It was known far and wide as the Chicken Ranch, a name coined back in the days when they'd accept chickens in payment.

All sorts of people went there: doctors and lawyers, politicians and lawmen, Aggies and UT students. Being equal distance between the schools, it was the only neutral place the rival schools would meet. Even high school kids from all the neighboring counties tried to go, often without success. But if they did get in, it was the stuff of legend. I guess they don't really check IDs at such places. It was rumored that the law went there, but I doubted our county sheriff did, if for no other reason than knowing Daddy's schedule like I did. Daddy was friends with the sheriff of Fayette County, like he was with all the county sheriffs in the surrounding area. They might be friends, but one sheriff would never interfere in the business of another county. So, the brothel in Fayette County was none of Daddy's concern. Mama, however, felt differently. She didn't like the sheriff of Fayette County and didn't mind saying so. She especially didn't like the fact that Daddy knew the madam at the Chicken Ranch.

The Madam had been to Caldwell to bail out her girls more than once, and Daddy was always accommodating. He never did rest well with a woman in his jail. Everybody liked Daddy, but especially women, and the Madam liked him a lot. The Madam, dressed in expensive and conservative garb, had, in front of Mama, told him with a big smile, that he'd be welcome at her establishment anytime. Reportedly Daddy's face bloomed red, and he said, "Thanks, Madam." Later he told Mama he wasn't being cute; he just couldn't remember her given name.

Once, at a fancy restaurant in Huntsville, Mama and Daddy ran into her, and she introduced Daddy as the "sweet Sheriff of Burleson County" to the expensively tailored man she was with. Mama worried who that person was for weeks afterward. A judge, a Texas Ranger, a congressman? That same night, Mama almost fainted when the Madam picked up their check. It made her mad at first, but always thrifty, she started thinking that as long as she had to speak to the woman, at least she could be compensated with the price of a good dinner. In the long list of experiences spared "normal" people (people who did not live in jails), associating with the Madam of the Chicken Ranch and having her buy your dinner and smile at your husband headed a long list that Mama might start in on if you gave her half a chance.

Nobody knew who was paying who, or how much, to allow the Chicken Ranch to continue, or even if money was changing hands at all. We all wondered, what with Fayette County so close to us. And then a time came when the whole thing got even closer to home.

My brother Bill went to work for the railroad right out of high school, but just lately had the bad luck to be in a train wreck in New Mexico, which, according to Bill, is an occupational hazard. He wasn't hurt, but when the bus that had come to pick up the survivors crashed and rolled down an embankment, Bill broke his leg. He was so proud. In his short life, he'd already wrecked a bicycle, a moped, a motorcycle, and been in two car wrecks—and here in one night, he'd added two new types of wrecks to his list: train and bus. He said he was going for a record and wanted to ride only in trucks until he could add a pick-up truck wreck to his record.

So Bill was home recovering, living again in the jail. He was bored, and about to drive us all crazy, until he went to work as a driver for a lawyer, one Forest Wine. The best lawyer in Burleson County, he was brilliant, some said. Although rich and successful, he had been terribly crippled in an accident as a boy. He might have been handsome, with that thick silver hair and square jaw, but with his withered body, his head seemed disproportionately large. His piercing blue eyes scared me as a child, but Mama always told me not to show it, since he evidently thought his deformity made children shy away from him. He had to walk with crutches and braces supporting his shrunken legs.

His office was just across the square from the courthouse. He would lurch across the street, pitifully limp up the stairs, always when the jury or witnesses gathered in the rotunda where they could see him, making a sad impression soon undone by his "go for the throat" courtroom tactics. He could not drive a car, so Bill had hired on as his driver. It was the perfect job for Bill, for Forest was as wild and crazy as he was brilliant and successful, fulfilling Bill's job requirement that no job ever be dull.

Forest was a patron of the Chicken Ranch. Mama said there were lots of women who would have relished a chance with him, but he couldn't believe it himself, and instead regularly traveled to LaGrange, now with Bill driving him up there. When Forest went to the Chicken Ranch, he might stay overnight (a costly undertaking), so Bill was left to languish in the "parlor" of the establishment, where he was, after a couple of weeks, adopted by the many girls who worked there as a sort of buddy, or mascot. These are Bill's own words I'm quoting here. He told me that he had a "code of conduct" that precluded his "participation," a practiced talk which I took with a grain of salt, thinking it might be meant for our mama. He, so he says, slept on the couches in the parlor, made friends with each and every girl over the months, and was made privy to their sad, sad stories. That part I believed. Bill, despite his hellish treatment of me as a child, had become a softie of the first magnitude. Show him an underdog, and Bill would become the champion.

At times Forest did not want to stay at the ranch. On these occasions, he would bring a girl home to spend the weekend at his lavish home on Lake Somerville. One weekend, Forest, wilder and somehow drunker than usual, had brought two girls back to Caldwell. Bill said the drive alone was a lesson in life. Back in the county only half an hour, trouble erupted. Forest took the girls to the Ranch Café, hangout for half the law in Burleson County, and that night, two tables were occupied by minor law: not the sheriff, not the police, not the highway patrol. Rather, there were constables, security guards, and that oddest of all lawmen, the "special" deputy, an official hanger on, made official by only the smallest of margins. Bill was nervous, with the girls and Forest and the lawmen all in the same room, but ordered the enchilada plate, and made conversation with the boys, whom he knew well.

Forest, meanwhile, three sheets to the wind, as the drunkest of the drunkest call it, decided to eat no food and to accompany the girls to the ladies' room, a cramped, one-stall affair near the kitchen. After an uncomfortably long stay in there, with the lawmen watching the door all the while, there came a strangled cry for help. Forest came crawling out of the ladies' room, hardly coherent, more from drink than from injury, Bill would later say.

"I've been struck," Forest called out in his robust courtroom voice.

Right behind him, wielding a heavy green glass ashtray high up over her head, emerged one of the LaGrange girls, yelling, calling Forest a "pervert," a "deviant," a "sickie." Bill was impressed, more by the girl's vocabulary than the irony of the whole thing.

The truth of what transpired in the ladies' room of the Ranch Café did not come to light, but the lawmen assumed a drunk Forest Wine was being rolled for his thick wallet, while the girls claimed he asked for significantly more than he paid for. Whatever the truth, the three of them, Forest and the two girls, were hauled to our jail and locked in three separate cells.

I saw them go in. A particularly rabid special deputy, Harvey Trunk, completed the lockup, informing Mama of the charges with more glee than usually accompanied an arrest. Public drunkenness for Forest, and attempted robbery for the whores, which is what he called them. Robbery was a major crime, not a misdemeanor like prostitution. This deputy, deputized by a local constable for poll watching during the last election, was proud of his first big arrest. He probably already pictured himself testifying in district court.

When Mama came into the kitchen with him to complete the paperwork, she gave me the raised eyebrow look. I rolled my eyes in return. Later, Mama said to me, "Baby girl, we've been around here too long when we take the side of the whores."

Not long after, Bill came in. When he heard of the charges against the girls, he was amazed. He told me how hard it would be for the girls to make bail on such a big charge as attempted robbery, and whatever had occurred, these particular girls (he knew them, he said), were not thieves. Tough and hard, true, but not thieves. He thought that Forest, once dried out, would back him up on his assessment. Mama said he would have to just talk to Daddy, her usual reply.

Sometime that night, before Daddy came in, Bill went into the cup towel drawer, where the big steel keys to the jail doors were kept at the bottom, under the lacey towels we never used. He opened the big jail doors, let the two girls out of their cells, risking God knows what in charges himself. Hearing the commotion, I woke up and walked out onto the driveway in my flannel pajamas, and while Bill told me to get lost, the girls were nice to me. One was older, maybe thirty, in a tight pink shiny dress. After a little small talk she said, "Go to college, kid." At that piece of advice, the other one, very young for a prostitute, I thought, and dressed like a schoolgirl but with hair bleached white, laughed. They piled into Forest's big Cadillac, and Bill drove them back to LaGrange, leaving them in the capable hands of the madam. She expressed her undying gratitude and an open invitation to visit anytime on the house. When Bill told the story later, he loved emphasizing that part, ". . . on the house."

Next morning, Harvey Trunk barged into the jail, waking me and everybody else within a block with cries of "Where are my whores? Where are my whores?" Fortunately, the melee served to wake a severely hungover Forest Wine, who also croaked a heartfelt "Where are my whores?" Mama ordered me back to my room while Forest told Daddy a totally different story of the evening before, one that included no robbery attempt at all, but that was obviously perverse enough that no one would ever share the details with me, and I usually found out everything.

Standing in the kitchen doorway, Mama heard the whole story, and worried out loud about Bill, and the risk he took releasing the girls. When she heard about my talk with the two girls in the driveway the night before, she worried about me.

Me, I worried about the girls, and how they got to be whores, pretty as they both were, and how things could have gone so wrong for them, if not for luck and my brother Bill. At my age and experience, choosing to become a whore looked like the worst choice a girl could make, if a girl had a choice. I worried if these girls had had a choice. I wondered if the Chicken Ranch had ever caused so much worry and concern before in all its years, and I thought it probably had.

Twenty

Falconer

"*I*'ll be out of here soon and this kind of thing will never happen to me again."

I held back my tears. I knew these words would make Daddy feel bad, too, but I said them anyway. I was as mad at my daddy as I'd ever been, and even if what happened wasn't his fault, I wanted him to know how he was wrecking my life, whether he was trying to or not, and this wasn't the first time. This was what passed for teenaged rebellion in our family.

It was Friday night, the last football game of the year, followed by the biggest dance of the fall in the high school gym. The floor was sprinkled with sawdust, and I personally had helped string twisted orange and white crepe paper from the ceilings, one corner to the other and back again. I'd rushed home after the game to prepare for my third date with Falconer Maddox. I had to change out of my baton twirler uniform into a brand-new blue plaid pleated skirt and mohair sweater that took me two trips to Bryan to talk Mama into buying for me.

I was in love with Falconer, who was an older man, my brother Bill's age. He was handsome, classically handsome, I told Peggy Worsek. He had dark hair and eyes, and cheekbones that made him look like an Indian, a Comanche in my fantasies, like the ones I'd been told lived down on the Brazos just a hundred years ago. I wished he were a little taller, but he had a couple of inches on me, so I could wear my little stacked heels if we ever went to church together, and I was hoping we would, since church with a boy meant it was serious.

Falconer was a college man, going to Texas A&M, even if he was a day student and still lived here at home with his parents, just up the street from us like he had since we were kids and he'd been my big crush in fifth grade. Still, I was in love, and like I told my mama, I really meant it this time. Falconer had won my heart surely, on our first date, when he'd taken me parking on the Deer Lick Road and performed every single one of the Smothers' Brothers comedy routines, from memory, doing the voices and everything.

On our second date, when he'd asked me to sit on his lap in the wagon-wheel rocker in our living room, I was a goner. Being a big, tall girl, I felt a little self-conscious about squashing a boy, but Falconer didn't even squirm, just sat there smiling, holding me in his arms and breathing in my hair, until I got worried his legs were going to sleep and pretended I had to go to the bathroom. When I got in there, I smiled at the mirror and said "Falconer" over and over in a whisper while I staring at myself, my mascaraed eyelashes, my teased up hair, thinking I looked really fine, and wondering was it love that did it?

Tonight, waiting for me to change, Falconer had been sitting in the living room with my daddy, talking about Daddy's job as sheriff, and his calls, riding patrol, and all that. All the boys showed such interest in police work and the jail, which drove me crazy. The city police brought in a prisoner, so Daddy had to go out to open the jail door, leaving Falconer watching through the front curtains. Then the phone rang, and Fates be damned, Falconer answered it. It was a call for Daddy, and Falconer took down all the information, and from the first touch of pen to notepad, I knew I'd lost him. There'd been a big wreck down at the Y intersection, two eighteen-wheelers. One a cattle truck, and the other a car transport loaded with foreign sports cars. Loose cows were running all over the highway, and a couple of the sports cars had broken free and were stuck upside down in the ditch. When Daddy walked in the door and Falconer told him the news, I heard the insinuation in Falconer's voice even before he asked Daddy could he go along, and maybe be of some help, directing traffic or chasing down cows.

Daddy saw me standing there in the doorway, in my new blue outfit that made my eyes look almost blue, and he raised his eyebrows in question. I shrugged my shoulders, knowing already that my love for Falconer, and my visions of dancing with him under the dimmed gym lights, were no match for the excitement of a big wreck, with cattle and sports cars and flashing lights and sirens. Falconer did have the decency to come over and take my hand, saying he'd be right back and we'd make it to the dance in time for the last set. But as I watched them drive off in Daddy's car, I knew Falconer would be there 'til the last cow was rounded up, and every one of those sports cars towed into the wrecking yard. I thought I might really love him because I was hoping he might get to drive one of those sports cars.

I couldn't blame Falconer. I remembered the first cattle trailer I'd seen wrecked, out on the farm to market road at Second Creek, probably when I was ten, and it had been great fun, with spooked cattle all up and down the road, and people chasing after them. And I'd even seen a car transport trailer wreck, with six shiny new Fords torn up and spread over a hundred yards of pavement, and I'd been excited about that, too, and that had only been a year or so ago.

No, I couldn't blame Falconer. But Daddy was a different story. Every boyfriend I'd had got to liking Daddy and riding patrol, so much so that I ended up a lot of my dates sitting in the living room with Mama, waiting on Daddy and my date to get back from a ride through Freemantown, or a quick check of all the beer joints in the county, or a wreck, or a ride to the river and back. Things start off innocently enough, while my date waited for me, like Falconer, or brought me home and came in for a Coke in the kitchen. They'd start listening to the police radio up on the refrigerator, hear Daddy taking a call on the phone, or watch when some lawman brought in a prisoner to be locked up in the jail. Then they'd talk to Daddy about what they heard or saw, follow him out into the carport to watch the pat-down, the search, and the handcuffs coming off. Pretty soon I'd go to bed and maybe they'd notice, or maybe not. Some old boyfriends, after we'd broken up, would still come around and ride with Daddy, and they were always sweet to me when they did, like they were grateful to me for the introduction. A few were looking ahead to careers in law enforcement.

This transfer of attention to Daddy didn't seem to happen with my brothers' friends. Nope, just my boyfriends, and I was beginning to wonder if it was a plot to keep me from having a serious boyfriend, which Daddy always warned me about anyway. To his credit, he tried to downplay the excitement angle to these boys, telling them how dull law enforcement could be, how much hard work it took, especially late at night. He talked about the dangers, and how it was no fun at all taking on the troubles of everybody. But the more he talked, the more their faces developed that entranced look, and even if Daddy tried to discourage them, they wanted to go with him, whatever the call, or merely to ride patrol, or even to go for coffee with the highway patrol down at the Ranch Cafe.

But tonight, Falconer was the last straw. Even if Daddy had gotten my okay, with his little eyebrow raising and my shrug and eye roll, this was the big dance, and Falconer was my big love. When the patrol car rolled in at 2:30 in the morning, I'd been dozing in my blue mohair sweater. Falconer didn't come inside, and I guess I was glad, since my hair was squished flat on one side where I'd been sleeping on it, and who knew if my mascara had run. I watched out the front window as he got out of Daddy's patrol car, shook his hand, and headed to his Ford Falcon with a grin on his lips. He'd had a good time on our third date, without me.

We'd lived in the jail half my life, and it was really all I knew. I'd accepted the jail life with some minor brushes with discontent along the way, mostly seeing Mama's aspirations for a normal life go wanting. But never before had I been livid about it, like I was tonight. I stood up and waited for him to open the door. As it opened, I said, "Why does this always happen? Why do they take off with you?" I was getting loud, something we never did in our family. To get mad at Daddy and yell at him how I'd be glad to get out of here, and go off to college, it must be love that's wrong with me.

When I'd gotten it all off my chest, Daddy sat down wearily in his chair, motioned me to the arm where I always sat when we talked. He wrapped his big arm around my shoulder and said, "I'm sorry, Dolly. I know the jail hasn't been an easy life for you, or your mother."

Something twisted in my chest, and tears filled my eyes. Right away, I wanted him to stop. My life hadn't been that bad, and it was just love for Falconer that made me act up this way. I was worried that Falconer liked the jail, and Daddy, not me. Before I could get that out, hard as it would have been to say, Daddy went on. "I'll make it a rule, no boyfriends ride with me. No police talk with your dates. Okay, Dolly?"

I couldn't have adored him more than I did right then. I leaned into him and smelled his particular smell, cigarettes and dry-cleaning fluid and soap, thinking I'd never forget that smell.

"Daddy, I'm dreading going off to San Marcos to college." That wasn't entirely true, but I felt like I wanted him to know I loved our family. And him. In truth, I wanted to go for a thousand reasons more important than his taking my boyfriends out on patrol, and I could tell him about them later when I was grown up, and we could laugh about this whole thing. I often pictured how I'd tell him things when I was grown up.

Falconer called me the next morning and said he was sorry about us not making it to the dance, and did I want to go to church with him the next day? My heart swelled in my chest, and I was almost happy again. Turned out, his church, the St. Mary's Catholic, was a little scary to me. I got the feeling his mother wasn't so pleased that I'd tagged along. When I smiled and asked if my head covering was adequate, she gave me a little nod and turned away without an answer. But nothing could dampen my excitement, not even his mother. Adding to that wonderful Sunday, I noticed we were almost the exact same height in my stacked heels.

After church, he brought me home, and stood outside with Daddy and the highway patrolmen who were taking all the DWIs to the Justice of the Peace so they could return home and suffer their hangovers in peace. I stood in the carport by the washing machine. I could see Daddy was suffering, trying to get Falconer to go into the house, without being mean or anything. But Falconer was not to be discouraged. When Daddy claimed he had to take off, hoping Falconer would take the hint, Falconer seized upon the nearest highway patrolman, asking, and getting permission, to ride along up to the courthouse with the DWIs. As they left, he walked past me with a huge smile. "I've never been to court," he gushed.

By midafternoon, Falconer came back and once again asked me to sit on his lap in the living room. I thought his interest in my daddy's job a little excessive, but with his breath in my hair, feeling my weight press down on him and him still smiling, I thought I could live with it.

I told Daddy it was okay for Falconer to spend time with him, and we juggled our dates and Daddy's calls and riding patrol and, finally, court.

Falconer went to nearly every trial held in District Court, sometimes cutting classes to do so, and every chance I got, I'd go with him. We both liked the witness testimony and the lawyers' arguments. We'd argue ourselves over who was a good witness, and who was not. Even if he wanted to linger in Daddy's office at the courthouse a little longer than I did, we had fun there.

The day I left for college, Falconer, about to graduate from college himself, broke it off. "We're just going in different directions," he said standing by his car. "We're going to be living a hundred miles apart." I couldn't believe this was the Falconer I'd known since I was a child, the Falconer who'd made me laugh and had me sit on his lap. I kept it together while he spoke, but afterward, I cried, though I held it in until he'd driven off up Fawn Street and couldn't see me.

I thought I was heartbroken for a few days, until I started my classes and got too busy to think about him. Once in a while, though, I pictured Falconer with his notepad at the district courtroom, sitting in our regular place over on the left side, by the door.

My first trip home, at Thanksgiving, Daddy said he hadn't seen Falconer since I left, and he hadn't been up to the courthouse either. Even though I was over Falconer and happier than I ever thought I'd be at college, the news made me feel good.

Even though I knew Daddy spent his days trying to see inside of people, and was darn good at it, it surprised me when he said, "It must have been you all along."

Daddy sure knew how to comfort a person.

Twenty-One

Dance Hall Romance

$\mathcal{M}$ama loved to dance. As far back as I can remember, she'd grab me up for a Texas two-step down the farmhouse hall, or for a waltz around the dining room table. She'd always lead, and she was a wonderful dancer, with good timing and a mastery of all the dances known to Texas dance halls. She came by it naturally, growing up a mile or two from Deanville Hall, one of our county's storied dance halls and my own favorite as a teenager. My grandma's church didn't approve of dancing, but she never tried to keep Mama or her brothers and sister from the halls. In fact, my mother's brother, Uncle Andy, had a band, playing pedal steel guitar at dance halls all over Texas. He learned to play after my grandma answered his Christmas wish for a six-string when he was just a boy. My mother and her sister danced their young years away at Deanville and all the other dance halls around the county like all their generation did.

Texas Dance Halls are legendary. They came about back in the day as community centers for the German and Czech immigrants around central Texas. As these groups spread out over the state, the community halls devolved into dance halls. Our county alone had Deanville Hall, Frenstat Hall, and SPJST's Snook Hall. Within easy driving distance were KC Hall in Bryan and Smetana Hall, both down Highway 21, Swiss Alp Dance Hall in LaGrange, and Round Top Dance Hall in Wesley. I was always told Wesley was the Czech word for joy, perfect for a dance hall location. There were the famous ones, Gruene Hall down near New Braunfels, Luckenbach, and Senglemann Hall in Schulenburg. Kids from high school on up danced away their Saturday nights as soon as they were old enough or brave enough to drive or catch a ride. For the younger kids, the Knights of Columbus Halls near the Catholic Churches held dances with no beer sales.

The halls hosted famous country musicians. They weren't the Beatles, but I personally remember Loretta Lynn, Bob Wills, BJ Thomas, and even Willie Nelson showing up. Famous musicians hardly ever came to our area for concerts, so these dance halls served as our only brush with stars.

For Daddy, the dance halls were a matter of keeping the fights down to a minimum and making sure no drunk drivers swerved their way home after last call. He also kept an eye out for underage drinking. His appearance at a dance hall served as a calming influence, probably quelling drinking, underage or no, and maybe even halting fist fights. He might show up at several hall dances on a summer Saturday night, making an appearance and moving on to the next. Because of these duties, he was not as enamored of hall dances as most folk in our county, including me. Or even as my mama would have been, given the chance.

Daddy wasn't that much of a dancer. He tended to slow dance only, shuffling along in one place. When I was little, I would stand on top of his feet and move with him in what I thought a unique father daughter dance, not realizing little girls all over the world learned to dance on their daddy's feet. Only a few times did I see Mama and Daddy dance together, and I always wondered if she was holding back her desire to lead.

During college, I would come home for the summers, prime hall dance time of year. I had a dance buddy, J. B., a friend I'd dated in high school, but by now we were mostly friends, and even better, dancing friends. We'd hit all the local dance halls on summer Saturday nights, ever since high school. Recently, as we'd take off from the jail, I'd detect a bit of envy on Mama's face. She'd always ask us who was playing and where and would they play her current favorite song. When I mentioned it to J. B., he asked, "Well, why doesn't she come along with us?" I immediately wondered the same thing. Why hadn't I thought of inviting her myself? Of course, the sheriff's wife dancing at a hall dance on a Saturday night, right before an election year, didn't create the picture of a family supporting the family values Daddy espoused. His daughter going was bad enough.

Over the next few weeks, I proposed to Mama that she come to Deanville with J. B. and me. She was absolutely against the idea at the start, but I kept up a weekly litany of who was playing and why nobody cared if the sheriff's wife danced at a hall dance, probably wouldn't even notice her. I told her that I had gotten Bill to agree to cover the jail for a night if she came along. Bill loved the idea. He'd danced a few rounds with Mama in his time and wouldn't mind being the man in charge at the jail for a few hours.

A few weeks later, a poster at Piwonka's grocery advertised that Mama's favorite, Ray Price, was set to play at Deanville Hall in two weeks. She'd seen him there years ago, with then little-known Willie Nelson playing guitar. She'd fallen into dancer's love with Ray and Willie, especially with their collaboration on "Faded Love." She sang that song any time she had a chance and did it justice. Mama could carry a tune, even while she was dancing.

I proposed a plan to Mama. She could wear my short blond wig as a kind of disguise. As time got closer, I heard Daddy planning to go to the other end of the county to cover a dance at Snook Hall on the night Ray Price was at Deanville. We could go, have J. B. swing Mama around the floor a couple of times, and be home before anyone missed us. Mama was doubtful, but excited.

"She looks so pretty," J. B. worried when she tried on the wig. "What if guys try to cut in to dance with her?" he asked. "Should I step away, or not?" We talked about the possibilities for a long time, much to Mama's amusement.

On that night, we took off late enough that there would be a crowd for Mama to fade into, but early enough to get home before Daddy came home. At Deanville Hall, Mr. Beran manned the door, taking money and stamping hands. His smile at me suggested he recognized Mama even in the blond wig, but he stamped her hand without a word. Not wasting any time, J. B. swirled Mama out onto the floor.

A big tin circular building, Deanville Hall had tin window panels propped up with poles to let in the fresh air. Hot in the summer, and cold in the winter, Deanville dancers, moving around the center supports in a circle, reflected the weather: shorts in summer and jackets in winter. At the tables arranged around the sides, couples rested and hopeful singles waited, looking out at the crowd for that special one. A raised stage for the band filled one side of the hall, which was so big that one or two circles per song was about usual, unless a polka or a fast Texas swing played. Some couples danced such choreographed and practiced routines that people backed off, giving them room to show their stuff.

In the blond wig, Mama looked wonderful, beautiful and mysterious and young as she and J. B. waltzed to "Waltz Across Texas," an homage to Ernest Tubb, another favorite of Mama's. I worried she might be trying to lead. But she seemed happy, laughing as she danced, as I thought she might have done many times as a young girl. They danced to every song, never once taking a break, as I had told J. B. to keep her going as long as he could.

I was sitting at a table near the stage, enjoying Ray Price. We were going to leave after the next dance, and I thought Mama had had some fun. I was feeling pretty proud of myself. Then I saw him. Daddy, standing at the door, talking to Mr. Beran, looking at Mama from across the hall. He was smiling what I thought was an adoring smile.

Mama didn't see him until he walked up to her and J. B. and held out his hand. She took it without a word, and I held my breath.

Hand-in-hand they walked out onto the floor, Mama in that ridiculous blond wig and Daddy in his summer suit and tie, probably his first time on the dance floor at Deanville. I wondered where he'd left his hat, but then I saw J. B. holding it, looking sheepish, probably wondering what penalty he'd suffer for secretly taking the sheriff's wife out to dance on a Saturday night.

Mama and Daddy danced slowly to "For the Good Times," a song Mama would treasure all her life, the two of them not even making it halfway round the center pole. I watched closely, and they didn't seem to talk at all, but they looked like lovers to me. Then when the song was over, he walked her back to the table, took his hat from J. B., and gave me a look that I couldn't decipher. Did he wink? Then he headed out the door.

We followed soon after, driving back to the jail with very little to say. Sitting in the back seat of J. B.'s Chevy sedan, Mama took off the blond wig and sighed audibly. I asked her if Daddy seemed upset, and she said no, he'd said that he knew she loved to dance, and was sorry she hardly got do it anymore. All three of us sighed.

When he came home late that night, I heard them talking softly into the night. I worried until their laughter trickled into my room. Mama came into my room and asked me for the wig. We both laughed as she put it on.

Next day, J. B. told me Mama was an excellent dancer, and she didn't try to lead like I did.

Twenty-Two

Istanbul to Texas

When they found me in Istanbul, Daddy was already dead, buried for a week. I was obsessed with the exact time he died, and later figured it out to have been sometime during the ride on that olive oil truck from the Greek border to Istanbul. Life was exciting and fun then, and as far away from Caldwell, Texas, as a person could get, using any measure, not only distance. Nobody knew me. I wasn't the sheriff's daughter there.

The truck had been old and slow, with pom-pom fringe around the windshield in the cab and bright colored holy cards pasted all over the dashboard. Cheryl, my longtime friend and college roommate who'd joined me to hitchhike across Europe and the only person I knew who could look stylish, glamorous even, out of a backpack, sat next to the loud Turkish driver who seemed to be ranting at us in his harsh-sounding language. We'd been traveling for some time, *Europe on $5/Day* tucked in our backpacks and our hitchhiking expertise at the ready. This driver was upset we'd mistaken him for a Greek.

Once in Istanbul, before I knew Daddy was dead, I'd sent him a postcard, telling him the trip was educational. I'd learned that Turks hate Greeks, and Greeks *really* hate Turks. When the driver quieted down and his hand wandered to Cheryl's thigh, we switched places. He tried the same thing with me. I'd been angry but kept wondering how he'd gotten to be so confident to attempt such a thing with us both. After some unintelligible shouting back and forth, the driver pulled over and Cheryl and I climbed up on top of the polished stainless steel olive oil tank where the hot wind blew us raw, and the diesel fumes burned our lungs.

During the night, the rain soaked us, and we juggled our packs to keep them from rolling away. I pictured falling asleep and sliding right down under the big truck tires, and that lecherous driver stopping to examine my dead body, getting to touch me after all.

As strange as this experience was, it was strangeness I was after. I didn't know that my life was changing forever at that very minute, back in Caldwell, in a way that would make me shy away from strangeness for many years to come.

My brothers found me through the American embassy in Istanbul. When I got the message to call, I played my usual game when I was afraid of what lay ahead. I made a list of the worst things it could possibly be, forcing myself to choose between imagined horrible possibilities. The first item on the list was that something happened to Mama or Daddy. And I made myself decide. Which would be worse? Mama or Daddy? Mercifully, I didn't have time for much of this punishment before the call went through, but as I walked into the booth, I made myself watch my shaking hands.

"It's Daddy," my brother Walter said, his voice cracking as he said it. "He's dead. They already buried him."

I sank to the dirty floor of the Turkish call center and I heard someone moan like a cornered animal, low in their throat for a long, long time, before I realized it was me.

By the time I got back to Texas, the flowers on his grave were starting to brown in the June heat, even under the cool shade of the big pecan tree on our family lot at the Masonic cemetery. Mama and I had come directly there, straight from the highway into town. I couldn't wait to see Daddy, as though he might be in a hurry to see me, too.

My anxiety had started at the airport, like my head was reeling with thoughts and memories, jumping from the past to the present and back again and again. The feeling grew as my brothers went on and on about how I'd gotten a TWA clerk in Istanbul to take a check on a small-town Texas bank, drawn on the account of a dead man, signed by his daughter, whose name appeared nowhere on the check. They knew from experience I could be a persuasive talker but were amazed at the caliber of this feat.

But now I hardly spoke at all. When we finally got away from the airport and into the car, Mama patted my shoulder and touched my hair, and I winced as if I'd been hit. I could see my recoiling hurt her, but I couldn't help it.

At the gravesite, I opened my mouth to talk to her, to tell her what I felt, but instead I'd pull in the hot, dry air with a kind of gasp, or maybe a sob, and then sigh it out again. She watched me closely while I stared at Daddy's grave, piled high with flowers and wreaths smelling of decay. With the toe of my sandal, I scratched at the fresh brown dirt of his grave, already dry as dust while Mama told me what had happened. Loss scraped her voice. I wondered how long she'd sound like that.

Daddy had gone out on a disturbing the peace call to the home of Grover Mitchell, a pudgy middle-aged man who lived on the edge of town with his elderly mother. I knew Grover; I knew everybody in Caldwell, even now in 1970 after being away at college for years. Grover had thinning brown hair, combed over his head like spiderwebs to cover his bald spot. The kids made fun of that. I knew his mother, the tiny Miss Mary Mitchell, my brother Walter's first grade teacher. She looked like you might expect your first-grade teacher to look, hair in a gray bun, wire-rimmed glasses, always with a flower pinned on her collar. She must have had a husband, but he'd been long gone before my time, and everybody called her Miss Mary.

Grover was threatening the little old lady and had shoved her down a few times before she called the jail, crying softly, afraid of her own son and ashamed to tell it. Daddy had been out there a few times in years past when Grover was drinking. The first two times Daddy went out to their house that day, Miss Mary had pleaded that he would not arrest "her boy" (a "boy" well into his fifties), and Daddy did not. The third time, he arrested him despite Miss Mary's protests, her with bruises all up and down her arms, and walking with a bit of a limp.

Daddy took him to the jail, and pushed him into the smallest cell, Mama said, yelling at him loud and harsh, in a way Daddy hardly ever did. Then he went down to the Ranch Café to get a cup of coffee with the highway patrol-men and fell down dead on the smooth gravel as he opened his car door.

"It killed your daddy to see a man treat his mother that way," Mama said, without irony.

The story was so commonplace and everyday from our years in the jail. But this story held such heartbreak and loss for me, for us, that it was almost unbearable to hear. Still, I didn't cry.

We got into the car, Daddy's sheriff car, the newest in a long line of black unmarked Chevrolets. We drove out through the cemetery; past the familiar graves and tombstones I'd seen all my life on Sunday afternoon drives. The marble and granite markers dating back a hundred years stood amongst beautiful trees of all kinds, lovingly cared for by families left behind. It had always been a friendly place, a family place, never scary. There had been no ghosts.

We drove down Buck Street, the main road into town, stopping in front of the Stilman house, a white frame with blue-black trim. Small and neat, the house had a large front porch with a swing hidden from the street by pink crepe myrtle. A gas light out front burned day and night. I remembered walking under that light to knock on Mrs. Stilman's door and shout out "trick or treat!" She always dropped the most delicious popcorn balls into our bags.

In the car, I looked at Mama, thinner than I remembered, in a puckered seersucker black dress. I wondered if I should be wearing black, too. Had she been wearing it every day? Dark circles rimmed her eyes. I doubted that she'd been sleeping. I raised my eyebrows as if to ask what we were doing there, at the Stilman's.

"It's ours," she answered quietly. "Your daddy and I bought it the week before he died. I moved our things in here yesterday."

I turned to peer at our new house through Daddy's dusty car window. Our new house that Daddy would never live in. I sighed one of those invol-untary sighs that seemed to be the only sound I could make now that I was back in Caldwell.

Mama had been busy, almost frantic, my two brothers would tell me, in the days since Daddy died. Her husband was dead, her daughter hitchhiking somewhere in Europe "God knows where," she'd say every time they wondered where I might be. To spare me pain, she'd told my brothers (and to stay busy, they thought) she'd moved us, lock, stock, and barrel, into the new house on Buck Street. A regular house. Seven blocks away from the jail I'd grown up in, where we'd lived all those years. There would be no police radio blaring on top of the refrigerator in the new house. Nobody knocking on the door all hours of the night. Nobody lurching in our doorway, bleeding. The only tears shed in our new house would be our own.

"Let's go on down to the jail, Mama," I said. Finally, I was able to get a word out, and despite Mama's best efforts to keep me away, the jail was where I wanted to go. "I appreciate your getting us moved, Mama, and I love the Stilman house, always have." I was talking a mile a minute now. "But I'd like to go to the jail. I want to see it. I saw the grave, now let's go to the jail. I need to feel like I'm really home."

She pulled the big black car out onto Buck Street, slowly.

I asked her, "Is he still in jail?"

"Who?"

"Grover Mitchell." The name came out too loud and hard.

"He got out the very next day, like usual," she said, giving me a sideways look that meant she was still worried about me. "But he got picked up again Thursday night, after your daddy's funeral, drunk and disorderly, at the West End Bar."

After a pause, a long one while she stared at me, she asked, "Why are you asking after him?"

"I just want to see him," I said, my voice hard.

Mama pursed her lips but didn't say a word. I must have sounded crazy, barely talking all day, then wanting to go to the jail, wanting to see Grover. I didn't know why I felt this way, so it's a good thing she didn't push me for an answer. I couldn't have said why.

At the jail, in the living room, I dropped into the maroon leather rocker with wagon-wheel arms. Mama had bought this set of furniture the first week we'd lived in the jail in 1956. "It looks like Texas jail furniture," she'd said. Now, fourteen years later, it was worn, but still serviceable. Mama perched on the arm of Daddy's green leather recliner where he'd slept many a night in his suit and boots, waiting for calls.

The jail, familiar as my own mother, surrounded me as naturally as did the air. I was home. Through the open door, I could hear the prisoners' voices from their cells. Someone barked out a laugh. Someone else, a muffled sob. Nothing had changed; everything had changed.

Twenty-Three

Guilt, Dreams, and Pills

I never did see Grover Mitchell, and finally, I hoped I wouldn't. Mama had seen him only once herself, at Daddy's funeral, leaning on Miss Mary's shoulder, her patting his head right on the bald spot. It was the last unflattering thing Mama ever said about Grover. And me, I guess I still felt that since Daddy was dead, I had to blame somebody, to hate somebody for it. Somebody like sad old Grover. Somebody besides me.

I knew, of course, I wasn't to blame for his death, any more than Grover was, but the thoughts kept coming that maybe I was, at least in part. My taking off backpacking around Europe was certainly a new addition to Daddy's constant stress. Any talk of hitchhiking had washed a look of real anguish across his face, followed by horror stories of doomed hitchhikers. He had worried about language, lecturing me about using body language and tone of voice to communicate, especially the word "no!" His stories about men being the same the world over, these words from a man who'd never been more than one state away from Texas, seemed cynical for such a compassionate man. Though I had laughed at the time, I thought now he'd been deadly serious about his concerns. I'd given him more to worry about, and he'd already had more than his share.

For days I cried in bed, and asked myself, "Why?" I was asking, "Why did I go? Why did I feel I had to get so far away from the small-town Texas he loved so much?"

The day I'd left Texas for the trip to Europe, he was dragging the river for yet another body, and got home minutes before I had to head to the airport. His smell of tobacco and Dial soap enveloped me as he held me close in a hug like he had thousands of times before, and like I thought he would a thousand times more.

"Be careful," he said. "And come home safe."

He might have said, or maybe I was adjusting the memory for the maximum punishment, "Do you have to go, Dolly?"

In the rush, I couldn't remember if I'd said I loved him. I usually did, whenever I left him to go anywhere, much less halfway around the world. No matter, I was sure he knew. At least, I told myself so. I wished I hadn't gone. I shouldn't have gone. Guilt stuck in my belly. Why had I always been obsessed about traveling? Daddy had teased me about it since I was a little girl when Bill and I were going to ride around the world.

The worst of it was I'd never asked him about that sadness that almost always lingered in his eyes. Never asked him if he had dreams that never came true. Never told him how proud I was of him. I'd been too absorbed in my desire for the different, the exotic, the foreign, to see what a treasure I had right here at home. I should have been looking homeward instead of outward to some imagined far-off horizon.

I'd been home a few days by now, most of them closed up in the bedroom of the new house on Buck Street, the curtains pulled tight to dim the bright sunshine. I told Mama I was reading in there, but I wasn't. I was sleeping, or trying real hard to. Or I was thinking, or trying real hard not to, since my mind swarmed with pictures from the past. I'd always had a tendency to remember only the good times—and now those were the ones that hurt the most.

Mama knocked on my door, and when I didn't answer, called out, "You ought to get out a little; go for a walk or something. You can't stay holed up in there."

It was her third visit to my door that day, and I didn't want her to worry. I had plenty of guilt already, so I pulled on jeans and an old Caldwell High School T-shirt, put a forced smile on my face, and headed out the door, Mama smiling after me. I hoped I wouldn't run into anyone who might want to talk to me.

Right around the corner was the Methodist Church, where we'd always gone on Sunday nights, Sunday mornings being too crazy around the jail.

I'd gone to Sunday school in the basement and taken organ lessons from the long-suffering Miss Bea on the big pipe organ in the main sanctuary. She'd thought I might be able to master the organ after I'd failed so miserably at the piano. She'd been tenacious, and kind, but, in the end, wrong. When I played for the evening service one time, I hit some terribly wrong notes, even on the simple hymns.

It was our church. A stained glass window in the East entry hall was dedicated to my grandfather, who'd died when Daddy had been a baby. A silo blade had cut him nearly in half, as he stood right in front of the dairy barn, the same barn I loved so much as a kid. And Daddy's funeral had been in this church.

I tried the side door; it was always unlocked. I crept into the sanctuary through the choir door. I sat, first on the organ bench, then on Daddy's favorite pew (left side, four rows from the back, where he could come in late, or leave early if he got called out). Where "as it is and ever shall be," had been said every week, and seemed like a lie now.

As I settled in that pew where I'd sat beside Daddy through so many services, I thought up deals to make with God. I would stay home, help Daddy out at the office, make sure he ate right and got rest. I'd dedicate my life to Jesus, become a missionary in Africa. Whatever it would take, if only things could go back to the way they were before, back to when I'd felt secure in this world, when Daddy was still in it. As it was and ever shall be.

I remembered making deals with Jesus when Bill had been shot and backing down from them when being nice to him had been more than I bargained for. I smiled for maybe the first time since coming home, surprised that I still could. I had always admired resilience but wasn't sure that I had it.

After the church visit, I felt a little more peaceful. So I'd started going there every afternoon, if the church was empty. I asked the preacher for permission to play the big pipe organ and would sound out a few easy hymns, no sharps or flats, before sitting in the pew on the left side, four rows from the back. I rested there. I breathed. I made no more deals with Jesus, though some days, I'd fall asleep.

I was having trouble sleeping at home, at night, probably because of the dreams that kept me turning on my bed or jolted me awake. I dreamed that phone call had been a mistake. I dreamed the call was a horribly bad joke my brothers had played. Soon, the dreams got more intricate. I would see the funeral, the flowers, photographs of the mourners, and yet all of it led to the same conclusion, that he wasn't really dead.

I dreamt he'd been taken hostage by terrorists who'd faked his death. That he'd gone undercover with the FBI who'd faked his death. He would come to my room himself, stand at the foot of my bed and tell me in his own gentle voice, "I'm alive." I would wake up and wander dazedly through the house, checking each room to see if he was there.

At Mama's insistence, I went to see Doc Fetzer. He wasn't a psychiatrist, but he had a reputation around town as a counselor who kept confidentiality, desirable, if rare, in a small-town doctor. In his office, where my only other visit had been to have my ears pierced five years before, I found myself as shut down and unable to talk to him as I was with Mama. But I did tell him how I'd been unable to sleep nights. I didn't go into detail about the dreams.

Doc Fetzer called my mama and told her I was suffering from depression, and she told him that that wasn't news. What was he going to do about it? My grandma had said I was "blue," but I told her if you had to put a color to how I felt, it'd be gray. The fact that my frame of mind was a topic of conversation didn't help matters.

On my second visit, Doc Fetzer gave me Seconal, big red capsules that put my mind at ease for those few minutes before they dropped me into a dreamless, if not completely restful, sleep. I woke up tired, but thankfully with no visions of the comforting, ghostly Daddy.

One day, I took a Seconal during the day. It had been a bad day for both Mama and me, as we sorted out Daddy's clothes, folding his suits, which smelled lightly of dry-cleaning fluid, heavily of Daddy. I caressed the black one, the gray one with a darker stripe, the dark blue, the brown, the stockman's suit with the yoke that he wore in the County Fair parade every year riding one of Bub's Appaloosas. There was the light gray summer suit he'd died in. Mama wondered aloud who else these clothes, tailored to fit Daddy's bulk, could ever fit.

She planned to send out his boots, six pairs of Tony Llamas in all the basic colors, to be shined before giving three pairs apiece to my brothers. Each right boot had a worn place just above the heel from pushing the accelerator down to drive from one far corner of the county to the other. We nestled his ties in a box, some stained with coffee, or a Ranch Café dinner, recalling which one of us bought this one or that, and was it Christmas or a birthday? Mama managed a laugh over the loud modern ties I'd bought him during the sixties that he never wore but kept on his tie rack just the same.

I didn't laugh. Envying Mama's increasing strength and resilience, I went to my room and swallowed the big red capsule without water. I didn't sleep, but I felt much better. In the floating drowsiness, body heavy, mind light, my thoughts were not so jagged and cutting. I could relax into the warmth of memories and smell the sweat in Daddy's felt Stetson hatband and feel something like a pleasant memory. It still hurt, but not so much.

I found that when I took the pills, in the warmth of near sleep, I could let my mind go, give up my fight to control and keep things in line like I'd been doing for weeks now. I could close my eyes and think freely, like in my dreams, and my mind would not go to the bad places, only the good. Like I'd done automatically, and often, as a child, I could think happy endings. I could think what might be.

I enjoyed these Seconal fantasies so much that during that first week, I began carrying a couple of the capsules in a plastic baggie in my jean pocket. That Saturday, Mama washed my jeans with several pills in the pocket. As I hung the jeans on the clothesline out by the redbud tree in the backyard, I found the baggie. I thought of the dwindling number of pills in the bottle. The fear of running out swarmed me. I turned the bag up to my mouth to drink the reddish pink, slightly soapy liquid down. My stomach twisted, probably from the detergent, but also from a big dose of self-disgust. I vowed to take no more red capsules.

That night, I dreamed Daddy had faked his own death, and even while that dream was being dreamed, I could not figure out why he would do such a thing. That turned out to be the last dream.

Mama knew about the pills, of course. She couldn't help but know. I'd been sleeping for nearly a week, most of every day, and if I wasn't sleeping, I looked like I ought to be. I bumped into the furniture, and slurred my words like the town drunk, Wooley Hearne. To her credit, she let me be. Maybe she thought all that sleep would do me good.

But even my indulgent Mama, who was grieving herself, had her limits. The next thing I knew, I was sitting in the porch swing next to Miss Ella Darwin, knowing full well I'd been set up for a little counseling by the best-known do-gooder in town. I thanked the Lord I'd run out of Seconal before this encounter. Miss Ella was tougher than Mama.

Miss Ella was a social worker; a real social worker, with a master's degree from a fancy Eastern University, and she really did do good. She helped a lot of people and worked hard at it. She had to, since she was the only social worker in Burleson County. In the county, Miss Ella was known by all as "The Welfare Lady," which didn't go nearly far enough to describe her efforts. I'd spent many high school summers in her office at the courthouse, watching her clients come and go, talking about them and their problems; about racism and poverty before I fully understood them; and about my own problems. I'd had my first philosophical arguments with Miss Ella, about God and man and the universe. She'd helped me come to grips with death before, back when I saw Al Sorensen's body in a terrible state of decay. With her white hair (she'd gone gray long before her time) pulled straight back and tucked in a bun, she might have looked old, but Miss Ella was forever young. She dressed flashy by Caldwell standards in capes, big hats, black stockings, and tall boots that were not Western. I could talk to her about anything. Anybody could. It was her talent, and her job.

"What are your plans?" she asked, pushing the swing with her toe that emerged from buffalo sandals from India. She'd been asking me that question since I was ten. I had no answer today, for her or for myself. I had planned to be in Europe right now. In fact, at this moment, I told Miss Ella, I would be in Spain, and I had planned to stay there through this next year, to see what might come my way and practice my Spanish. That hadn't been much of a plan, I admitted to her, but back here in Caldwell, I didn't even have that.

"Everybody needs a plan," Miss Ella said, as I'd heard so many times before. "Makes all the difference. You've got to make a plan."

When the silence went on a little too long, Miss Ella told me her plan. She was about to retire, after forty years, and wanted to travel. I could picture her, inquiring about the plans of every stewardess, bus driver, and hotel desk clerk she met.

I looked at her, eyes open wide, surprised and a little sad at yet more change. I guess I had thought she'd be in the courthouse forever, her office right there by Daddy's. She put her arm around my shoulder and got down to the business at hand.

"Everybody dies," she said. "I'm going to. So are you, and your mama, too. It's just a part of life, the end part. Maybe not the best part, but still a part of life. We've all got to come to grips with it."

Pity showed right there on her face, along with some disappointment. They were the same things I was seeing in Mama's face, and it was just as hard for me to take from one as from the other. I could see that Miss Ella, like Mama, was surprised I wasn't handling Daddy's death better. We'd been right on top of tragedy, and grief and hurt, ever since we'd lived in the jail, so you'd think I'd be good at it by now. I had thought I was. But other people's pain, hard as it was to witness, paled by comparison to the real thing.

"The world keeps turning," she said, "and you've got to live in it, and do a good job of it, like you always have, like your Daddy did. Make him proud of you." She sure knew what to say. I took a deep breath, sat up straighter, and tried to at least look like I was coping.

We made a plan, just a little one, that we'd get together to talk about her travel plans for next spring, and then I watched Miss Ella walk off across Buck Street, under the big live oaks, her African print caftan bright even off there in the shade. I thought she walked as though she had a plan. I sat on the swing, without one.

Twenty-Four

Mama Is Sheriff

*M*iss Ella was right, I needed a plan. I needed to look ahead, not back, even if I couldn't quite do it yet. My grandma kept saying "get yourself a nice young man," and then she'd add, "One just like your daddy." I wasn't sure I was ready to replace him. But if I were, would I look for someone exactly like him, or did I want to be like him myself? I thought I might. Miss Ella had told me once that people become what they want others to be, and right now I wanted everyone, not only me, to be like Daddy. This kind of thinking was swirling around when Bobby Whaley, definitely a nice young man, who was a bit like Daddy, and my boyfriend in college, came to visit.

"Sorry about your Daddy," Bobby said as he walked up on the porch, and he smiled his little boy smile. He meant what he said, but the smile marked a long-standing joke between us. The first time Bobby and I had gone to the jail for him to meet my parents, as we headed away from Caldwell in his brother's red Healy convertible, he'd asked me, "Aren't you a little old to be calling him Daddy, instead of Dad?" I'd asked him right back, "Aren't you a little old to be calling yourself Bobby instead of Bob?" We agreed right then that Daddy would always be Daddy to me, and that Bobby would always be Bobby.

Bobby and I had been on and off now for more years than things like that usually go on and off. We liked each other, so we'd never get quite mad enough to end with a complete break. During the times I'd moved back home to the jail, he'd come there to see me, sometimes staying the weekend. Gradually he'd started going out on patrol, and occasionally on calls, with Daddy. This had been happening since I started going out with boys at sixteen. At first, Daddy didn't take them on actual calls—and he'd bring them back to the jail if he got a call while they rode patrol, especially if he knew their mothers. After high school, when my boyfriends got older, and he wasn't likely to know their mothers, he would let them go along if they were not too "lamebrained," his word for a good many of my boyfriends. Bobby, though, was one of the good ones, Daddy liked to say. He was smart, didn't talk too much, and knew when to get out of the way. He was also strong and muscular and could help out just by standing in the background, looking powerful, and maybe holding a flashlight. Even during times when Bobby and I were off, not on, he'd come over and ride with Daddy.

"The Whale was here last weekend," Daddy would say, the nickname from Bobby's last name. "Helped me out with traffic at a wreck out at the Lyons Junction." Then he'd give me a raised eyebrow look, like wasn't I sorry I'd missed the boy, and when was I going to do something about him and me, and didn't I know he was one of the good ones? Daddy could always say a lot with a look.

———

Now Bobby was here, bent and determined to cheer me up, and under normal circumstances, he could do it. He was one of the funniest boys I'd ever known, another reason we were still so close after all the breakups. He didn't tell jokes with punch lines, rather he told drawn-out, humorous stories, complete with characters and voices. Like Mark Twain in a college letter sweater. He also did a spot-on impression of Daddy, and wisely had never done it in front of him.

Since I'd gotten back, I hadn't seen Bobby, though we'd talked on the phone several times. Like everybody else, he didn't expect that I'd be so down, so obsessed with the past, so morose. I told him how I'd been living mostly in memories, and that they seemed bright and colorful, while the here and now seemed like a black-and-white movie. He didn't commiserate or pat me on the head. Instead he started in on a memory of his own. The last time he saw Daddy.

Several weeks before Daddy died, Bobby had been riding with Daddy and Granite Bailey, the security guard, on a Saturday. Everybody in

Caldwell knew that Granite was hopeless as a lawman, but Bobby hadn't known. He'd been shaken that night when Granite pulled his gun on a couple of young toughs. He threw the weapon from hand to hand "like Roy Rogers," Bobby said. Doing a perfect imitation of Granite's shrill voice and jerky movements, Bobby demonstrated Granite's twirling the gun around his finger, gunfighter style. Once Daddy had the boys locked in the car, Granite shouted, "And don't you forget it!" You'd have sworn Bobby's act was Granite, right there in the house on Buck Street. He had me laughing out loud. Later that night, Bobby had asked Daddy if that kind of dangerous gun play was common, or even permitted. "Heck, no, Bobby," Daddy had said. This time, Bobby did a low soft drawl that sounded amazingly like Daddy. "Granite's pistol isn't loaded. It never is. He agreed to never load it again after he shot himself a few years ago. He was practicing quick draws with his gun stuffed down in his pants, and the gun went off. Nicked the side of his manly organ. Bled a lot, and then it healed up with a 90-degree angle kink in the thing. Strangest thing you ever saw. He shows it to everybody. You're just lucky, son, he didn't show it to you." Bobby let out a perfect Daddy chuckle, low in his throat.

"It's true, Bobby," I said. "Daddy was always afraid Granite would forget himself and show it to Mama. Bill used to kid him about peeing around corners." A laugh slipped out of my mouth.

We were still laughing when Mama came in, sinking into Daddy's old recliner that had been moved from the jail to our new house.

"I took the job," she said with a sigh. "I'm the sheriff."

"What did you say?" I asked with gasp. Disbelief and shock took my breath away. My heart fluttered and threatened to stop.

"You heard me right. I am now the sheriff of Burleson County."

I couldn't speak. . . . I looked at Bobby, unable to say a word, and I think he was speechless, too. If anybody would have gone running out of the jail at the first chance, away from that life, I thought it would have been Mama, screaming bloody murder as she ran. But now she'd agreed to fill out Daddy's term? When an official died in office in the county, it was customary to appoint the wife to complete the term, if she was qualified. But this was the first time a sheriff had died. Mama would be the first woman sheriff in the county—and the only woman sheriff in Texas at the time, for that matter.

I could only think about her hopes for a normal life, a regular home. The "someday" house she and Daddy had started to build almost ten years ago at the farm, completing only the porch in the first few years. It still sat unfinished. But for all those ten years, every few weeks, Mama had gone to sit on that porch, walked through the unfinished house and drawn plans for its completion, planning her escape from the jail. The slow progress of the "someday" house was a joke in our family, to everyone except Mama.

She may have escaped the jail, living in a regular house now, but the calls, the not-so-normal life of other people's problems and disagreements, the late nights, and all of it would be very much the same. I couldn't believe she'd even consider it.

She had plenty of experience to hold the office, of course. She'd handled sheriff's business when Daddy was off in other parts of the county and had been in charge of the jail for all our years there. She wrote all the reports and wrangled the paperwork. Every day she fed the prisoners, talked with them, counseled them through the bars, stood in the jail hallway handing out advice along with black-eyed peas and cornbread. When they'd backslide and land in jail a second or third time, or turned into regulars, she was tougher on them than Daddy. She'd dealt with all other levels of law enforcement, as they came and went. And when the victims—the beaten wives, the children who'd been mistreated, or who'd lost their parents, or any other injured soul—showed up at our door, she comforted them as good as Daddy could. She even went on Daddy's calls with him a few times, but mostly she was the steadfast force who answered every call on the phone, on the radio, at the door.

Daddy talked about cases with her, of course. We all talked about his cases around the supper table in the evenings, whenever he made it in time. Mama had good instincts about the cases. She knew what to look for and where to look for it as the case developed. After the first few years, she kept little case notebooks, and more times than not, the facts would bear her out and we'd all have to admit she'd been right from the start. She didn't gloat, but it pleased her to be right so much of the time. Now she'd be doing it all on her own, for real, without Daddy.

"Mama, why?" I choked out, shocked at her pronouncement.

She settled her gray eyes on me and then on Bobby, and after a long pause, said, "It's what I know. It's what I'm used to." She reached for a tissue and dabbed at the corners of her eyes and said, "It's all I know."

The phone rang. Already, her job was calling. We listened as she stated a few quick words about where and when, and she took off out the door. It was all so familiar.

"Why on earth would she want this job, Bobby?" I wondered as I watched Mama drive off in Daddy's black Chevy. "She longed for a normal life as long as I can remember," I cried.

But then I never could figure out why Daddy took the job and kept it so long either, ill-suited as he was for it. There were parts of the job he could barely tolerate, that took so much out of him that you could actually see it on his face, in the way he walked. I hoped I never would see my mama walking that way. All Daddy had wanted out of life was peace and quiet and time to spend with his cows. He loved nothing better than going out to the farm, walking out among the cows, out of earshot of his radio. He might sit for an hour, if he was lucky, in the shade of the big mesquite on the bank of the tank, watching the cattle drink, switching their tails to keep the flies at bay. He said he got the best sleep out there, even if it was dozing in his patrol car, or leaned up against a tree. He got precious little of any of that. I hoped this house would protect Mama, give her a place to go, where she could get some good sleep, and be a little of what she'd always wanted.

I told Bobby, "I don't even know why Daddy kept doing the job. It took such a toll on him. Much less my mother!"

"He was great at it," Bobby said kindly but forcefully. "Even I've seen it. That's why. People trusted him with their lives. And he could do more with a quiet word than anybody I ever saw. He made a difference. Not many people can say anything like that about their life's work."

We didn't need to say another word. Bobby had said it all. The thought took root in my mind and gave me great comfort.

Bobby and I stayed at the jail that night, my first time to spend a night there since I came back. It was a busy night, and we stayed up manning the phones and opening the jail door all through the night, as prisoners came and went. Bobby handled the radio calls and had a grand time doing it. He left for home, talking about coming back to do it all again the next weekend, but it would be, I knew by the morning, my last night in the jail.

Twenty-Five

The Funeral

I was still raw.

I avoided the police radios, preferring to ride in the family car instead of Daddy's black Chevrolet, in case a call came through. I never answered the phone, not even at the Buck Street house. Mama, though, settled into the role of sheriff, as she had the sheriff's wife. Daddy's deputies helped her a great deal, especially Bub Wallis, who handled the night calls, and anything especially messy or scary during the day. Mama spent as much time on the phone and radio as she ever had, probably more, and worked in the sheriff's office at the courthouse all day long. Every couple of hours in the evening, she went to the jail for one thing or another.

She hired Byron Taylor, a widower and retired military policeman from Temple, who moved in as jailer. He slept in the back bedroom where Daddy had missed so many nights' sleep. After his first Saturday night, he came up to the Buck Street house to sit at the kitchen table with Mama, and I heard him say, "Don't see how y'all did it, all those years, with a family."

"Mr. Taylor," she said, "it gets to be ordinary pretty quick."

I thought how we had adjusted over the years, how jail life had become ordinary. We made light of the danger and joked about the stress, especially Daddy. But not so much Mama. I remembered how she'd moved us out to my grandma's in the early years, when she didn't think there was anything ordinary about living in a jail. I wondered how she was doing it so well now.

Hard to believe now, but there had been plenty of times when I, too, looked forward to the busy nights, times when I sat by the phone, or begged to be allowed to man the radio. Now, I would head out to the farm, sit by the creek under the cottonwoods for hours on end. No phones, no radio, and no people.

It was a Tuesday, down by the creek, with cows lapping at the tank and geese flying in a V overhead, that I finally looked at the pictures of the funeral and listened to the tape Mama had made. The books about grief that Miss Ella had given me said I needed the closure. So, I decided to have the funeral, all over again, down here by the creek. Daddy's second funeral. I'd lugged down Bub Wallis's portable tape player with the reel of tape, the big album with all the pictures in it, the stack of sympathy cards and the sign-in book with almost a thousand signatures. It had been Caldwell's biggest funeral ever, Mama had said with a tinge of pride in her voice. I laid out our plaid picnic blanket in the grassy spot near my brother's old hideout and stacked the funeral paraphernalia neatly around me. For a long while, I sat watching grasshoppers jump on and off the edge of the blanket. Maybe I thought Daddy's funeral would seep out through the covers of the albums and into my head to spare me having to look.

Finally, I got up my nerve, and started with the pictures, and they were horrible. Daddy in a coffin, from all angles. Close up, and far away, before it was draped with flowers and after. His ruddy complexion had disappeared into a waxy gray face. His red cheeks used to shine so, even when he slept, but this looked nothing like sleep. Daddy had been an active sleeper, snoring and tossing his head like he might be dreaming a sheriff's dream, or maybe having a good time, which was what I always hoped, and muttering to himself. I'd never seen him so still. He looked like a terrible mannequin. I realized I'd been holding my breath, and I had to look away, to be able to breathe again. I tried to see the cows, the tank, the grasshoppers. But I couldn't keep my eyes away. I studied the images of Daddy closely for a long time, so glad I hadn't seen the real thing.

I examined the cards, reading people's condolences, noting who'd sent flowers. I read through the long list of signatures in the guest book. There were so many, I couldn't imagine anyone who'd not attended. I pictured each person as I read the names, each sad face.

When I started the tape, I could hear muffled coughing, sounds of shuffling around in the church, but most distinctly, crying. I turned off the tape and wondered who had cried so. The grasshoppers sprang around, and a mockingbird chattered away overhead. I wondered how I wasn't crying now, when so much less had set me off weeping these past few months. Where had Mama and my brothers sat at the funeral? Had they sat down front, and or in our regular pew near the back? Up to now, I hadn't wanted to hear a thing about Daddy's funeral, even refused to listen when Mama or Bill or Walter tried to tell me details. But now I wondered. I thought Miss Ella would approve.

I started the tape again. More crying, perhaps Daddy's sisters or my grandma. Next I expected speaking or a formal opening or a eulogy. But instead a clear voice rang out, sweet and silvery: "There's a land that is fairer than day." Her voice quavered briefly, like that thing trumpets do when playing taps, but then she sang out strong and full, her voice lifting high, and my spirits soared along.

"In the sweet by and by, we shall meet on that beautiful shore," Sister Ocean sang.

I could picture her, tiny with her white hair shining, by the front altar of our church, her voice moving every single person in the chapel. And now it was real, Daddy's funeral down there by the creek. I was sure he would have liked the location, and that the mourners included a few of his cows who'd wandered over, attracted by Sister Ocean's voice.

After the sermon by Daddy's favorite preacher, the one with bright red hair and a Spanish accent, several people spoke heartfelt eulogies. Then finally Sister Ocean sang the first song I'd ever heard from her, "Shall We Gather at the River?" In her unearthly voice, she sang all four verses. I thought how if I walked to the top of the pasture, I could see the cemetery on the next hill over, the place Daddy rested. I rewound the tape and played it again, and again, as the sun slipped behind the hills and a cool evening breeze began to blow through the cottonwoods.

Twenty-Six

The Welfare Lady

*T*here had been so many caladiums at Daddy's funeral that Mama and I made a huge bed along the south fence of the Buck Street house, with the help of Wooly Hearne and my brother Walter, who'd come home to visit.

"The funeral must have put a strain on the local flower shops," Mama said, wiping a dirt smear off my cheek, and smiling at Walter.

We'd taken most of the flowers and the potted plants to the nursing home up by the railroad tracks, but Daddy liked caladiums, so we decided to plant them.

"The funeral was nice, Mama," I said, thinking how normally we were talking about everything now, and knowing we needed to.

She smiled again, patting dirt around a big red stem. "I was worried how you'd feel about not being there, not being able to say goodbye to him. I was afraid you might be angry, angry at me."

Her words hit closer to the truth than I could go, so I stayed quiet while Walter went inside to get us iced teas.

I dug deep into the dry dirt, breaking small clods with my hands "Well, it was a nice funeral, all in all, and you did what you had to do, Mama. It was probably easier for me, not being there, not knowing a thing till it was all over. You had the hard job."

Walter handed us jelly glasses, cold and wet. As we sipped iced tea in the yard, melting mud slid down the sides onto our arms.

"Guess who's back in jail?" Mama said.

Walter and I made it a game, going through the long list of old-time prisoners, looking at Wooly, one of the oldest, who hadn't stopped for iced tea but continued to dig a deep trench around the side of the house. I wondered what Mama was getting at. She gave us a clue. "Mr. Taylor says the jail has never been cleaner."

"Not LoBoy!" we both wailed in disbelief.

"Yep," she said with a sigh. "LoBoy. Got an early out in Sugarland for good behavior. Drunk and Disorderly. To Mr. Taylor, he's complaining that the food's not as good as it used to be. I gave him a good talking-to last night, just like your daddy would have, even if I do say so. Not sure it made a difference, though."

"Boy, the demon rum," Walter said, trying to make a joke, but I could tell he was a stunned as I was. How must that have been for Daddy to see the same people making messes of their lives, over and over again? Especially someone like LoBoy that we'd considered almost family. Still, he'd kept trying. When LoBoy had been made the trustee all those years ago, Daddy was trying. When he took LoBoy to AA, he was trying. Even a man headed for prison for his wife's murder was worth saving, worth the effort. Bobby Whaley had gotten it right: Daddy had made a difference.

Several weeks later, Mama was down at the jail, cooking prisoner food at the special request of LoBoy. He'd stayed in the jail, staying sober and cleaning like mad, just like the old days. Mama had let him out as trustee to run errands in town. When I turned into the back driveway, crunching gravel as I drove, I saw LoBoy, standing in the jail yard next to the two big German Shepherds that had replaced the aging bloodhounds years ago. He was, even I could see, drunk.

I called Mama out and she got Mr. Taylor to put LoBoy inside, into the cell for drunks, the one with the plastic cover on the mattress. Later that evening, hungover and sad, LoBoy told Mama he'd been sober for more than ten years, right up until a month or so ago.

"It was the sheriff that done it," he said. "He told me I could make something of myself, and I never wanted to let him down."

He and Mama made plans for an AA meeting for the very next day, and Mama said he looked a little better by the time she closed the big steel door on him.

Chapter Twenty-Six

"I won't let you down," LoBoy called after her, as she walked to the car where I waited for her, to drive us up to Buck Street, where we'd be away from it all.

But it wasn't like that at all. Instead of being away from it all, we spent that evening gathering materials for an AA meeting, calling people to set it up. This task made me feel good, the best I'd felt since coming home. Maybe we could make a difference. We were doing exactly what Daddy would have done, and it felt right.

Next day, after the AA meeting, held in the jail yard under the fig tree, I called Miss Ella Darwin. She was about to retire after forty years. Miss Ella had approached me with the idea of applying for her job. "Are you interested?" she said as soon as she picked up the phone. I was. She said she had already talked to the department about me, my background and experience, and assuming I did well on the test I'd have to take, the job could be mine for the asking. She didn't gloat, not right then, but I figured she would next time I saw her.

Mama wasn't too surprised either. "You're sure?" she asked. "You know the job will be almost like the jail. The jail, and more. You used to say Miss Ella's job was like your daddy's job, without the gun."

"I'm sure," I said. Just like Mama, this life was what I knew, my inheritance. The family business.

Six months later, driving LoBoy to another AA meeting at Reverend Jerome's Church in Hix, I stopped at the stop sign on the highway and waved to a client of mine standing at the corner. A pretty young woman, Eula Chandler had a stylish Afro and five young children, and was studying to be a hairdresser at Premier Beauty School in Bryan. Her mother, also a client, was keeping Eula's children and seven others in a newly licensed daycare center that we hoped might show a profit by year's end.

I pulled up close and noted the young man standing beside Eula. He was tall and handsome, very athletic, and I knew that Eula loved him. But he was living and working in Houston, not offering much support. As I mentally prepared an "absent father" letter for him, planning how we'd get him involved with his son, one of Eula's five, I waved at the two of them.

He turned his head, looking my way. Through the open window, I heard him ask, "Isn't that the sheriff's daughter?"

"No," Eula answered. "That's the Welfare Lady."

AFTERWORD

The sheriffs in these fictionalized stories, Reid and Willie Mae Philp, were very real.

Their legacy is honored in the Caldwell Civic Center Museum, where their service weapons are on display. Reid Philp is also honored in the Lost Lawman Memorial in Austin, dedicated to lawmen who died in service to the people of Texas.

They were dedicated public servants, loving parents, and wonderful people.

ABOUT THE AUTHOR

LAREIDA BUCKLEY was born and raised in Caldwell, Texas, and though this book is fiction, Lareida actually did grow up in the Burleson County Jail where her father *and* mother were sheriffs of the county. Lareida graduated from Texas A&M University with honors in 1968, with only thirty-four women in her graduating class. She attended the University of Hawaii's Graduate School of Library Science and has lived on Hawaii's Big Island for almost fifty years.